# Maria the Wanted

## V. CASTRO

**TITAN** BOOKS

Maria the Wanted
Print edition ISBN: 9781803366722
E-book edition ISBN: 9781803366739

Published by Titan Books
A division of Titan Publishing Group Ltd
144 Southwark Street, London SE1 0UP
www.titanbooks.com

First edition: February 2026
10 9 8 7 6 5 4 3 2 1

A CIP catalogue record for this title is
available from the British Library.

EU RP (for authorities only)
eucomply OÜ, Pärnu mnt. 139b-14, 11317 Tallinn, Estonia
hello@eucompliancepartner.com, +3375690241

Designed and typeset in Sabon LT by Richard Mason.

Printed and bound by CPI Group (UK) Ltd, Croydon CR0 4YY.

# Part One

*1*

## Juárez, Mexico—1995

Maria faced the warehouse, inhaling the last breath of fresh air she would enjoy until she trudged back out at dawn. Just looking at the poorly ventilated building made her feel sluggish, even before setting foot inside. *Ándale, Maria. Be grateful. It's only for a few more months. I don't know where we'll be, but it won't be here. Anywhere but here.* The financial and political instability was deepening by the day, giving Maria little confidence in what her future would be in Mexico with assassinations, currency devaluation, violent insurrections. She didn't recognize her home or what the world was calling the Peso Crisis.

The rusty front door let out an ear-piercing screech as she forced herself inside, the final rays of sunlight making her coworkers squint, each already at their sewing machines.

"Hola, chicas," she shouted over the clip-clapping of the machines.

Big Boss sat in his office watching some sports event on the crackling fuzzy TV. Pictures of naked women covered the walls, making Maria shudder. There he was, relishing his fistfuls of power while they all scrambled to make a living.

"You're late," he barked, barely sparing her a glance.

No cameras aimed their lenses at her, so she flipped the middle finger behind his back as she continued on to the middle of the factory floor. Maria never told her husband, Diego, that Big Boss still managed to sneak in his backside slaps or lecherous winks whenever he got the chance. This seemed like a small price to pay for a job—a job that would get them to the States. She yearned for change. Her mind seemed always fixed on the idea, as if a hidden part of her clawed from somewhere deep inside wanting to get out. These days, people lurked at every corner ready to suck her dry. If it wasn't Big Boss, it was the coyotes—and if it wasn't either of those, then there would be La Migra to deal with.

The coyotes. Their prices were as high as their promises to get you into the States with no problems. She toyed with the idea of taking extra hours at the bakery with Mamá, but she was so tired and sick all the time. Once Maria reached twelve weeks in her pregnancy, they would be across the border by any means necessary. No, she couldn't take the extra hours, as much as she wanted the money, because she would need every bit of strength for a journey that often ended in death.

It was the usual skeleton crew of five working that night. There were only five because the Even Bigger Bosses didn't like to pay overtime, but their quota had to be met somehow. At night, temperatures dropped, and it was quiet enough to listen to Selena Quintanilla or conversational English tapes on a cassette player and headphones while working. Tapping feet to 'Como La Flor' or repeating English phrases under her breath made the monotonous work bearable. Tonight they were making cheap ugly red ties, which would be sold at a price they could only afford after a month's wages. Even though this was the easiest shift of the day, there was nothing easy about maquiladora work.

What felt like hours passed. The muscles in her back and shoulders began to spasm, and sweat gathered underneath her braided hair. She didn't want to lose momentum to stretch or scratch her head, fearing Boss's attention for not making her count. Selena began to sing 'Bidi Bidi Bom Bom' when the screech of the heavy door broke the room's silent concentration. Maria turned to see Big Boss guiding three men inside, being careful to keep his distance as he did so. If Boss was afraid of these strangers, it couldn't be good. He pointed to the clock hanging on the wall, shut the door and then ran off. The revving of his car as he pulled away was distinct. There would be no one to help them now.

Two of the men were Mexican or South American: she could tell by their shiny silver-tipped snakeskin boots, dark jeans and the large hats which shielded their faces. The third had to be white. From what Maria could see he was handsome with wavy light chestnut brown hair, soft blue eyes and a perfect cupid's bow for lips. He was dressed like an American soap or pop star in a silk shirt, matching jacket and stylish dress shoes. The gringo walked the factory floor looking at the faces of the five women and his surroundings in mild disgust while the other two chuckled among themselves. The girls were dumbstruck and fearful because Juárez and its body count was notorious for good reason.

"Mujeres," one of the laughing men shouted out. "Let's have some fun!"

The other rifled through a stack of cassettes before choosing one for the tape player located just outside the office. He pushed play and turned the volume up as loud as the crappy speakers would allow. 'Devil Inside' by INXS started to play.

"This one's for you, gringo!" he yelled.

The other women were out of their seats and huddled together against the office's glass window. With a mother's instinct, Maria grabbed her belly. *No, no, no*, she thought. Not now, not before this little nine-week-old life had a chance, her little mustard seed of faith in everything that was good in this miserable world.

Before she had a chance to join the other workers, one of the strangers hurled himself headfirst into the group of women. These men, these *things* were not looking for sex: they were out for blood.

The nearly empty factory amplified the screams of their terror. Maria's coworkers tried to run for the door, but the men blocked their way. One made silly faces like you would to a baby, toying with them while dancing to the music.

Backing toward the end of the factory floor, she tried to make herself as small and unnoticed as possible. Her bladder cramped as fear seized every fiber of her being. If she recalled correctly, there was another door, a fire exit. As the two men in hats tore into her coworkers again she white-knuckled one hand over her mouth and the other over her belly, as if she could cast some protective spell over both. One for silence; one for safety. The gringo watched on, bored and impatient, checking his watch twice before placing his hands back into his pockets.

As if in slow motion, one of the now-bloodied strangers pointed straight at Maria. His wide smile was smeared with red, and white points protruded where normal teeth should have been. Maria ran toward the fire door, but a thick chain snaked around the handle, a large bolt latched on the front like an evil present wrapped with a metal bow. Prayers flooded past her lips as she pulled on the unrelenting chains.

"Your turn, amigo," someone called to the gringo. "We break bread tonight. Show us you're serious about our deal! Tizoc demands loyalty."

As they continued picking through the now nearly lifeless bodies, the blue-eyed devil with an angel's mouth looked at Maria with a weariness like he hadn't slept in years. She hoped whatever he had in mind would be quick. He didn't seem to have the same wild appetite as the others. He was handsome and had dressed nice, yet he had misery etched in his every expression. He grabbed a red polyester tie from one of the boxes as he approached her. The two others continued to feed and terrorize, but still managed to shout encouragements.

"You tying her up? Kinky! It's always the quiet types!"

Those blue eyes narrowed at this comment, suddenly coming alive, his anger obvious. Maria couldn't understand—if he disliked this pointless slaughter, then why was he allowing it? Desperate to survive, she searched for whatever she could find lying nearby to use as a weapon. All she found was a pitiful metal stool. The man walked toward her in a slow, calm manner, as if he was approaching a rabid dog just waiting to strike.

"Please don't fight me. You will only make things worse. We don't want them to become involved." His tone was slow and even. Somehow, she believed him. His voice proved he was not local or American. He had an accent you only heard in historic films set in a country far away. England. He opened pale pink lips to reveal two small points stabbing downwards. A gasp fled her throat as she dropped the useless stool and reached for the silver and turquoise cross around her neck. Didn't monsters despise the crucifix? At least that was the story always told.

He rolled his eyes, grabbed her wrists and pushed

the cross back to her chest. Her hands went limp under his cold vice-like grasp as he bound them with the tie. He was stronger than his voice and appearance made him out to be. But she wouldn't be taken that easy. Not like this, not here. If her life meant anything in this world she would walk out of here alive. Unable to break away, she resorted to biting his hand while stomping on his gleaming shoes as hard as her soft sneakers would allow. *Maybe* by the sacred heart of Jesus she could just make it past the others and out the door. Not a drop of blood from his skin or welp of pain from his mouth.

The stranger's eyes and voice trembled. "*Please*, I beg you. Don't do this. I will drain you and it will be over."

"Hurry, lover boy, we don't have all night," one of his companions joked.

He whipped his head back and smirked. "Let me have my fun, okay?"

When he turned back to Maria, his dead expression returned and his jaw clenched.

He pulled his bitten hand away to wipe away her saliva and proceeded to drag her from the door with the other with solid quick steps. Crouching on the floor, she did her best to resist being taken toward the hungry demons nearby. Her body tensed, every muscle resisting certain death. She wouldn't go without trying to fight back for her baby. She had to survive this. But the creature lifted her over one shoulder as if she weighed no more than a small child. More music played loudly, and she heard the breaking of shot bottles. The others must have found Boss's stash of tequila. Still bound and trying to wiggle away, she found herself being lowered onto the sewing table. The man looked over his shoulder, then back to Maria, completely cool and calm. From the weight of his arms holding her down, she knew the fight was over. There was no way out. How arrogant she was to think she mattered at all. The stupidity in her big plan to shake off this town and her unremarkable existence. Her mother had been right all along.

"Como te llamas?" the stranger whispered as he caressed her cheek like a lover. His eyes darted across her face as though reading a poem about heartbreak. But his ice-cold touch made her shudder with fear.

Her voice cracked, but she managed to whisper, "Maria."

He glanced back at his companions again then faced her again. In that moment something seemed to change in his eyes. Instead of sadness there was a spark of determination. "Do you want to live through death? I only give you a gift, a chance. What you do with it is up to you. Do you want my gift?"

Living through death? She wondered if he meant Santa Muerte. But what would he know of her?

"Sí," she answered with hope as small as the child inside of her. Maybe the sacred heart still burned. Her tears drenched the stranger's fingers. Maria's fear throbbed and writhed inside as she wondered what would happen next.

The stranger reached for a pair of scissors lying on

the table. With a swift motion, he sliced open his wrist. Before she could react, his body was leaning over her and two long needles for teeth punctured her neck. A roar of laughter and howling filled her ears as she screamed in agony. Warmth drained from her skin. Pinpricks of pain dotted her body.

This was the end. The end of Diego, their baby, the States, night school, a good job. This was the death of the only dream she had ever dared to dream. Maria could feel her eyes become heavy when a small tide of blood moved down her throat. She had to swallow it otherwise it would choke her with its viscosity. The taste of cold pesos made her gag. And that is what her life was worth in that place.

The gringo placed his hand over her lips. "Don't move until we leave. Your boss will be back soon, so I hope you enjoy your vengeance, Maria. Sometimes that is enough to get people like us from one day to another." A wicked smile, and then he closed her eyes with his cold hand. She kept them shut.

"We didn't think you had it in you!" The other two were still reveling in their killing spree. "You old vamps are all the same. You forget how to party!"

The heavy door screeched open and closed again. Maria lay on the sewing table, trying to still her quivering body and labored breath. The music stopped and she assumed they were gone, but the fear of seeing what they had done made her unable to move. Twenty minutes passed before the pain began. Deep cramps radiated from her lower belly to her back, like tiny fists armed with knives trying to punch through her guts. Waves upon waves of torment pulled at her body like a lethal undertow, then stopped just as suddenly as they had started. A pool of warmth settled between her legs. Her jeans were wet, and the truth suddenly hit her like a blow to the face. Her mustard seed—her spark of life—was gone.

Maria placed her hand over her mouth, sealing in guttural sobs of loss and grief. She lodged her fist between her lips to contain any sound. The heartache so deep, teeth broke the skin over her knuckles leaving little spots of blood. She hadn't realized saving her own life meant ending another. No longer able to contain the despair, she let out a soul-rending cry until the cords of her neck felt like they were about to snap. Maria grabbed her abuelita's turquoise cross and kissed it. Now she wanted to die. She wanted to fly away like a cicada leaving its shell clinging onto a branch.

It was then some other terror started to emerge with a fever. Beads of sweat formed at the small of her back and the top of her lip. Sweat continued to pour from her pores. Her gums ached, and she tasted blood on her tongue. Maria wondered if a slow death was the gift the gringo spoke of.

"*Please*, please take this pain, take me home. I *can't* do this, Lord. Why are you doing this?! What have I done? Hear me, dammit!" Nada. Not a sound. She responded to the silence by kicking the sewing machine from the table.

The front door creaked open.

"¡Aye! Dios Mio!" a husky voice cried out.

Maria knew exactly who that was. Big Boss. That dirty, pig-faced traitor probably sold them for gambling money and a six-pack of beer. The thought of him caused Maria's desire for vengeance to bubble and boil, coagulating into something hateful. Time to get up. She wiped away her wet mascara and eyeliner with the red tie still binding her wrists, then ripped it away like it was tissue paper. He would pay for this. Someone always pays.

Big Boss's gaze landed on Maria. His expression was that of a man who had seen the Devil, or a ghost, or a woman scorned.

Her gaze intensified as the small veins in her eyes grew. His heartbeat pounded between her eyes, a drumbeat that enticed her to come closer. With unnatural speed, she ran to him and sank her newly sprouted fangs into his neck.

Maria drank with vicious despair, digging her sharp teeth deeper as she thought of how Diego held her after lovemaking, how they'd never hear that first little kitten's meow of a cry from their child. She ripped off a chunk of his flesh and spat it out before throwing his body down like a devoured tamale husk licked clean.

Never in her life had she felt power like that. Anything seemed possible. What a small existence humanity was compared to this. The rush of taking his life gave her a pleasure not even experienced in sex. She wanted to do it again and again. She closed her eyes as the blood cooled in her body. She opened them again.

Until that moment, Maria hadn't taken in the gruesome crime scene around her. Blood and flesh speckled the sewing tables. The women's eyes were still wide open, their bodies the color of sunbaked dirt. This scene of injustice brought tears to Maria, staining her red eyes with black all over again. She felt shame over the emotions she'd experienced as she killed her boss. Blood tears felt like hot candlewax sliding down her face, threatening to singe anything they touched. This place was now unholy. She would cleanse it with fire, but not before the families of those that gave their lives to this thankless work had some sort of real compensation.

Maria snatched the keys from the chain attached to Boss's wallet and headed into his dingy office. Immediately, the full female nudes pinned to the walls sparked her rage again. She ripped the images down one by one, remembering each time the man had inappropriately pawed at her or her coworkers. If she had to murder someone it might as well be him. Sometimes people deserved exactly what they got in the manner they received it.

The safe sat under his desk, she was sure of it: she had often caught sight of his half-exposed backside shimmying out from beneath. The old safe was helpless against her newly acquired strength. Inside sat piles of cash, real and fake passports, odd pieces of jewelry and watches. A glint of metal caught her eyes, and she found another set of keys to his brand-new navy-blue Camaro. Rifling through desk drawers, she found his preferred method of punishment: brass knuckles. Many times she had seen the bruises and cuts on men and women alike. It seemed ironic they were engraved with crosses, the name *JESUS* splayed across the knuckles. She highly doubted that the prince of peace, the purveyor of "turn the other cheek," would approve. Nevertheless, she slipped them on her fingers. They were much too big. She would have to grip them tighter.

Nothing of value remained except the souls of her fallen coworkers. She kneeled beside them and said a prayer, crossing herself and asking God for mercy for their souls, forgiveness for the journey she would have to take and the strength to hear his voice when she needed it the most. Maria knew this was the end of whatever life she had lived before. Whatever she was becoming, it was a one-way ticket. Diego wouldn't want her like this. He deserved better. She took off her thin gold wedding band and tossed it into the midst of the pile of bodies.

Maria stuffed one of the unfinished ties into a half-empty tequila bottle and lit it with Big Boss's lighter. Before lobbing the firebomb into the office, she let out one scream, one name with every ounce of grief she had inside of her. "Gabriela!" The name of her unborn if she carried a little girl. This dream was as black as the smoke rising from the inferno she had started.

Maria drove away in the navy-blue Camaro as the factory exploded.

# 2

Adam walked with his hands in his pockets behind the two vampire murderers as they laughed and recounted their kills—these guys worked for Tizoc, overseeing this part of his territory. Adam wasn't a murderer at heart; he was only in the business of making money, just like his father. His sister, Adelaide, on the other hand— had she been here, she would have only encouraged more chaos and slaughter. Having fun with these two and probably seducing Tizoc again. It was her idea, after all, to investigate the narcotics business. Watching humans devour the stuff at parties in her Manhattan and Miami penthouses fascinated her. Not only did she want their secrets, she wanted to control their vice. "The rich are slaves to their vanity and egos while the poor are slaves to their basic needs. We are the true masters, my brother."

But Adam didn't feel like a master of anything. He was a slave to blood and hated himself for it. There was no joy in his life any longer. He wanted more. Of what he didn't quite know. Could vampires have the equivalent of a human midlife existential crisis?

After meeting leaders of various cartels and walking through thick jungle to see the process of drugs being manufactured, Adam wanted no part of it. He'd tried to convince Adelaide to relinquish the ugly, dangerous business, but there was no persuading her. She argued his white-collar crime was just as heinous. Maybe she was right. But it was she who had made him a vampire. Her love and hatred for him. Like the old saying, you can choose your friends but not your family. He would always remember the way she looked covered in blood in the darkness of Tintern Abbey with the dismembered bodies of the priests at her feet. Her malice burned brighter than a torch. That was his last memory as a human.

His final stop on this trip had been to the old vampire, Tizoc, the keeper of the corridor of crime in these parts. This man—not even a man—made Adam's skin crawl, especially when Tizoc had tried to convince him trading in flesh was more entertaining than drugs. He abhorred the lurid Polaroids of Tizoc's "recent stock" and the creature's gloating cruel eyes as he leered at the bound females. Adam had never been in love; however, he had been raised in the fourteenth century with certain values as a nobleman. Maybe if he had experienced colonization like Tizoc, he would be just as twisted and intoxicated with power, with the kill. The conquest had destroyed some part of the old vampire, who had watched everyone he loved raped or murdered. Adam became a vampire with sorrow in his heart when the Black Death raged across Europe; Tizoc burned with rage when he was turned lying in a pile of butchered bodies.

Centuries later, there was no honor or nobility in Tizoc's soul. If Adam valued his own life less, he would have taken great pleasure in ripping the man into pieces to be fed on by the animals of the jungle. Tizoc had insisted his two best agents take Adam to their usual hunting grounds in Juárez to show him some of the perks of doing business with him. Blood from young, frightened and nubile women tasted so sweet. Just grab them by the culo. You could do anything to them. They never saw the vampires coming and, best of all, no one cared.

In these parts—like so many other forgotten places in the world—killing and feeding was easy. The two vampire associates chose their factories at random—it added to the excitement. Tizoc knew all the little men managing the maquiladoras would jump to attention whenever he needed something. No one in his ranks dared disregard his orders.

But to Adam, the whole charade of visiting this bright place seemed pointless. It wasn't like he needed the money, the eighties had made him more cash than he could spend in decades. Adam felt right at home as a vampire in bull markets. He was content to be that shadow in the middle, brokering secret deals and then disappearing with his fistful of untraceable cash. True, he would return to a screaming, disappointed sister in New York, who lusted after the riches and excitement of the drug trade, but she would soon forget after a night of pleasure with any man or woman she fancied.

Once Adam had removed his family name from the slave trade all those years ago, he never looked back. Conning suits and fiddling with numbers was cleaner than the flesh and drugs business—easier. He couldn't kill these assholes he followed into the night, but he *could* return to help the poor girl he just turned—his first vampire. With any luck, she'd make her way to Mordecai and the Keepers. All of them better than he could ever hope to be. Regret had become a suit of chain mail becoming heavier and heavier. He stood for nothing and loved no one. Least of all himself.

The small home Maria shared with Diego was dark and still. Its familiar smell made her want to crawl into bed and pretend she had awoken from a nightmare. There were still many hours before morning, when her husband would greet her with pan dulce and strong black coffee. For now, Diego slept without moving. Maria crept into the kitchen where she could count the money from the factory and distribute it evenly.

To her surprise, she didn't need a single light to see in the dark. The only things she had to contain the haul from the safe were a stack of Diego's tube socks that waited to be put away. She packed each one with cash and tied it tight at the top. It was time to say goodbye.

She watched the man she'd thought she would grow old with sleep with his snoring mouth open and one leg dangling off the bed. These little things made her heart hurt. But now was not the time to hurt. She needed to harden to survive. To him, she would now become one of the many dead or missing, gone long before the seed of life had had time to take root. Girls like her were plucked like growing weeds in the spring and tossed into the wind.

She blew Diego a kiss before grabbing a plastic Fiesta grocery bag. She packed a tape player, her jeans, various underclothes, Diego's hole-filled San Antonio Spurs t-shirt his cousin gave him that acted as her nightgown, and of course the Selena t-shirt Diego had bought her for her birthday.

Before she walked out the door, she spotted Diego's black Stetson. It was a bit big, but she couldn't help taking one more thing to remind her of this previous life, an existence she wanted as bad as cracked earth longs for a storm. She placed it on her head. The way it shielded her eyes in shadow felt right. She was now a shadow. Maria shut the door to a path she felt she no longer deserved. She didn't look back as she darted away into the night.


Tizoc's associates smoked cigarettes next to their truck as they waited for Adam to catch up.

"So where do you want to go next?" one of them

asked. The white paper of their cigarettes had red stains from their bloody lips and hands.

Adam mustered a disingenuous smile. "Sorry to disappoint you, but can you take me to the airport? I have a direct flight back to New York City."

They stared at him with hard expressions and heavy eyes. Gorging on blood had sedated them.

"Sure thing. It was a good night," the one with snakeskin boots said. They tossed their cigarettes to the ground and got into the black Ford.

Adam climbed into the backseat, eager to leave their presence. It reminded him of how he felt when he was near his sister Adelaide. The toxicity of her venom weakened his heart. It was time he became his own man. Fuck his promise to his dying parents to look after her. She didn't need it, or him. His desire to not be alone in this long life had kept him close to her. Not anymore.

The drive was silent except for the radio on low. From the cheers, it sounded like a football match. He glanced at his clothing to see how much blood had spattered on him. There wasn't as much as on the other two.

When they arrived at the airport, he left the vehicle, calling, "Thank you, I will be in touch." Knowing he never would be.

Once the men disappeared into the darkness, he hailed a taxi. When he got into the backseat, he shut his eyes to try and remember the name of the road they had traveled on or the name of the factory. Images flew past his vision.

"Maquiladora Alto!" he said suddenly, with urgency, as his eyes snapped open. The driver gave him a puzzled look in the rearview mirror but pulled off anyway.

As they approached the factory, Adam could see an orange glow in the distance. Either the boss had got to the young vampire first and covered the evidence, or this Maria had indeed embraced her vengeance.

He handed a neatly folded fifty-dollar bill to the driver to continue on, but they were stopped when a police officer shook his head and waved for them to go in the opposite direction. There were too many humans around to make a difference now and he wasn't about to make his life more difficult by leaving a string of bodies to get to the factory.

"Aeropuerto," he said to the driver, who turned the taxi around to go back the way they came.

"Fuck," Adam cursed himself and those devils who did this. He balled his fists until the nails drew blood from his palms. As he breathed deeply to calm himself, he thought of another vampire he knew in Mexico—a woman, a very magical woman—but it was too dangerous for him to reach out with everything that had happened. Her husband had business arrangements with Tizoc; however, it wasn't worth the risk. And speaking to her might bring up old heartache. He pushed the idea away.

His mind switched to New York and Adelaide. He needed a plan to get away from her. His love for his sister had frayed faster in than previous years, and the oath to his father centuries ago to look after Adelaide felt like a tarnished relic, a dying factor of a past that no longer held any meaning. She didn't need looking after—she was one of the most ruthless people he had ever met. And times had changed since the fourteenth century. These days, it seemed no amount of blood, sex or money could bring the slightest of smiles to his face or joy into his marrow. There had to be a way out of the tangled life he shared with Adelaide. As the taxi reached the airport once more, he resolved to seek out the only man who might be able to help him.

Instead of boarding his plane to New York, he booked a flight to London leaving the same day.

Sitting in the British Airways First Class lounge, Adam listened to 'Behind Blue Eyes' by The Who, his favorite band of this century (and his personal theme song, if songs could contain the essence of someone's life). His eyes kept returning to his watch. Now he had made this momentous decision, the wait was borderline agonizing. It felt as if his sanity and future teetered on the tip of a fang. London had called to him for years. His bones missed the unpredictable wet gloom that sometimes made midday look like dusk. Walks through Hyde Park or along the South Bank made him feel at ease with the world. The cold blue sky of New York had become far too bright for him with his fiery sister always looking over his shoulder. Now, as disaster struck and he was filled with remorse, the smallest sense of hope was placed in front of him.

—

Maria wasn't sure how long she drove for; she only knew she needed to get away from people who might recognize her. The harsh Mexican sun was quickly moving high in the sky and she drove with tube socks covering her hands and hat worn low to protect her face.

Finally, she caught sight of an abandoned gas station on the side of the road. It looked like a good place to stop until nightfall when she could organize her thoughts. Parking behind the derelict building, Maria covered herself in a serape blanket left in the back of the Camaro. She had seen the movies; vampires can't go into the light. Mind you, the movies also said that crosses burned vampires, but curiously her little silver and turquoise cross lay around her neck as it had done for years. The gringo last night didn't seem a bit fazed by it, either. Maybe the movies and stories had it all wrong.

Her agitation rose with the temperature as hours passed with her trapped under the blanket. The afternoon Mexican heat was dry and stifling, unlike the crisp mornings. She realized she wasn't sweating, despite feeling every increase in degree.

At two in the afternoon, she decided to turn the car on for a blast of air conditioning, even if it meant the battery might die. She reached for the ignition, trying to stay under the scratchy serape. Short fingers wrapped in tube socks didn't quite grip the key, so, desperate in the stifling heat, she decide to risk removing the sock and going for the key as quick as possible. She didn't want to burn and make this day worse than it had begun.

As a ray of sunlight cast itself against her wrist, Maria pulled her arm back before it could become barbeque. But not even a rash appeared. She pulled the blanket off her head and stuck one finger into the light. Nada. She placed her entire hand into the light. Her mood elevated with this sudden stroke of luck. The movies were wrong. But then it struck her, if vampires could walk in the daylight, how many were there out there? She could be just as she was except for the bloodlust.

Maria jumped into the front seat ready to drive off. She held onto the hot steering wheel. "Where are we even going?" she said to herself out loud. Her stomach growled like a waking animal. She looked down at her belly and touched it. There was nothing in there except hunger.

In the hierarchy of needs, blood had suddenly risen to the top with a nagging bite inside of her. That first feed had sharpened her brain, instincts and physical strength. She had accomplished all she wanted to after the factory bloodbath without even thinking. Now the blood high was slowing down like a sailboat without wind.

For the rest of the day and the next, Maria drove with no destination in mind in a hunger-induced vertigo. She only stopped once to refuel as her body didn't feel the need for sleep. When she paid she kept her hat low and tossed money on the counter. The scent of human blood oozing from the pores of the person behind the cash register made her want to rip their head off their neck. Instead she bit her lip and ran back to the car. Her trembling hands gripped the steering wheel while she fretted how to quench her growing desperation to feed. Her chapped lips and gums ached. She didn't want to kill, despite the physical elation when she did; she couldn't run into Diego's arms expecting him to make everything okay. As her body grew weaker, her mind became ever more desperate as she contemplated her limited options. It dawned on her that this was how thieves are made. She had to steal from a hospital. There was no other way. Hospitals around here had no real security, so how hard could it be?

She had a little gas left in the tank but could use more. She would stop at the next gas station and ask. This was risky because it required her to interact with a human pumping blood that made her salivate. *Think of it as a test*, she told herself.

A wave of relief calmed her racing mind when she saw the tall gas station logo on a sign glinting in the sunlight. She pressed on the accelerator to get there faster. With a quick turn of the steering wheel she veered toward an empty pump. This one had attendants. A man on the right began to clean her front window and the other pumped the gas. She swallowed hard as she fumbled with more cash than was needed. It didn't matter. She couldn't wait for change. The windshield washer moved to her side window. She rolled it down expecting to reach out and hand the man the money. Instead he leaned in close. She licked her lips, his neck in view. His sweat smelled sweet and she wanted to peel his skin like an orange.

"¿Donde esta el hospital mas cercano?" she asked in a shaky voice, trying not to make eye contact or show the teeth she could feel growing the longer he stood there, tempting her with his beating heart and scent.

"Diez millas."

She shoved her hand outside the window with a fistful of money. It made him stand upright again. She clenched her jaw, wanting to cry out or drain them both. The other attendant must have finished filling up her tank because he now stood next to the window washer counting the cash. Before they could thank her, she left on squealing tires, leaving a plume of dust in her wake.

Ten miles. She only had to make it ten miles and there should be a sign, like for most hospitals.

A few minutes later, she saw it. She tried not to drive too fast as she followed the signs to the staff parking lot at the rear of the building and pulled up. Now it was time to wait until after dark, under that scratchy, smelly serape so no one would notice her. Maria prayed someone would come out for a smoke break and leave the door open. For now, she closed her eyes. Not consuming the two gas station attendants felt unnatural and had taken all her energy and self-control.

# 3

When Maria rewound the tape of memory coiled in her mind, she could just see her grandfather's half-built little house she and her mother had shared with him, her auntie, and sometimes her uncle, who showed up when he was in between jobs or luck. If not for this house, they would have been homeless once her mother had enough of her father constantly disappearing into another woman's arms, rolled-up joint or bottle of tequila. Years of her mother's sobs behind closed doors or slick promises slithering out of her father's lying mouth had become tiresome for them both.

From the age of six, Maria stayed far from their fights after watching her father push her mother into the bathtub while he was high or drunk, demanding sex. These two angry strangers scared her as they viciously tore each other to pieces with their words. She didn't understand what they were saying, only that she wanted no part of it nor be the cause. It finally took a severe miscarriage that left her mother in the hospital for two days to be the sign it was time to move on for good. Just one child was enough for Mrs. Muñoz. Sometimes her mother made Maria feel she was too much work with not a lot of reward, as she was a precocious little thing who looked just like her waste-of-space father. Maybe she would have been better off not having Maria. Mrs. Muñoz also had no tolerance for daydreamers, and Maria was a chronic daydreamer.

This feeling of not being wanted fully sunk into Maria's consciousness when she was about eleven and she realized she was all but forgotten about in her mother's daily routine. The impending threat of raising a teenager loomed over Mrs. Muñoz, and it seemed she didn't like it one bit. Maria felt like another body just passing through the small unfinished waystation of a home that the family liked to joke was their version of 'Heartbreak Hotel'.

Maria often wondered what drunken fumble or sweet nothings had brought her parents together to create and keep an accident they seemed to never have wanted at all. What spectral hand had aborted her mother's first pregnancy at the age of sixteen but passed over her? At least her parents tried to make a go of it for a few years, she supposed. But during the sporadic times she saw her father after the separation, Maria was always left with disappointment and growing indifference. He usually had bloodshot eyes or smelled of tequila, and was with a different sancha on every occasion. Their meetings were awkward with few loving, warm thoughts coming to mind when Maria tried her best to hug her father.

His smell, his sense of entitlement when seeing her, his hand open for *any spare pesos for her dear father*— it all tasted like rotting food in her mouth. How these countless women could stand the sight of him was a mystery to Maria. He possessed as much charm as a scorpion. By the time Maria was fifteen, he didn't bother calling anymore, and Maria didn't seek anything from this empty man with nothing to give.

Maria didn't mind making her way to and from school alone. It was all she knew since she could remember. She would daydream through lessons to ward off the boredom. She daydreamed about what she would do when she was grown and where would she go. Would it be like the stories on TV or the glamorous photos in the magazines her auntie left lying about? It didn't matter as long as she wasn't miserable, without love like her mother. Sometimes she would do her homework, but no one cared to ask if it was completed by the time she went to bed. What good did school do for anyone they knew? School cost money and time. It didn't put food on the table or gas in the car or provide water on a hot day.

Maria's mother worked in the local bakery, taking as many shifts as she could get, which meant starting very early and long hours. When she returned home she didn't have the energy for domestic matters or the chitter-chattering of a child. Mrs. Muñoz wanted to watch her telenovelas and sleep before she had to get up and do it all over again for a meager paycheck that still left the fridge mostly empty—except for the twenty-four pack of beer waiting to be consumed.

The shining light in Maria's life was her great-abuelita on her mother's side. Maria would race to her house with excitement to make homemade tortillas and listen to her chatter on about life. Until Abuelita was quite old, she ironed clothes and made Christmas cakes in used coffee cans for extra money. There was always a warm smile on her face. She gave Maria her silver and turquoise cross to keep her close to God and family. It was her abuelita who also gave her an illustrated Bible to ease her insecurities and fear at bedtime. "Whenever in doubt, Maria, just pray. It doesn't matter where you are or what you have done. Your voice matters." Abuelita always knew how to banish the monsters. In the end, God blessed Abuelita with ninety-nine years on this Earth. Maria was eighteen when she said goodbye to her.

When not going through the motions at school, Maria played with her friend Rita, who lived next door. Maria found the transition to living with multiple family members in a crowded house difficult at first. Someone was always getting up for work or coming home. All at different times of the early morning and late night. Everyone's possessions took up space in the closets and on the floor, giving the house a claustrophobic feeling. When she learned that a little girl the same age lived so close, Maria took it as a sign for good things to come. She felt grown up, coming and going with no supervision. Sadly, that first venture into independence became spoiled when the older cousins of her best friend would visit. The youngest one, a twenty-year old ranch hand nicknamed Paco, enjoyed teasing Maria and took every opportunity to pinch her twelve-year-old rear. He would stick out his tongue and laugh with a leering smile. The smell of lukewarm beer, cigarettes and body odor made Maria feel sick when she passed them in the front room. Maria had a strange fear when those man-boys were around. She could never quite understand what that unshakable shiver down her back meant.

The last time Maria walked into that house the cousins were playing cards and drinking. Maria and Rita dashed into the kitchen for cold sodas to take outside. As the refrigerator door opened, an overwhelming stench of raw meat blasted their faces. On a plate lay a skinned goat head with its eyes still open in their sockets and a purpled tongue hanging out from between its teeth. Congealed blood and fat pooled around the severed head. Various other animal parts surrounded it in sealed containers ready for cooking. Maria stumbled back against the wall and screamed in fear. The cousins let out a roar of laughter.

Rita smiled. "Mother is going to boil it then shred the meat later. She says the head has the most flavor. Don't be scared. We'll save you some."

Maria wanted to burst into tears. Instead, she ran out the door before a hand could reach out and grab her backside. She returned to an empty house. All she wanted was her mother or anyone to hold her and tell everything was okay.

As Maria aged, friends came and went and year after year the faces she knew best dropped out of school. There was always a good enough reason to drop out, especially when the lure of cartel money was so strong. The only motivation for Maria to finish high school was to escape her mother's home. It was school, or find a crappy job for crappy pay, or work with her mother in the bakery.

After graduation, nothing worthwhile came along, so Maria had to make do. Standing side by side with her mother at the bakery, the daydreams of her youth evaporated second by second. Mrs. Muñoz assured Maria those aches and pains in her fingers and back would go with time. Maria prayed to Jesus she would never just get used to the arthritic cramps of kneading dough. Maybe it was her imagination, but she could swear her mother wore a satisfied smirk of *I told you so* whenever Maria slipped on her apron. In those bakery days, she felt as small and weightless as sieved flour.

The only satisfaction of the bakery job was handing out the leftovers to the local children. She loved watching their little faces light up at this small act of kindness. Mrs. Muñoz would suck her teeth and ask why she didn't at least charge them a few pesos. Her mother's greed incensed Maria, making her desire to leave even stronger, despite not knowing how or when. The kids loved it when she would call Mrs. Muñoz *Bruja* behind her back, then pretend to be a witch as she chased them around.

Maria hoped to discover some talent to take her away from her lonesome, banal existence. She danced around her bedroom listening to Selena's upbeat music, imagining what her life could be like. Selena brought childhood magic back into her mind. Most of the popular bands in Mexico at the time were all male. Selena was different. So different to Vicente Fernandez, for sure. Mrs. Muñoz would chastise her for thinking there was ever any other way for them.

"If you don't want to survive, Maria, then just leave and see what becomes of you. Who do you think you are? You think it will be as easy as *María la del Barrio*? That is a TV show and this is real life. There's no rich uncle to take you from this landfill, now or ever."

Maria started to believe she was right. She felt she wasn't very good at school or anything else. But then her abuelita would reassure her. "Your destiny will appear when it is needed most. Not just for you, but for others as well."

The sun was finally setting, creating enough darkness to give her cover in the shadows. Maria could feel the tiny veins in her eyes start to throb; grave hopelessness scratched beneath the surface of her skin. Cloying hunger and memory mocked her at her lowest point. She couldn't wait any longer.

As she walked toward the hospital, a male voice called from behind her.

"You lost? You don't look like you work here."

Maria continued walking with her head down, afraid of some man calling to her in the dark. She felt suddenly ashamed—she hadn't washed or changed her clothes in days.

"Wait, slow down, honey, you want to score? You look like you need it bad. I can help you out, for a price, of course. I take payment upfront."

The male voice was close behind. She could smell him and hear his heartbeat. Before she could quicken her pace, his breath was on her neck as he grabbed her hips. Maria tried to summon her new powers and wriggle free, but in her starved state she had none of the strength she had used on Big Boss.

"Why you fighting? You should be used to this, you junkie bitch."

As his heartbeat became louder she could feel herself begin to change. Her desire to feed blinded her to all else. The man grabbed her around the waist and pressed a sweaty hand over her mouth. Big mistake. She bit into the fleshy part of his palm. Liquid relief quenched an angry thirst. Almost instantly, she could feel the gears of her brain and body start to move again.

The man screamed out, not expecting any fight from this easy target. He tried to pull his hand away, but her fangs were metal claws caught in his flesh. Using his free hand, he punched her hard in the torso. This only caused Maria to bite down harder. His blood belonged to her.

He fell to his knees. The blood flow from his palm was insufficient for her hunger so she let him go but, before he could recover, his wrist was in her mouth. Her strength grew with every free-flowing gulp. Her heartbeat, which had been a feeble pitter patter, now roared between her ears. Breasts which had been sore from preparing to feed a child now tightened around the nipples, flush with blood. She rolled the liquid sustenance in her mouth, caring little for the dribbles coating her chin.

Her nostrils flared, as she recalled he had just called her a bitch. *Who's the bitch now?* she thought while crushing the bones in his other hand with one knee. The sound thrilled her. The blood brought her close to orgasm as it rushed through her body. Every sensitive part of her had become engorged with it.

Maria's meal was still pumping blood when her now-acute hearing alerted her to the back door of the hospital opening. She dragged the man's body behind the darkened line of cars and continued to feed. For a singular moment, she understood the men back in the factory. This thirst was like a black hole, all-consuming, ready to drag everything and anything into its body without question or concern. She felt no pity or heartache while she fed, only the revival of her flesh. And it tasted *good*. The warm syrup had all the sweetness of a prickly pear with the spice of roasted chilies. There wasn't enough to fill the pit in her stomach. The tap was dry.

Maria looked at her dead prey and her bloodied clothes. She realized this was her second kill—she had ascended from thief to murderer in a matter of minutes. Digging her hands into her hair, she whispered, "What have I done?" as she tried her best to compose herself. *He was trying to assault you. One less predator*, she told herself. How long could she go on like this—loving the feed but hating herself afterwards? But this was who she was now.

The voices outside the hospital disappeared. Maria assumed they had finished their cigarette break and gone back inside. Pools of blood had gathered in her white canvas sneakers; they squelched with every step back to her car. She had once seen a horror film called *Carrie* about a girl covered in blood by a bunch of mean girls at a party. In her mind, this is what she looked like. Before reaching the car door, she caught her reflection in the window. She wasn't far off.

Maria glanced back at the body, then looked at herself again. The need for answers was all that mattered now. She had to find the gringo and she had to find him *now*. What exactly was she? Who was she? She covered the front seat of the Camaro with the serape and drove off, satisfied in body, with her mind and soul feeling like shattered bone in a bag of skin.

Maria drove a few miles to the next town, identical to the last one, to clean up as best as possible. She planned to find a market in the morning. She found a quiet park with public bathrooms and a water fountain in front of it. Once changed, she tried to sleep outstretched in the backseat but found it impossible. Sleep seemed a distant memory. A restlessness refused to leave her body or her mind. The fresh blood invigorated her. If only the dogged questions tormenting her would stop. Perhaps she could rest her eyes, if only for a moment. The exhaustion of trying to understand her transformation was relentless.


Hours later, the morning sun warmed her eyelids while breaking a deep meditation. The blood rejuvenating her cells in the sunlight made her feel as if her soul might burst through her skin to a place where all her questions would be answered. Despite not sleeping, she was fresh with a renewed strength in her body. The market would be open soon.

As she drove closer to the center of the town, she looked at her reflection in the rearview mirror and realized dry blood had matted her hair. Her feet felt sticky. She hadn't thought to bring another pair of shoes when she left home: her blood-soaked sneakers and socks would have to be thrown away. She would have to walk barefoot. Fuck it. Any vestige of caring what people might think as she passed was long gone. She parked on a side street and removed her shoes and socks before getting out. She followed the aroma of humans to the market. Each step on the scorching pavement was painful without shoes to protect her feet.

A woman with cataracts and deeply grooved brown skin sat on the hard ground selling candles. Maria thought of her dead great-abuelita. What she wouldn't give for five minutes with her now. She folded a one-hundred-dollar bill into the crepe-paper hands of the woman and decided on a red candle with the burning heart of Jesus. Maria needed all the help she could get.

She scanned the various stalls in vacant recognition. *Where do you even begin to look for a ghost?* She had killed the Boss, burned down the factory. All that was left was the stolen, macho-ugly car. *The car!* A mustard seed of hope tumbled in her belly. Something that was lost had been replaced with an unseen guide when she needed it most.

Two stalls away were boxes filled with secondhand shoes. The car could wait because she couldn't carry on picking stones and glass from the soles of her feet. Peering inside the boxes, she found they all contained shoes that were too high and impractical or not her size.

As she was about to leave, she spotted a pair tossed aside on a table, as if the sacred heart had willed her to find them: steel-toed square black cowboy boots with a buckle around the ankle. She fell in love with these boots as she inspected them. The leather felt worn but tough to the touch; a hard knock on the toe reassured her the steel was still intact. Before she would have passed them with an admiring eye but wouldn't have dared to wear them as she knew Diego wouldn't approve. She remembered how vulnerable she felt the night before. These boots were a perfect match in size and attitude. Today was a new day, with no Diego or anyone else to offer their opinion. Maria had her new secondhand boots and Jesus; now to find some answers. She headed back to the car.

The unopened trunk of the car stared back at her like they were in a Mexican standoff. Her trepidation over the unknown future was crippling, so she held her unlit candle to her chest and prayed in the dirt. Then she took a deep breath and pulled open the trunk. Pornographic magazines, which she tossed in the bushes, empty tequila bottles, a full tequila bottle, spare tire, car jack. Nada.

She returned to the driver's seat, dejected and frustrated. One hand held the candle; the other clutched the full bottle of tequila. Maria opened the bottle and took a large gulp, which she hoped would take her tears down to the bottom of her bowels. Instantly her stomach seized from the liquid as if a cocktail of bleach and acid had been poured into her system. Throwing open the car door, she vomited the yellow stuff out. Instantly all was better. New vampires and booze didn't mix.

It was better this way. Whatever path she was on required a clear head, without alcohol-induced mistakes. As she had learned growing up, only regret was found at the bottom of a bottle. She needed Selena. The tape player she took from home had fallen to the floor of the passenger seat when she parked. As she reached down, a small, crumpled piece of paper lay next to the headphones. Was this her Hail Mary? The unfolded note read:

> T called. Monterrey boys coming up for a little fun before the guest heads back north. Make sure you leave after they arrive and clean up after they're gone. Don't disappoint him.

"Monterrey," she whispered. Something felt right. God did have time for sinners. Maria started the car and drove out of town toward the highway.

# 5

Maria arrived in Monterrey in 1995 without a single clue where to start her journey or what form that journey would take. The little motel on the side of a desolate road was supposed to be for a few days, but days became weeks and then a sign appeared in the registration office looking for a maid. She grumbled at the appearance of the wanted sign. *How typical.* But her money wouldn't last forever. This job would only be for the short term. How come the most temporary situations required the most temperance?

When Maria felt in utter despair, she lit a sacred heart candle and prayed even if she didn't quite believe anymore that something existed out there. It was a good story to tell herself. The thought of wandering into some convent and throwing herself on the sisters' mercy crossed her mind more than once. Maybe that would illicit some reaction from some god. But there was always something little and nagging saying, *No, that isn't the way. What if you are wanted,* needed *for more.*

In her worst moments, Maria wondered why she was spared. What the hell was that Englishman thinking? Every day felt like a pointless exercise in breathing. Those solitary sleepless nights alone in her motel room stretched her patience. All the harsh words spoken to loved ones, all the mistakes, all the emotions that drained from her body along with her blood, swirled like a greasy dark cloud in her mind night after night. Drowning herself in a bottle wasn't an option, as she had found out parked on the edge of the market. There was nowhere to hide as a vampire. Every thought and emotion drove itself clean through her heart until it emerged from the other side.

For months she cried herself to sleep in Diego's t-shirt, trying to take in the last of his scent. She would live a life of celibacy to forever preserve what they had shared. As time went on, as it does with or without our consent, little scales started to form over Maria's wounds. She only had herself, and her mission to find her creator.

To satisfy her hunger she resorted to animal blood, bought in secret for double the price from a local butcher. It kept her alive and strong enough, but she could tell the synapses in her brain didn't react with the same luminosity that human blood gave, and her body felt slack. Hope dwindled with every shit-ringed toilet or cum-stained sheet that greeted her in the mornings, waiting to be cleaned. In this time of purgatory, she saw managers come and go, the angel Selena murdered for no good reason, technology change in ways she never thought possible, a Black President in the States, talk of a mighty wall being built—but Maria stayed the same. She would catch her reflection in the mirrors of the bathrooms she cleaned. Not one gray hair or any crow's feet around her eyes. She had something in her blood people would probably spend good money to have—if they were okay with taking lives.

She felt she might as well be in a coffin riding out the years. Birthdays, holidays and New Year's Days came and went without fanfare, because what was the point of marking a day in the year that meant something to everyone except Maria? She wondered if anyone brought her empty grave tamales and rice on Día de los Muertos.

The first time Maria ventured into a church was one Christmas, when the agonizing pill of loneliness lodged itself particularly deep in her throat. The crucifix had no effect on her, so maybe God would strike her down for entering his house as this thing she had become. Nada. Her death wish was met with silence. Perhaps *that* was the sign—everything could be considered a sign. God didn't care or didn't exist. Maybe God was a vampire too.

After that first Christmas, Maria continued to go to church. Watching people kneel in prayer or light their candles made her feel like she was a part of something bigger yet unseen. She wasn't the only desperate soul yearning for a voice, a change, a hand to provide some salve to her burning questions and heart's desire. God didn't drive her to Hell; there was only the feeling that she was right where she needed to be as much as she disliked being there. Maria couldn't understand or explain the little crystals of confidence that sparkled when she closed her eyes to rest.

But Maria needed more than prayer and cleaning up after others. Eventually, her restlessness kicked her brain in the ass to finish what she'd started. She made a pact with herself to become fluent in English, so she could confront her maker in his native tongue when she finally met him. At least this new goal was bite-sized and in her control. Maria devoured everything and anything she could get her hands on in English. Her higher education came out of the secondhand stalls at the market, ranging from random years of torn *National Geographic*s and dog-eared *Cosmopolitan* magazines to Stephen King books and raunchy romances, which made her blush, to musty-smelling encyclopedias on all there was to know inside and outside of Mexico. When an old VHS player cropped up, she took the opportunity to watch as many American films as she could find still in VHS. *Revenge of The Nerds* was a great distraction when the desire to give up hardened like lead in her bones. For the first time, Maria owned a library card and used it regularly. Loneliness was not so painful with a book nearby.

She started scouring the newspapers for crime

stories. Eventually the internet made the job of searching for anything that seemed impossible or couldn't be explained easier. Not a single detail could be taken for granted. The world Maria learned about as she became more connected was both sordid and fascinating. Maria had no connection to anyone, but she could peek into the lives of people not unlike herself all over this big world she was just discovering. How the hell was she going to find one gringo vampire in a world of billions? The depressing weight of the impossible task drove her from the library on to the streets.

After work, Maria spent her nights walking the through the town with her hands in her pockets and oversized hat worn low. Every male face gave her a little twinge of hope. *Maybe the next one: all it takes is one familiar face from that night. If you exist, God, guide me to the face that will unlock the next door.* She sat for hours in the local bars, pretending to sip the same bottle of Coke until it turned to warm syrup. If the factory demons were like her, they would look the same as they did all those years ago. Same night, different bar, same outcome. Nada. It was now 2019 and she still searched.

One Saturday, her only day off, morning came and Maria felt like she had rested on a bed of cacti. She lay on her back, telling her body to get up, but her mind wanted to stay right where it was until something, *anything* would happen. Jesus's sacred heart was at its last little flame from burning all night. She would have to buy more. Maria had also finished her latest stack of English and Spanish reading material. That should have been enough reason to shift her out of bed, but it wasn't. That Saturday morning was a dark prickly morning without the small comfort of coffee.

She told herself, "Five more minutes, Maria, then ya!" Then she finally summoned the ganas to move with the thought of her great-abuelita encouraging her. Maria didn't want to make any more excuses for herself. The busiest market day would provide some distraction to her frustration.

The market was heaving as usual. She still wore her old Selena t-shirt, but she had removed the fraying sleeves and the image of the now-deceased Selena had long faded. Today a man with telenovela good looks passed out fliers. He handed one to Maria. The flier advertised the use of boxing equipment, private tuition and a small ring for sparring. An image of a large fist with the word FIGHT BOX on the knuckles caught her eye, along with a picture of Oscar de la Hoya and a masked Lucha wrestler wearing all white with angel wings on the back of his white boots. The word ANGEL was on his belt. Maria wondered if the wrestler was this same guy who handed out the fliers because he had a tattoo of the Archangel Michael slaying the Devil on the side of his right calf. The tattooed man called out to Maria as she wandered past, moving more slowly than the rest of the dusty bodies bustling through the market.

"Come check it out with your man."

"I don't have a man, and I don't have any money." Maria handed the flier back and moved away.

He jogged up next to her. "I hope you don't mind me saying, but you look like you're searching for something that can't be bought at one of the stalls."

This made her stop. She turned and looked into his eyes. He appeared tired, soft bags hung under his eyes. "I could say the same about you."

"You wouldn't be wrong. I'm not too proud to admit there aren't enough hours in the day to make a new business work and this business *has* to work. It won't be long before I'm out of dreams and cash."

"You want help with your business?" she said, none of her previous defensiveness in her tone.

"Are you looking for a job? I just need a bit of washing, tidying up, checking in clients when they arrive, the basics to keep everyone coming back."

Her momentary feeling of hope evaporated, and the frustration returned. "You mean women's work," Maria sneered. She could feel her vexation about to explode on this poor unsuspecting hombre.

The man laughed. "Are you calling me a woman? Not that there's anything wrong with that—I've been doing it since I opened. It's difficult to be out here looking for customers and keep an eye on the place. I can't pay a lot, but I have a spare room if you need somewhere to live rent free."

Maria considered this random stroke of change, sudden and unexpected like the proverbial thief in the night; however she wasn't exactly sure how to receive it. She looked at his face, trying to decide if she could trust him. His expression had the expectation of a young fighter, but his eyes were worn like those of someone who had been through many defeats. Yet he still hadn't given up. Like her. She hadn't given up on life. She figured there was nothing left to lose because all was lost twenty-two years ago. Since then, not much had changed. Maria didn't get creep vibes from this angel fighter, either. Her one prayer centered around getting out of that bedbug-infested motel.

They stood there in silence, others going about their business around them as if they didn't exist except to block the main path. Both of them seemed to be searching for a way forward in their lives. Maria's dynamite was diffused a little. Maybe it was time to take that leap of faith.

"No questions when I come and go, and no going through my belongings. I am also not interested in any romantic ideas you may have."

His eyes lit up and a large grin spread across his face. The man offered his hand to shake on it. "We have a deal, then. My name is Jorge. Your business is your business and my business is all that matters to me."

# 6

Maria pulled up to the gym after closing as Jorge had requested, so he could spend time showing her around. As she walked in, the reek of sweat and dirty laundry hit her. Even though it hadn't been long since the grand opening—based on the sign outside—everything seemed to be held together by duct tape. The center was dominated by a ring with a red mat and black ropes. To the left were rows of punching bags, speed bags and a pile of jump ropes. The back of the gym had a mirrored wall consisted of various machines stacked with weights. Free weights on a shelf lined the furthest corner.

Jorge fiddled with a boxing glove in a box. "Glad you made it!"

"Thank you. This is some place."

"It's all I have in this world and it means a lot to me—hopefully others too. My vision was for this to be a gym for the people. I do my best to keep the place together because it's my wife and my baby."

"How did you get into boxing?"

He smiled as his gaze crossed framed photos on the wall. "I've always been drawn to sports. I was told I had the physical build to succeed at most things if I tried. My body and brain were hardwired to move in perfect coordination. Boxing and wrestling were my favorite from my first lessons at five years old. But you get older... my dream was to make it into the showbiz kind of wrestling that would offer fistfuls of money for fast cars and women, and enough to provide for my entire family to facilitate their dreams to flourish, too."

Maria understood this. Youth makes possibilities seem as limitless as the Mexican sky over the desert. She walked over to the photos to have a closer look. They showed the highlights of his career. One showed him winning a match, holding a large belt over his head. Blood streamed down his neck from beneath his mask. Another was with a group of wrestlers dressed in full costume and masks. It was a pageant of bright colors and muscles on show. He wore the same costume as the luchador on the flyer.

Jorge followed her. "Promoters and coaches all said I was going to make it big. *Jorge Machado—The King of Lucha Libre*." He chuckled, but the smile didn't last long.

"What happened?" she asked.

"In the end it only took one dirty fight to end it all. Nothing is immune to corruption, including entertainment... That's when I got my Saint Michael slaying the Devil tattoo, to cover the scars from my shattered leg. The hours upon hours the tattoo took didn't compare to the post-surgery recovery. I lay bedridden for weeks wishing I could disappear. I had so much shame. I thought I wasn't so special after all, dropped by everyone but my family."

Jorge's story moved Maria. The pain in his voice was palpable. "But it looks like you have done alright. You made this dream happen. And that is a great tattoo."

"Yeah, it's a reminder that I overcame the worst disappointment in my life. The doctors said that, by the look of my knee, I was lucky to still walk with little pain. The money I saved from my short career I used to buy this place along with some secondhand equipment I found along the way."

They stood in silence for a few moments, staring at the wall of photos. Then Maria placed her bag on the ground.

Jorge noticed. "Enough about me. Let me show you where you will stay. My father and brothers helped me build a little two-bedroom casita by the side of the gym—so much for fast cars."

"You don't know where your path will lead you."

"I suppose not." He exhaled and grabbed her bag.

She went to follow him but stopped in front of the elaborate stereo on a wooden bench near the kitchen. "This is a nice piece of equipment."

Jorge's face lit up. "That's the most expensive thing in the entire gym. My second passion is music. In another life

I would have started a band… not a soft one like Menudo, but a stadium-filling, groupie-attracting explosion of rock like AC/DC, Def Leppard or Led Zeppelin."

She shook her head and smiled. Maria liked this Jorge. Despite his broken body and dreams, he had picked himself up and vowed to make it one way or another.

Maria spent the days making sure Fight Box smelled more like cleaning supplies than sweat, singing along to Guns N' Roses' 'Sweet Child o' Mine' or whatever she or Jorge decided to play. She fixed equipment by hand or searched the flea markets for cheap replacements. A few of the regulars tried to chat her up, shirtless and sweating; it only took one of her *don't mess with me* looks to make them think twice. They respected Jorge, so they gave her the same respect; besides, she didn't look like the "up for a fun time" kind of girl. Maria dressed plainly for comfort while working and didn't bother with makeup.

Instead of a smile, she greeted them with a little nod. It wasn't long before Maria oversaw the collection of gym fees. The punters knew they couldn't sad-talk or bro-talk their way out of payment. When Maria approached you with an upturned palm, you paid.

Only the street boys got in for free. She might have been a vampire, but the cartel was the worst blood-sucker of them all. How she hated those rats. Maria and Jorge agreed: better they mess around in the ring, instead of the pushers looking for new clients or small hands to deal their poison. Maria would pass the boys a few pesos for extra work she pretended to be too tired to do. Although it wasn't much, it was the least she could do. If only she could do more.

The little girls thought it was funny that she worked in the gym. It was a tough smelly place for a pretty lady to be working at, with mostly men. Maria handed out sweets when school was finished, and the girls would grab a rag to help her to clean up to the music that filled the gym from open to close. Sometimes they would braid her long hair with ribbons in the traditional folklorico way. No one left without knowing who Selena was or her importance. God rest her soul—Selena's memory still brought warmth to Maria's heart and tears to her eyes. Anyone who dared to strive for more deserved that honor.

In the little girls she saw the daughter she longed to meet. Of all of them, she had become closest to Esmeralda. She was only six years old, but her brown eyes with little wisps of hair between her brows gave the child the look of a soul much older.

Esmeralda had started tagging along to the gym with her father, Carlos, when she saw Maria there. Her mother worked at the launderia in the evening so she would sit in the corner of the gym with a few books and her only doll. It was a fuzzy Monchichi with patches of shorn fur and a missing arm which she cherished with all her heart. Maria enjoyed the company of the inquisitive girl who wanted to know about everything faster than Maria could answer.

A double portion of animal blood kept Maria's hunger at bay, even when someone bled in the ring. She didn't want to take the chance of lashing out in hungry desperation. What Maria didn't want to admit was there was still a creeping urgency to find her gringo creator. The longer she waited, the more animal blood she needed. Her strength was still greater than a human, but the aches and pains were settling in over time.

One day Esmeralda came in as usual, but wasn't her usual sunny self. A large red welt protruded across the back of her leg. Carlos dragged Esmeralda to a bench and sat her down forcefully with a menacing look in his eye. "Don't you dare act up on me tonight. You hear? Just like your mother," he spat as he walked away.

Maria watched from behind the kitchenette door. Her belly twisted, and she could feel the points of her teeth growing. Maria closed her eyes for a count of five, *Lord give me the strength,* before taking a leftover concha to Esmeralda.

"You okay, mija?" Esmeralda's heartbroken eyes pulled at Maria's soul. "Eat this. It's sweet, just like you."

Little Esmeralda brightened a bit and wolfed down the pastry. Small flakes of sugar coated her face and mouth. They smiled and laughed together as Maria dusted Esmeralda's face.

Carlos sparred with another guy in a ferocious rage. He didn't just fight; he taunted his opponent, trying to coax a response. His rival wasn't biting so Carlos declared himself the victor before tossing his gloves at Maria's feet.

"Let's go, Esme. We need to pick up your mother." The little girl waved goodbye with her big beautiful eyes.

Maria followed Carlos with a snarling stare. Her eye caught Jorge's: he was watching her. He came over to her.

"He is not a nice man, and he works for men who are even worse, but it's none of our business. If anything, speak to Conchita first," he said, quietly.

Without thinking, Maria threw the hardest slug she could manage at the nearest punching bag. The bag flew horizontal in the air, breaking the chain. The few people left in the gym glanced toward the commotion without much interest but Jorge stepped back, stunned, his eyes wild and his mouth forming a big smile.

"Maria! Whoohoo! That was incredible."

Maria was astonished by her own strength, even without human blood. Then she panicked that Jorge might wonder how she was capable of such a feat. "I'm sorry. I'll pay for that."

Jorge inspected the chain. "Don't worry. It was rusty anyway." He looked seriously at Maria. "What you need is direction."

Maria shot him her one of her famous *back off* looks. She didn't take orders.

He held up his hands, not wanting to follow the flight of the bag. "I mean, technique. You have a lot of power, woman, you just need to learn a bit of technique. And don't apologize for showing what God gave you. None of these hombres would, and you got more power in one fist than their entire bodies!"

Maria could live with that. She looked at her fists and remembered the reclaimed brass knuckles, thinking how satisfying it would be to put that Carlos in his place.

"When do we start?" she said.

After the gym closed, Maria and Jorge got to work. He reinforced the punching bag with one of her flea market finds of scrap metal, bolts and double chains. Then Jorge sat next to Maria with wrist wraps. "Let's start with your right."

She watched intently as he showed her how to wrap her hand. When finished he wrapped the left. "Now we get to the basics of footwork, different punches. Then speed drills, your defense, and something a bit fun—the jump rope."

She felt slightly overwhelmed but was ready for this challenge. It invigorated her with purpose. Jorge showed her a few moves then stopped to watch her repeat it.

Maria's fast vampire mind sucked the knowledge in with a speed she didn't anticipate. When her body moved, it felt natural, like she had done it her entire life. She relished this side of being a vampire.

This didn't go unnoticed by Jorge. "Wow, I'm

astonished. You've never done this before? You're better than I ever was."

She stopped and flashed him a smile. "Determination."

"I would have said a great love gone wrong—or pure hate."

She didn't want to tell him her secret, but she felt this was true: most people were a simmering cauldron of both and everything in between.

From then on, after Jorge went to bed, Maria spent hours at the speed bag or with the jump rope. When lost in their rhythm, she found she could think. She borrowed an old iPod from Jorge and spent her nights listening to Stevie Nicks, Santana, Kiss, David Bowie, The Ramones, and Heart. As if skipping promised to bring her closer to the answers she sought, she jumped to 'White Wedding' by Billy Idol until she could feel the skin on her toes break. Her eyes focused on a creased poster of Apollo Creed with his dukes up, telling her to keep going. Training became her prayer in which she searched for a plan to find her vampire creator.

Maria had needed to drink even more animal blood since she started training. Her body needed to recover from the exertion. She paid the butcher triple for his silence and speed in providing her meals. It took up most of what she earned at Fight Box, but was worth it.

It was a Thursday night when Esmeralda ran into the gym, her face dirty except for the trail of tears that streaked her cheeks. Maria embraced the little girl to calm her enough to find out why she was in such a state.

"Mamá!" Esmeralda screamed.

The little girl, hysterical with fright, pointed to the door. Maria knelt and quickly inspected the little girl's body, to check if she was injured. Fresh welts slashed the back of her legs.

Jorge touched Maria's arm. "Don't even think about it. It's none of our business."

Maria shot him an angry look. She stood, meeting his eyes and gritting her teeth. The taste of copper laced her mouth from biting her lip so hard. Something dark and vengeful pulsated inside of her. It sizzled like water on a hot cast iron comal.

"How bad does it have to get before it is our business?" she hissed. "Nobody, I mean *nobody*, tells me what to think or do!"

She led Esmeralda into her room and tucked her into bed. She held her hand and looked into the little girl's eyes.

"Your Mamá will be okay. Stay here until I come back." She kissed Esmeralda's forehead, then grabbed her +*JESUS*+ knuckles and wrapped her left hand. With steel-toed boots and black hat in place, she walked out the door before Jorge attempted to halt her. They both knew there was no stopping her.

Maria ran toward the house little Esmeralda had told her about when they first met. All she could see was Carlos. Without feeding beforehand, she worried about the level of self-control she possessed. She wanted to teach Carlos a lesson, not slaughter him. Then again, a man who lays hands on a woman or child gets whatever comes his way—just like Big Boss. The idea of consuming human blood stoked the already blazing furnace in her heart. Maria smiled, welcoming the dark cloak of righteousness as it took take control. This was no time to feel guilty.

Maria arrived at the house to see fighting through the curtained window. The two bodies looked like shadow puppets at war, with the argument loud enough to be heard from the street. Maria approached the scene with a belly rumbling from angry hunger. One kick knocked the door off its hinges.

Conchita's left eye was already puffy, turning a shade of violet; her clothes were torn and spotted with blood from a split lip. Complete surprise came across Carlos's face at the sight of this tiny woman in a big hat at the entrance of his home. Maria ran toward him hitting him fully on the jaw with *+JESUS+*. Blood sprayed from his mouth as he fell onto the coffee table. A steel-toed boot kicked him in the side. Maria wasn't afraid to kick a bully while he was down. In fact, for a millisecond, it felt as if all the stars and planets were aligned and the world had been set right. All the bruises and broken bones of her coworkers and friends, all the stories of missing, abused humans flashed in her mind as she kicked him again. It felt good to lose control.

He cried out in pain, trying to guard his face with one hand.

She paused so both of them would remember this moment. The fear in his eyes made her want to hurt him in ways he would never forget.

But in this intoxicating moment of revenge, she didn't notice at first as Carlos reached for the back of his jeans. Then, she caught a flash of metal and instinctively swiped at the gun barrel to knock it from his hand. A shot rang out, and a shock of pain made her realize the bullet had hit her. She glanced at her thigh to see a small hole through her jeans and flesh. The sight incensed her. When Carlos saw the thick red veins in the whites of her eyes, a high-pitched cry escaped his mouth and he dropped the gun. Her dusty black boot pummeled the weapon in one stomp.

Maria brought her nose within inches of Carlos's whimpering face. She wiped the blood trickling from his lip with her fingers and licked them to reveal gleaming white fangs. How irresistible the umami of fear mingled with blood tasted on her tongue. The experience was intoxicating. Frightening. There was no limit to what she could do to the helpless humans in the room. Moving closer to the scent of blood, she glimpsed her turquoise cross reflected in a shard of broken glass. The story of a weak and hungry Jesus and his temptation by Lucifer in the desert brought her back into herself. She didn't really believe in the Devil anymore; however, she did know evil. What would innocent little Esmeralda think?

"You listen to me, and you listen real good, hombre," she snarled. "Get your things and leave. You're dead to this family and dead men don't come back. If I get so much as a whiff of that chickenshit machismo, I will do more to that pretty little pout. Comprende?"

Maria smelled ammonia. She looked down to see Carlos had pissed himself from fright. He nodded his head, scrambled up and limped out the door.

Conchita fell to the floor, grateful to be alive.

"How can I repay you? Thank you!" she cried.

But Maria wasn't looking at Conchita. She replied distantly, "You can thank me by not asking for forgiveness and don't give that piece of shit a second thought. What he did wasn't your fault." Her stomach moaned as she looked at the trail of blood Carlos had left behind. As much as Maria had wanted to drain his black heart of every drop of blood, he was still Esmeralda's father and fathers were sometimes hard to come by. Maybe one day Carlos would seek Esmeralda's forgiveness. Maria would not be the one to take that opportunity away. She'd made the right decision to not kill him. But she realized she had given away her secret in the heat of the moment. She could feel Conchita looking at her as if she could read her mind.

Conchita rose from her knees and walked into the kitchen, returning with a knife and coffee cup. Slashing into her palm she squeezed blood into the vessel. Then Conchita raised the cup to Maria while bowing her head like an ancient priestess offering a sacrifice for a good rain.

"What are you doing?" asked Maria.

"I am not afraid of you. You are not of this world. Let me thank you with a sacred gift—lifeblood."

Maria couldn't turn away this remarkable gesture. She needed it. She cradled the cup in gratitude, drinking every drop. Conchita crossed herself, whispering more prayers to the heavens. As she finished, Maria clasped Conchita's bleeding hand.

"Esme is at my place. She is safe. Rest and get your home together. I will bring her back tomorrow."

Conchita wrapped her arms around Maria. "Your secret, your dark magic, is safe with me, mujer."

"Thank you for your kindness."

Maria left swiftly, striding into the night.

# 7

Jorge paced the gym when Maria returned. He stopped and looked at her disheveled state and the wound on her leg.

"Are you okay? What did you do, Maria?"

She smiled in sly contentment while looking at her blood-soaked, wrapped left hand. "What should have been done a long time ago." She walked past Jorge into the bathroom to clean up.

It had been so very long since Maria had tasted human blood. Since she'd torn into the man who tried to attack her at the hospital. In the moment she'd felt sorry for taking his life. Not anymore. And she didn't feel bad for kicking the shit out of Carlos. As she showered, hot water bounced off skin that had regained its collagen. Strength returned to her body and the wound in her leg completely closed. Thighs touched in their fullness, regaining lost power. The arms that worked all day and trained all night became chiseled with muscle.

There was a thickness to her hair that wasn't there before. Every cell inside her body tingled with a song of hallelujah. Human blood, even small amounts did more than that of an animal.

Refreshed, she changed into Diego's threadbare San Antonio Spurs t-shirt, which would soon be cut up for cleaning rags. Esmeralda shifted when Maria gave her a kiss on the forehead. Maria made a bed on the floor with spare blankets. As she lay there watching the young girl sleep, she thought of what her life would have been like if that fateful night in the maquiladora had never happened. Had Diego really been the one after all? She felt confident and full of power, more than she had ever in her life. And it wasn't because she could rip a man to pieces. It was because she had the power to choose. Conchita offered her blood to her like she was a god. And compared to ordinary humans, she was.

She closed her eyes and thought of Diego. A life that was not meant for her, but that had shaped her.


The day Maria met Diego was still a vivid memory, unlike the blurred patches of her parents' existence. Her mother's car had broken down again and they began to suspect their usual mechanic was purposely not fixing it properly so they would continue needing his business. Maria found a new garage and decided to go herself. Maybe she could sweet-talk a discount.

Tejano music blasted from the garage's speakers as

men worked on vehicles. Maria approached the first mechanic she saw, wanting to get this over with. There was no reason to feel shy, but she did anyway. The man was hunched over the open hood of a car wearing a thin tank top translucent from sweat, his mechanic's overalls were pulled down to his waist. Black grease covered his hands and defined forearms. Maria mustered what confidence she had to speak to him.

"Excuse me, I need a little help with my car. It's at my house and won't start. Is anyone available to have a look?"

The man lifted his eyes toward her soft voice. He was a few years older than her, but still handsome with thick black hair and a light stubble covering his face. Maria continued to feel self-conscious as he looked at her.

"How about you give me your address and I'll come by after work? I'm Diego."

Maria wrote her name and address on a scrap of paper for him and then walked toward the bus stop. She didn't dare look back as she felt him watching her leave—at least, she hoped he was watching.

Diego kept his word and got to work on their car that afternoon.

"You need a new part, not just running repairs. That's why it keeps breaking down. I've got extra parts at home and can come back tomorrow after work."

Maria was afraid of this. "How much will it cost?"

Diego rubbed the sweat and grease off his forehead. "I don't think I can do it for less than two beers and dancing on Friday night."

Maria wondered if, without warning, someone had switched the sun's heat to maximum scorch. Her cheeks felt slightly sunburnt. "No, please, I have to pay for something."

"A date with you is payment enough. I can always make money, but I don't always meet a pretty girl like you."

Maria's heart fluttered with flattery at the thought of a date with this man she found herself attracted to. He seemed strong, hardworking, confident; his good looks didn't hurt, either. Everything her father wasn't.

She wore her best-fitting jeans, boots and a loose blouse with just a hint of her sexiest bra peeking out. The Selena red lipstick accentuated her mouth, causing her mother to give her the glare of someone who had swallowed a jar of pickle juice. Only loose women with trouble on their mind wore that shade of red. Maria was past caring what her lonely, bitter mother thought.

Diego picked her up in his refurbished black vintage truck that looked recently cleaned and waxed. He was a different man: shaven, smelling like cologne, dressed in his best with boots shined for a night out. Mostly, she liked his black Stetson.

He looked at Maria, then her clothes. "Baby, with a body like that you should be in a dress, or at least a skirt."

Maria wasn't sure how to react. His words were the tiniest of stings like a quick vaccination to the arm. "I don't really own many dresses or shoes to go with dresses."

Diego smiled and placed his hand on her thigh. "Never mind. You're still gorgeous. Let's have some fun."

They spent the evening drinking and dancing at his favorite dance hall. His cumbia was perfect with not a single misstep. His large belt buckle pressed into her belly as they danced, hips so close as he took the lead. Diego listened to her every word, his eyes never straying from her face. He paid for everything. When the music stopped, he invited her back to the house he owned.

Maria already knew what this would lead to. This night was unlike any other dates before tonight. Her first few sexual experiences with boys were exciting to start with, only to finish with her wondering what all the in-between class gossip was all about. The boys were left on a bug-eyed high after the chance to look at her breasts. Maria didn't find their greedy hands or slobbery mouths pleasurable in the slightest. Her mother's harsh words didn't help: *Don't you come back to me ruined, Maria. There are enough putas in this world.* Those words played in her mind as she walked out the door. Mrs. Muñoz thought by not talking about sex it wouldn't happen, leaving Maria's knowledge to come from TV or schoolyard chatter. Maria hoped it would be different with a real man like Diego. *He* was different.

Slightly drunk, she stumbled out of her jeans and into Diego's bed. She became tense with the realization they had been dancing. What if she smelled funny? Did she remember to shave her legs? What if he wanted to

72

do things she had never done before? How could she pretend to enjoy it if she didn't? She smiled, hoping he wouldn't notice any of the insecurities that punctuated her thoughts on pleasure.

"Just relax, you will love this." His hands were gentle as he undressed her. Diego wasn't slobbery or too eager in his desire. She relaxed her body, telling her mind to *cállate already* so she could feel the things all the girls at school talked about, but had never happened to her.

Diego and Maria were never apart after that first night. When his shift finished early on Friday nights, he liked to go dancing. As his lady, Maria needed to look the part, too. He took her shopping for dresses and shoes only to be worn for him. Once, when they were out with friends, *his* friends. She told him she wanted a hat like his.

"Baby, why you want to hide those beautiful eyes from me? Men wear hats."

Maria thought maybe he was right. She didn't want to be mistaken for a man. She was his woman, after all, and there was nothing she wouldn't do to keep it that way. Diego did allow her to buy any lipstick she adored. Maria still loved a deep red like Selena. But at home or at work she wore white sneakers, jeans and little to no makeup.

The life they were creating together made Maria feel loved, cared for, like she was wrapped in a downy cloud of comfort. Maria was living a Selena song when they were together. There was nothing Diego overlooked when it came to her. He never raised his voice or hand, or demanded anything of her. He was a man who had to be in control, never drinking more than two beers at one time. Diego only made sure Maria knew what he wanted and what made him happy. She obliged, knowing he would come home to her every night to compliment her cooking or how clean the house was.

The sex was as exciting as an unflavored raspa. Maria couldn't let him know the only way she could orgasm was with herself, when the shyness and worry of imperfection didn't exist. A friend from the bakery instructed her in a low whisper during a lunch break how to do it in the bath or shower. At first, Maria was too embarrassed and ashamed to want to feel such things. Her body wanted something else.

When Maria summoned the courage to explore every soft corner between her legs, it took longer than she expected to feel pleasure rather than think about pleasure. She explored until she found the right rhythm and pressure along the engorged ridges of her slick insides. She closed her eyes, allowing a little rope to wrap itself into a tight knot until she let go, allowing her body to be awoken by a cataclysmic rumbling of unearthed joy. Maria finally knew what the talk was all about. She couldn't wait to try everything and anything with Diego. All those doors of self-discovery were large enough for the two of them to explore together.

When she tried to introduce her hand during love-making, Diego brushed it away. "That's my job, just relax. I know what I'm doing." Maria was determined to make it happen naturally with Diego, but gave up after she failed to orgasm, and he asked, "Is there something wrong with you? I know women's bodies and I'm doing everything right." His words stuck to her like thick cactus needles. She flopped around in bed all night, worrying he would leave to find someone better, more experienced, prettier. *Is this why men leave?* So instead she would pretend to feel ecstasy and enjoy how he held her afterwards. What they shared was bigger than screams and moans. All that was bullshit to make the telenovelas exciting for people like her mother. She would forgo the pleasure of someone's body for the comfort of someone's arms. It seemed she would be the keeper of her own pleasure from now on. Diego had taken her from her mother's home. She owed Diego everything. Her father probably didn't even know where she was now.

Three months into the relationship, Diego proposed. After a Sunday morning of lovemaking he brought her black coffee, pan dulce and a ring on a plate. Maria nearly knocked over the coffee when trying on the band. She didn't hesitate to say "yes" through her tears of a prayer finally answered. There would always be someone to run home to.

Mrs. Muñoz was less enthused about the marriage; any union was probably doomed at some point. Their kind of life could be hard, and hard lives didn't make for lasting love. Love was *never* enough. She told Maria to work a bit longer before becoming pregnant. That would be another world of worry. But Maria ignored her mother's unsolicited advice and skepticism. Diego carefully laid out their life like he did her outfits on a Friday night. He made life easy for her. At least her mother gave her a guide to the kind of mother she wouldn't be. Maria knew she had a lot of love to give and a family was her heart's desire.

Neither of them saw the point of a long engagement so the wedding was a month later. Maria spent all her savings from the bakery to make herself into the perfect bride for the perfect husband. Her mother made the cake as a wedding gift; Diego's favorite dance hall hosted the reception; Diego's extensive family paid and prepared the food.

After the ceremony Diego's mother, Matilda, took her aside. "You need to eat enough in these coming weeks. A lot of women want to be so skinny to look good in jeans, but you want to be ready for babies. A honeymoon baby is a sign of good luck for a long, happy, lasting marriage just like mine. God blessed me with four sons and good health. Dreams do come true for people like us."

Maria could only smile. She knew Matilda meant well; however, something stirred inside of her causing unease. Had she moved too fast? In the distance she could see Diego with the friends she didn't like. Some of them were in a gang called the Culebra Kings—CK for short. They had been friends since they were kids and he didn't want to break ranks with them. The Culebra Kings were the first name that came to mind with any local crime. Diego knew too much about them to make them enemies, but also liked to have their support if needed.

The wedding night was like any other night. Maria cried next to the kitchen window watching the clouds cover the moonlight. This was the beginning of the rest of her life, yet it somehow felt incomplete.

And then the dream changed, like breaking clouds allowing a small crescent of blue to peek through. They couldn't afford a honeymoon so, on Maria's birthday, Diego bought tickets to an upcoming Selena Quintanilla concert. Maria jumped around the house with wild screams when Diego presented her with yet another surprise. She spent the weeks leading up to the concert making sure everything was just right in their home to show her appreciation. She felt dumb for doubting it. The beer was cold and the lovemaking as frequent as he pleased.

Maria sang until her voice went hoarse. Nothing else existed during the concert, not even Diego. Selena oozed beauty, power, confidence, talent, and heart. Every note Selena sang was like she was singing for her alone. Her infectious smile made Maria feel like anything was possible. If Maria could be anyone, it would be Selena.

Somewhere between beer-filled plastic cups and fevered dancing, a mirage of what life could be like in the States appeared. The strobe lighting hit her like a thunderbolt of ambition. Delirious with hope, she wondered if she could find her way there; go back to school for hair or cosmetology or learn how to create the beautiful costumes Selena wore on her enviable figure. She wanted a little stage of her own. Until the concert Maria had settled on the idea of making a home with Diego, with him at the top of the table. She would have to find the courage to pull the tablecloth from the table without disturbing the dishes.

The following day she brought up the idea of moving. "I want this, my love. Let's start our life afresh. Mexico will always be in my heart but watching Selena sparked something inside of me."

By the way Diego stabbed at his food against his plate while refusing to look at her, Maria could tell he was not happy. "Maria, my family is here, my friends are here, my job that provides us with enough to live is here. What more do you want? You want a baby? Have a baby."

"I do. Not here. I know nowhere is perfect. But I want more options. The news is bad. The economy. Who knows when things will pick up?"

Diego chugged his beer and left her to cry over the meal she had run home to prepare.

Later, Maria lay wide awake in bed feeling unsure of herself. Diego placed a hand on her shoulder.

"Hey, I'm sorry about earlier. I drove to Marco's house to see if he could get you a job at one of the factories. The pay is better than the bakery. Plus, he knows a guy who knows a guy who can get us across the border."

Maria turned toward him. "Those factories are dangerous."

"Well, if you are asking me to leave everything behind, I'm not leaving without everything I earned over the years. You'll have to pay for us to get there."

"You don't think I'll do it. Do you?"

He gave her a soft smile and stroked her head. "No. Pretty and quiet girls like you want a nice man and an easy life. You need me to tell you what you want and need. I think you need to see for yourself how foolish it is getting ideas in your little head."

The sensation she felt on their wedding night returned. She had no choice but to prove him wrong. But first she hoped the wave of sickness she had been feeling lately would go away.

"Fine, Diego. Believe what you want. I'll take the job."

# 8

Maria's reverie was disturbed by Jorge and Conchita talking with Esmeralda in the background. She was almost afraid to see them. What would their feelings be in the light of day?

Maria lifted herself from the floor to find out if this was the day she moved on. When she opened the door, the three humans turned to her.

"There she is." Esmeralda ran to Maria. "I was telling them how you are my best friend and you're going to save the world."

Maria cleared her throat with a sudden inability to form words.

"I wouldn't say the second part, but I can be your best friend."

Conchita and Maria exchanged glances. Despite Maria knowing she could trust Conchita, the previous night had been a jumpstart to her dead heart. Something inside of her had shifted and nothing would ever be the same.

It didn't take long for whispers to circulate that there was a new enforcer roaming the streets at night. No one knew if she was a demon or an angel, or perhaps a mythical mix of both. Maybe the woman in the black hat was one of the old gods who wandered this land before the lash of the cross was introduced. The only thing anyone knew was that no human could run from their devious deeds if Maria and her fist caught you in their sights.

More and more women around the town bore a scar across their palms. They were a sisterhood who protected Maria's identity. A small blood sacrifice was what they had to offer in gratitude. The institutions people were supposed to rely on were crumbling, corrupt farces. Maria was more than satisfied to trade hope for blood.

The women and occasional man would wait until the gym closed for the evening before approaching Maria with their stories of injustice. Without a word she would guide them to the kitchenette then shut the door behind her. Jorge would glance in her direction, then look away to find some task to occupy himself. She knew his experience was that people who asked too many questions or didn't recognize their station didn't last long: that's why he remained silent. He didn't know that the guy who usually came around for his "business tax" hadn't bothered to collect for months because she'd broken his right knee as a warning to stop coming around the gym.

Conchita started spending more time at the gym with Esmeralda and decided to take Maria up on her offer to learn self-defense from Jorge in case Carlos tried to return. The two seemed to work well with each other. The night Maria burst into their house, Conchita had confronted Carlos over his treatment of Esmeralda. This time it meant leaving him for good. It was one thing to slap her around; it was something else to touch the only thing that mattered to her in this miserable world. As her words reached his ears, it didn't take long for his rage to reach his fists, and it didn't take much for him to overpower her. Conchita agreed to train because she didn't want her daughter to grow up feeling scared or hopeless. Conchita wanted to raise a fighter, a problem solver; a woman who would never give up.

When not righting the wrongs of this corner of the world, Maria would lie in bed listening to night sounds, trying to will the universe to provide a way forward, some clue to the devil who made her. The conflict between leaving to continue her search and staying to help those who had no power continued to torment her.

One night, frantic knocks bombarded her bedroom door. When she opened it, a bloodshot-eyed Jorge stood next to a larger, older version of himself.

"Maria, you have to help," Jorge cried, his face gray with worry. "They've taken my niece, Sofia. She's only thirteen! She didn't return from school today. Her friends said she left them at the corner shop to go home just after five. My sister-in-law is too distraught to speak so she sent my brother Ernesto here. The local women told her to come to you."

The man with Jorge looked even more distressed. Without speaking, Ernesto unwrapped a ceramic bowl and pulled out the large bowie knife holstered to his belt. He slashed both palms, squeezing until the veins in his arms and neck bulged. His laser gaze looked past the ceiling and screamed the most grief-stricken cry Maria had ever heard. She knew this pain: that sense of cavernous loss and longing. She had made that very same cry the night life was given and taken from her. No daughter would be lost tonight—or any night, as long as she had fire in her veins and power in her fists.

"What are you doing, brother?!" Jorge looked terrified and confused.

Maria knew she couldn't keep her secret from Jorge forever. She grabbed the bowl to chug the sweet blood juice. Immediately she felt small red veins in the whites of her eyes swell. Jorge's eyes widened when he saw the little points protruding from Maria's mouth.

She looked at the spent, pale father while grabbing her black hat. "What else do you know?" she demanded.

"It was the Culebra Kings... sometimes they are called the CK."

Maria's heart stopped. But she couldn't think of her past or Diego now.

"Keep going."

Jorge placed his arm around his brother as he began to cry again. "I'll tell you what we know, Maria."

The Monterrey CK was the local gang who ran the streets as part of the larger Culebra Kings cartel. They drove around town with music blasting from open windows in oversized shiny trucks with even bigger tires. The Kings would call out to girls they admired as they drove around. Held hostage by their fear, the girls couldn't ignore them nor give them attention in case they stopped and came calling for you. It was this same gang that took protection money from the small business owners, provided the town's many poisons and kept the veins of vice open across this part of the country.

The gang hung out at a go-go bar on the outskirts of town called Zuma Zuma. Maria decided she would start there and see where the trail led.

Jorge wrapped her left hand and gave her his leather jacket to make her appear larger than she really was. Maria also pinned her hair in a braided bun to conceal she was a woman. Before she left, Jorge pulled her aside.

"I knew you were different, but I never believed someone like you existed. I mean, I don't care what you are because you have given hope to so many. I've seen the faces of those who sit in my kitchen. More than that, you have been a good friend to me. Thank you and be careful."

Maria hugged Jorge in silent appreciation, feeling their friendship solidify. She didn't feel any surge of expectation for herself; she only hoped to rescue this innocent girl.

Jorge and Ernesto entered the kitchen and lit a Virgen de Guadalupe candle. The glowing heart of the Virgen de Guadalupe was the only light in the building and their whispered prayers the only sound. Ernesto gripped his rosary between clasped hands, causing blood to trickle from his palms onto the crucifix, forming a small pool on the table.

Maria pulled up to the bar. The music and laughter resurrected images from the night of her terrible transformation. Before entering, she took a deep breath, kissed her +*JESUS*+ brass knuckles and ran her fingers over her turquoise cross. She silently pleaded, *For the love of whatever is good in this world, please be alive.*

Her oversized hat sat low as she entered the rowdy bar, allowing her to reach the rear without being noticed. Heeled, dancing feet on podiums either side of her guided the way. Strobe lights cut through smoke that burned her eyes, reminding her of Rita's house with the butt-pinching cousins. The crowd thinned out as she neared the restrooms, giving her room to breathe.

Once past the first door she could see large boots and an even larger belt buckle dead ahead.

"Hey, where you going? You passed the bathroom, hombre," said a husky male voice.

Maria raised her head and flashed a wicked smile.

"Who you callin', hombre?" A knee to his groin followed by a single punch from +*JESUS*+ put the man out cold. *That was too easy.*

No one had noticed the commotion in the corridor. With the strength Ernesto's blood had given her, she pulled the man into the bathroom, pulled his jeans down to his ankles and sat him on the toilet.

Now it was time to see what was behind door number two.

To her surprise, the previously guarded door opened with ease. A large, stern-looking man sat behind a desk. His body was tan and well built: his bare arms were sculpted muscle and the outline of his chest could be seen from under his thin white tank top. He had the face of a king with a square jaw, high cheekbones and a narrow, hooked nose pierced with what looked like bone. Deep almond eyes stared at a glowing iPad. His glossy black hair was worn in two long braids with a folded bandanna around the forehead. She could see thick red veins in the whites of his eyes. Long bark-like nails clicked the screen each time he swiped against the glass.

*He couldn't be.*

His eyes moved from the iPad to Maria's face and then body. As he rose from the chair and walked round his desk, his frame dominated the room. He wore faded jeans and a turquoise belt buckle in the shape of a snake, and snakeskin cowboy boots. Even in casual dress, he carried himself like a man of regal birth.

"It's nice to finally meet you. You're a wanted woman, you know." His voice was deep and sultry. Each word measured. This was no ordinary man from the streets.

Maria searched for words as her brain moved from one thought to another faster than she could speak. This wasn't what she expected.

"You know who I am?" she managed at last.

He frowned and walked closer to her. His height was substantial and he had to tilt his head downwards when he spoke. She could smell the blood in his body beneath the hint of aloe vera on his hair and skin. It couldn't mask the sour vampire blood she didn't want to consume.

"Well, I knew there was a rogue vamp since the incident at my brothel in Monterrey. I didn't know it was a woman—a very beautiful one at that. I'm Tizoc." He offered his hand.

Maria shuddered at the memory of that night. But she felt no remorse. She looked at his turquoise-ringed fingers with suspicion, deciding not to take his outstretched hand.

"Maria."

He brought his hand back and folded his arms across his chest. "How old are you, Maria?" Seeing her confusion, he added, "I mean, when were you created?"

Maria had to think about a number that no longer mattered.

"1995. I was only twenty-three when…" Her voice trailed off, remembering that second birth again.

"You're a pup! But created at the perfect age. You will forever be fresh, firm." He let out a low, growling laugh as he moved even closer. "I'm nearly six hundred." He gave her a smile that showed just enough teeth and looked more beast than human. The point of his nail found its way to her crucifix. "You prefer the new gods, I see."

Maria stepped back before his finger could move any lower.

"What brings you here today, little pup? Are you already lonely? There comes a time when we all seek our own kind."

She walked around the office, searching for any obvious clues and keeping her distance. Maybe this man could lead her to her creator. The walls were bare save velvet paintings of the tragic legend of Popocatépetl and the famous *Dogs Playing Pool*.

"I'm looking for two people."

Tizoc's interest was clearly piqued. He returned to his desk and leaned on the edge as though waiting to make a deal they would both benefit from.

"Do you know a gringo vamp?" she continued. "Dresses sharp, handsome, wavy light brown hair, blue eyes? He might keep the company of two Mexicans or South Americans."

Tizoc gave her a secret smile, like he was already pleased with the outcome of his next move. "There are only two I have met like us that might qualify as gringo. One, an ancient named Mordecai, and the other named

Adam. But they haven't been here for years. Adam is English and Mordecai... well, he probably fell from the sky or sprouted from the ground. It's been centuries since I've seen that worm. Why do you want to know?"

She ignored this question as it suddenly dawned on her that Tizoc might be *T* from the note in the Camaro. She also remembered her creator had an accent. Maria kept calm, knowing she had to contain her excitement. Poker face, it was called.

"I'm also looking for a girl. She's only thirteen. I think the boys that hang around here might have taken her."

He walked back behind the desk. There was his deal.

"We trade in girls. We have clients, orders to be filled. If I give you this girl, what do I tell my clients? Before you know it, everyone will want their girls back, then I'm out of business. Besides, wasn't it you that shut down my brothel? The superstitious idiots who survived were too afraid to reopen, fearing the devil would return, and the girls believed an angel had saved them. They refuse to work and don't touch any of my product anymore."

Maria didn't bother to disguise her disgust. She felt her feed rise from her belly. "I don't have time for filthy, drug-dealing, slave-making traffickers. Tell me where she is."

In turn, he didn't bother disguising his own malicious indifference, making her warm blood cold. She could tell this man had seen death and suffering, and cared little about either.

"I tell you what, little sister. Let's make a deal. I will see if I have this girl, but you have to promise to quit your little vigilante act. The women of this town bear your scar."

Maria's eyes widened and her previous calm vanished into fear. Tizoc seemed to read her like tea leaves.

"Oh yes, that is what made you known to me and *only* me. A little do-gooder too afraid to go in for the kill. Instead, they whisper about you like you're some God-sent saint. A real-life Jesus Christ for them to worship and give them hope in this shitty world. I didn't make it this long through dying civilizations, invaders and wars—without one eye always on the peasants. If you'd made me wait any longer, I would have found you myself."

Maria let out a soft *huh* while looking at her brass knuckles, before returning Tizoc's hate-filled gaze.

The girl was alive and she could be found.

Maria threw herself toward the hulking warrior, knowing it would be a fight to the death.

With the element of surprise, Maria knocked Tizoc from his chair onto the ground. Two solid punches contacted his face as she straddled him, until he overpowered her by lifting her up by the sides of her arms. He threw Maria down next to the desk, pinning her to the ground by the shoulders. His nails dug into the dirty carpet as he sat bestride her, trapping her body in a cage she couldn't escape.

As his knee pressed against her crotch, she could see

his jeans tighten around his growing cock. His strength took her back to the night she became a vampire: then she didn't have the strength she did now, but this ancient vampire was *very* strong. Maria couldn't fight the pressure of his grip and it was beginning to hurt.

Despite the pain in her arms and between her legs, she noticed he wasn't increasing his violence. She silenced her panic, not wanting this demon to get any kicks from her incapacity. He would never get the pleasure of her tears or her body. She relaxed her muscles and asked God for a way out, any small crack she could break through.

Tizoc's fangs were long and the spider veins in his eyes began to grow. "Don't make me hurt you. We should be lovers, not enemies. Don't you see, we will own this world soon enough. It has been deemed by the feathered serpent himself. Now, if you promise to play nice and be mine for as long as I please, we can forget any of this ever happened. You can even have the girl as a gift from me. There is so much time for our kind to fill."

Tizoc buried his nose into Maria's fallen hair. He smiled and whispered, "Be mine, Maria the Wanted." He then took her bottom lip into his mouth with a sensual tenderness that didn't match the viciousness of his eyes. His hands slipped down her arms and to her breasts.

Maria felt the sacred heart burning bright inside of her; this was her chance. Maria kissed him back, tasting a hint of his sickening blood.

Snapping back to her disgust for this vampire, she

drew his attention to her lips and slowly eased her brass knuckles directly under his chest. Maria's fangs grew, puncturing right through his lips and tongue. Tizoc roared in pain, jerking his body away, chunks of his tongue flying into the air.

Taking this sliver of a chance and using every ounce of strength, Maria thrust her brass-knuckled fist into Tizoc's chest. Bone scraped her skin before hitting his organs. Her fingers felt around like a claw to locate the one thing he needed as much as his head—his heart. The organ beat against her palm as she curled her hand around it. The wetness of his blood excited her as much as the thought of ending his life. With one hard squeeze, she yanked the organ from his chest. His eyes looked at her in horror as she lifted his heart in front of his face.

"This is mine now, asshole."

Tizoc fell backward with a heavy thud.

Maria got to her feet, holding the still-pulsating heart from her hand. His blood smelled repulsive, unlike that of humans—another curious fact to her. The taste of his blood was also of something that had been long decayed and left for the maggots. He may have survived six hundred years of change, but he couldn't survive Maria's will. She stuck the bloody muscle back in his chest and wiped her hands on his shirt.

Knowing time was not on her side, she rifled through the desk, looking for any clue about the missing girl. In a drawer she found keys, an invoice for watermelons, customs papers and a large stash of rolled-up cash.

The oddest find in the pile was a business card with a shooting star and bold black lettering: *DIABLO'S, Acapulco's finest Tequila and Dancing*. It could be nothing or it could be everything. She grabbed a brown leather tote hanging on the door, dumping the contents on the floor: a glittery bikini, impossible lucite heels and a ruffled red dress. She kept the dress and left the rest, packing it with the contents of the desk, including Tizoc's iPad.

As Maria turned to leave she realized there was the small detail of the large vampire's dead body. If anyone wandered in, they would immediately raise the alarm. This gigantic man wouldn't fit anywhere where he wouldn't be found, and she couldn't take the body with her. The only exit was a large window. Maria wrestled with the catch and then hefted and rolled the body outside into the wild thick bougainvillea that crawled along the walls of the building. There were dumpsters in front of the wild bush that would also provide some cover.

Maria then frantically tried put the room back to a normal state, using her t-shirt as a rag to clean the blood spatter. Her sense of urgency turned into panic as she followed Tizoc's body out of the window and stepped on his bulk. She glanced around before kneeling in the dirt next to his head. Her will was all she had and it had to be enough. She balled both fists and looked at them before hitting the ground. The punches created a small crater. Using her remaining strength, she hit the dirt again and again to make a bigger hole. It was big, but not big enough to bury him. She snapped off a large branch from the bougainvillea and used it to dig faster and deeper.

Soon she had a shallow grave. She rose to her feet and tugged on Tizoc's arms to drop him inside. With quick kicks, then on her knees with her hands, she covered the body. As a human that would be impossible. And in that moment it hit her that maybe she was meant to be more than a human. Now she had to use that strength to find Jorge's niece.

The young woman could be anywhere or in transit. Once that happened she might be impossible to find. Or, in the worst-case scenario, she had already made it into the hands of someone who wanted to harm her. The thought stoked Maria's fury.

With parts of the body still visible, she covered him with dry leaves and flowers. Not a twinge of remorse pulled at her heart. He didn't deserve any better. Not really. How many fallen women from his vile business were disposed in the same manner? Maria remembered the fear and exhaustion in the eyes of those who came to her for help and the stories on the internet that made her leave the library in a slow burning rage.

She closed the window behind her and zipped up the leather jacket to hide her blood-splattered, dirt-encrusted body. God must having been taking prayers that night because, as she turned to walk away, she saw a large truck with a smiling winking sun parked behind the bar.

The logo on the truck matched the invoice she'd found in the desk. She remembered the keys she'd swiped from the office. She fished around the bag until she felt them, then walked toward the cab and unlocked the door. A quick search didn't tell her anything of value, but the little mustard seed stirred inside her belly telling her not to give up. She made her way to the back and pulled open the heavy double doors. A blast of suffocating heat enveloped her body. Boxes of watermelons were stacked inside. Unsatisfied, Maria jumped into the metal oven. Behind the boxes, she found fifteen girls huddled together, faces stained with mascara, tears and sweat. Maria's fists clenched when she realized the sick bastards that did this hadn't bothered to leave water for these women. She searched their faces. Some appeared dehydrated and puffy-eyed from crying. All looked exhausted, but otherwise unharmed. Upon the sight of her, the ones closer to her moved back. She looked like she had been dragged through Hell's graveyard, all covered in blood and scrapes. Her hair was a tangled mess.

"Is there a Sofia here?" she called out gently. A small hand waved from the back. The girl slowly moved closer to Maria. From the shadows within that truck, Maria could see she had a resemblance to Jorge and his brother. "Your dad and Uncle Jorge sent me. Stay by my side. You don't know me, but I'm taking you *all* home."

"Wait. I think I have heard of you."

Maria turned to a voice coming from her left. A woman in her mid-twenties rose to her knees.

"What have you heard and what is your name?" asked Maria.

The women spoke to each other in hushed tones. Maria could hear the desperation and fear. She couldn't blame any of them for not trusting her.

"Consuelo. My neighbor came over one evening to speak to my older sister. I thought it was just gossip, but she spoke of someone who liked the dark and made bad people pay in exchange..." The young woman stopped.

"I will not harm you and I expect nothing from you. Let me take you from here."

More whispers from the crowd.

"I trust you," said Consuelo.

"So do I. My uncle is a good man."

Maria scanned the back of the truck. It broke her heart. "Can we go now?"

Heads bobbed, giving her the go-ahead.

"I will close this door again, but don't be afraid. I promise you will be safe."

Maria drove the truck to the closed Fiesta supermercado in town. She couldn't believe she'd outwitted that old vampire who didn't deserve another breath. More importantly, she had done what she set out to do and found another clue to follow. *So close, speak to me, show me, I'm ready.*

Maria opened the doors once more.

"I only have one phone, so everyone make a call and make it fast. Sofia, call your father first."

Each girl received a stack of cash while they waited to be collected in the parking lot. Mothers, fathers, sisters ran to the truck and into the arms of their missing loved ones. Each family handed Maria a glass bottle. By the end she had a box beside her stacked with soda, milk and beer bottles filled with blood. She made sure to clasp each of their bandaged hands as thanks for their token. Before they left, Maria made a makeshift sign with the word *FREE* and propped it on the boxes of watermelons. Sofia and Maria would return to the gym on foot, so Maria left the truck in the parking lot with the keys in the ignition. Someone would take it sooner or later.

Except for a small flickering light, the gym was dark. Both men were still in prayer as they entered the dim kitchen with the Virgen de Guadalupe candle at the end of her life.

"Papá!"

Ernesto looked up from his blood-caked rosary. "Mija!" Father and daughter embraced, Jorge joining in too, while Maria watched. She felt a sense of peace descend as her head spun from the night's activities.

Even though she had a box filled with vessels of blood, she forgot to drink after the fight. Maria's eyelids drooped and her legs could no longer stand the weight of her body. She collapsed to the ground. Jorge ran to Maria first. Ernesto tried to squeeze his fist, but nothing came out. Jorge grabbed the knife from the case attached to his belt to slash his palm, urging Maria to drink. Maria began to come back to life. Jorge slashed the other palm and held it to Maria's mouth once more. She took what she needed without greed and closed Jorge's hand. "Thank you."

# 9

Maria lay in bed the next day. She knew it was time to go. It felt too soon to move on, but she had to leave before someone started cracking skulls to find her. The boss always had another boss and so on. A six-hundred-year-old vampire going missing would be questioned by whomever he worked with. She also felt a pull to find other vampires. They couldn't all be bad. Her creator's eyes had told her that.

As she made preparations, Maria guessed Jorge could hear her stumbling around. He probably suspected the inevitable. She gathered her meager belongings and cleaned the room until it looked like no one had ever been there. Except maybe a ghost. She slipped on her sleeveless Selena top and jeans. It would take Selena and a prayer to leave her little family.

A soft knock on the door realigned her thoughts back into reality. Jorge stood in the doorway, unshaven, with bags under his eyes from the emotional exhaustion of the previous night. He looked past her at the half-filled box and leather bag.

"I know you have to leave. Can it wait until tonight? A few people want to say goodbye."

Maria gave Jorge a sad half smile and nodded. What difference would a few hours make? Jorge was a brother to her and a friend. She'd watched him struggle with his perceived failure; she wanted him to succeed, to find love and, when he's old, to think back on their time together as a good memory. He was her unexpected angel, offering a safe haven when she needed it the most. He'd given her the tools she needed to fight all the things she thought were wrong in this world.

Someone thought to bring the Camaro back. It would have to be packed for a road trip that might not have any end, if it survived that long. She had had multiple parts replaced in all the years she had been driving it. By some miracle, the car was still on the road.

Jorge and Maria spent the day passing each other in silence, ignoring the clock as they busied themselves in their usual tasks. When she finished cleaning the kitchenette, dusk had just begun to settle in. Time always moved faster when all you needed was for it to slow down. The few customers were ushered out early by Jorge with the promise of free hours as compensation. Maria looked out the window to see small dancing lights approaching the gym. She ran to the front door, grabbing her brass knuckles from her back pocket, worried this might be her reckoning. But Jorge was already greeting people. The gym was soon filled with the familiar faces she had helped during her time in Monterrey, holding multi-colored candles adorned with saints. The gym transformed into a church.

Esmeralda broke from the crowd and hugged Maria. Maria stroked the little girl's hair, tears filling the corners of her eyes. Conchita approached Maria, cupping her face, ready to speak, but only sobs emerged. Jorge embraced Conchita, allowing her to bury her face into his shoulder for comfort. He didn't care who noticed his wet eyes. Even men cried.

Esmeralda gave Maria a small velvet pouch. "For you." Inside was a tiny, folded piece of paper with a brown thumbprint, various heart and flower stickers randomly stuck to the paper, followed by *Te Amo*. Maria noticed the Band-Aid on Esmeralda's thumb, giving it a light kiss. With an innocent giggle, Esmeralda gave Maria a large grin.

Regaining her composure, Conchita wiped her face. "She insisted, so I let her give her thumb a little prick with my sewing needle. Please, there's something else inside. It's not much, just a reminder of us."

The little pouch also contained silver hoop earrings with small winding markings all the way around. The top of the earring that covered the pierced lobe was the head of a snake. Maria thought of Tizoc as she placed the earrings into her ears.

"This is too much. Thank you!" she said, choking with emotion. When had she last received a gift of friendship, of love? She thought back to her goodbye to Diego and how it seemed so much easier than this, as if saying adios to her old life had been predestined and she didn't realize it before. She wanted to stretch herself over and around her friends and give them the freedom to live in peace as every creature deserved. Maria's wayward path was leading elsewhere.

Others brought mismatched bottles of blood. The leathersmith's wife laid a pair of soft brown cowboy boots at her feet. Maria had roughed up the market owner for trying to raise the cost of their stall to the point that the family would have been left on the brink of starvation. Maria traced the white stitching across the soft leather with her fingertips. These people had very little, but their generosity was like gushing water from a stone. She wondered why that was always the way. By the end of the procession Maria had a menagerie of blood-filled bottles to add to those from the previous night.

"I have something, too." Jorge went into his room and returned with a plastic bag. Maria looked inside and pulled out a secondhand smartphone. "Look in the music app," said Jorge.

She pressed the icon then threw her head back in laughter. It was preloaded with the music they listened to while they worked. There was Daddy Yankee, Santana, Shakira, DLG, Stevie Ray Vaughn, Pitbull, AC/DC, Neil Young, Metallica, Guns N' Roses, even Dire Straits. In the photos she found wonderful pictures of the people she didn't really know that well but had grown to love. At the bottom of the bag lay fresh packets of wraps for her hands and a jump rope.

Maria hugged Jorge one last time. His voice cracked as he spoke into her ear. "My friend, I won't forget you. Maria, you've been an angel to me and the community. Someone I could depend on and love like a sister. I would've given up this business if not for your encouragement."

Maria broke from his embrace. "I feel the same, Jorge. I hope we will meet again. Walk me to my car?"

He wiped his wet eyes and nodded.

Outside a few men packed the bottles of blood in two coolers while the women gathered around, touching any part of her body they could lay a fingertip on and praying. Maria drank in their blessings. She felt washed in love for others and herself, like the love she felt the moment she found out she was expecting. In silence she prayed for forgiveness for the bitterness she felt on her most desperate days. Maybe her life was worth something. Only time and judgment would tell.

Once the car was packed with her gifts, Maria said her final goodbyes. The sainted candles were at the end of their lives. The women lifted their scarred palms toward Maria. She waved back before driving away.

"All right, Adam. Where are you?" she whispered as she pressed her boot to the gas pedal.

# 10

Maria had never seen the ocean before. She was looking forward to experiencing the sensation of sand and water between her toes. 'Free Bird' by Lynyrd Skynyrd played as loud as the volume of the aging car would permit. Jorge's affinity for rock and roll had rubbed off on her as he played music from lights on to lights off. She had soaked in the new sounds and lyrics like she had absorbed books in the motel. Loneliness is a spirit. It has a soul. It needs certain things to stop from becoming a monster. The further she drove listening to the song the harder her foot pressed on the accelerator like she chased the devil, or maybe it was the other way around. She wondered if each life had a predetermined number of times a heart could break and start over. How many times could it bleed out like the sound of an aching music note.

A lot of music would be needed to get through the long drive along dangerous snaking mountain roads, keeping count of how much she spent on gas, and the one thing that truly mattered—how much blood she consumed. The two coolers would have to last her as long as possible, until she found some other trusted way of receiving sustenance. She tried to forget these details and focus on the sense of joy that came with forward movement—joy that was greater than her feeling of terror of the unknown. This journey would be the farthest from home she had ever dared to venture. On those dark nights on the road, her little mustard seed said this was only the beginning.

Maria drove straight to water once she reached the Acapulco city limits. The sky was just beginning to disrobe its darkness into milky white wisps of cloud when she made it to her destination. Tall hotels twinkled in the distance like Christmas lights. Beyond the hotels, rocky tree-covered hills created a dark silhouette against the sky. There was no one on the long, curved sandy beach except a few bums unconscious from drinking or who knows what else.

Maria pulled off her boots in childish anticipation, almost tripping over herself to be rid of them, and walked toward the clear water, thinking about absolutely nothing except the delicious new sensation of sinking bare feet into sand. A salty breeze blew through her hair while her toes kissed the edges of the waves. All her senses were in overdrive, consuming the freshness of the breeze, the coolness of the water and the ferocious beauty of the ocean which could only be tamed by God. She couldn't imagine a lifetime without experiencing something so magnificent. Was there even a world behind her? All that mattered was what lay before her.

Maria's oneness in the moment was disturbed by her little mustard seed causing her to shiver. She could take care of herself, but a bad feeling was on the horizon. This bauble of beauty felt like it was being cradled by some dark claw that could squeeze the life out of everyone in the space of a heartbeat.

Maria found a dilapidated motel on the outskirts of Acapulco. She didn't think she would find herself in a place like this again; however, this time it was only for a very short time. Although it wasn't ideal, she didn't want to bring too much attention to herself without knowing what lurked here. The blood she had been given needed to stay cool for as long as possible and some of the rooms offered kitchenettes, which would suit her basic needs. So many years had passed without a hint as to where she might find her creator; now that she was on the road to discovery, she didn't want to waste another minute. She tried to temper her expectations, but the jitters of hope and impatience wouldn't allow her to sit still. She would take a look at Diablo's that night.

Maria trawled through her single bag of belongings to find the dancer's dress she had taken from the bag in

Tizoc's office, a Wet n' Wild red lipstick bought out of habit, and a tube of outdated drugstore mascara.

Steaming water filled the grimy tub to baptize her into a life as a true vampire on whom nothing would grow, nor a drop of sweat would ever form on the top of her lip.

After the soothing bath, she put on the off-the-shoulder red dress. It was form-fitting but not uncomfortable; it fell a bit on the short side, only reaching mid-thigh. Maybe she would be the only one to notice. Now wasn't the time to feel self-conscious. Her body would stay this way until the day she died; better get used to it. The new cowboy boots gifted to her before leaving Monterrey were the only footwear she had brought with her so they would have to work. Maria looked into the mirror, liking what she saw. For the first time, her reflection started to mirror how she felt inside. *Not bad at all, lady.* She grabbed her bag and wandered into the waning light.

The main drag was alive with traffic and people buying and selling on the streets. Men whistled as she walked past, blowing kisses, but this was as interesting to her as cigarette smoke blown into her face. Wafts of roasting corn, spices, and tacos filled her nose, reminding her of the life she had shared with Diego. She had always made sure the house smelled like simmering food when he came home at night. Funny—this was the first time in a long time she had thought of him. The memory wasn't sad; it was only a picture her senses flipped to in her mind. She glanced back to a raspa vendor offering her a red syrupy cone of ice. *Hmm, if only that was blood*. Hunger ached within her: she needed to ration what she had brought with her.

Diablo's was at the end of the main street, on the corner, with a red neon sign featuring a flickering white star. Two large tattooed men with pistols on their hips guarded the door like sentinels ready to strike. Expressionless, they glanced in her bag and waved her in. DLG's 'Muevete' began to play. As if orchestrated, the entire crowd began to howl. The music's frenetic salsa energy was their reward after hard work and worry. There were no outstanding debts, demanding bosses or crying children on the dance floor. Tonight, they danced, drank, made love. Bodies gyrated close to each other. Sweat drenched the backs of the dancers; hair was pulled up or stuck to skulls. The bar smelled of body heat, clashing perfumes, and stale beer. Maria weaved through the bodies unnoticed, just as she liked it. The feeling of invisibility among the maze of people made it easier for her to spot anything out of the ordinary.

Every stool at the bar was empty. The bartender, a young woman close to Maria's human age, danced to the song while wiping glasses. Her fuchsia lipstick matched the hibiscus flower in her hair. She stopped her little dance to lean across the bar and take Maria's order.

"Drink?"

Maria mouthed *cola*. Her jitters returned as she searched the faces of the crowd. They continued to move in sweaty, sweet oblivion. Skirts flew to the rhythm in a pageant of colorful flowers. Nothing seemed out of place. She grabbed her Coke, deciding to look a little harder. Maybe there was a back room like at Zuma Zuma where she had discovered Tizoc. Nada. The bathrooms were clear and there were no obvious back rooms. Maybe the nice bartender knew something.

*Just a sign, Lord. Anything will do. This can't be it. I can feel it.* She wandered back to the dancing bartender.

"Can I get you something more potent?" The young woman pointed to a bottle of tequila.

Maria frowned, wishing she could do a shot the size of half a bottle. "Doesn't agree with me."

The girl leaned over the bar. "Paloma!" she called. "My name is Paloma. You waiting for someone? A date?"

Maria shook her head. "No date. I'm new in town, but I am looking for someone. A gringo, wavy hair, the palest blue eyes you've ever seen?"

Paloma seemed to search her memory for a few seconds as she started to wipe glasses. "I can't recall anyone who matches that description, but you see a lot of people come through here."

Maria forced a smile, grabbed a napkin and mimed for a pen. Paloma quickly obliged.

"Here's my number. If you see anyone out of place or hear anything unusual, call me."

As Paloma reached for the napkin, her hand brushed against Maria's fingertips.

Maria spent the next few days exploring the city as dark clouds thundered through her insides. She was hungry, frustrated and wanting to forget the mounting *what ifs*. As time passed it was becoming urgent for Maria to secure a supplier of blood.

Ironically, there was no shortage of spilled blood in this town. Armed local police patrolled the streets night and day, trying to hold back the tide of drugs and death. The poor were not just poor; they were tired. Tired of the bloodshed, tired of unanswered prayers, tired of endless hunger. This wasn't just Mexico. There was a film of grime across the entire globe. As Maria had learned, hunger isn't always in the body—it can be in the mind, the soul. Hunger in the body was the easiest to cure. She had seen on TV the people in Venezuela breaking under some fake government led by someone no better than Tizoc. Those people were not just hungry, they were being starved to death. They begged for life and a single man took it upon himself to serve an entire nation a death sentence. If she was ever near this man, she would allow her uncontrolled hunger to devour him breath to bone. She missed patrolling the streets for trash to take out.

Things weren't great in the States, either. There was going to be an election soon and one of the candidates, Mr. Horace Kilburn, was a bad hombre desperate for power. His fat fingers were always pointing somewhere while his spittle was acidic. He divided people with a fury that had not been seen in a long time. From what Maria read in her history books, anything divided becomes weak and susceptible to whatever disease that comes its way. It's in those times the real danger prowled. She hoped this man wouldn't be President. She wanted her vision of *anything is possible in the States* to remain preserved, as if in a picturesque snow globe you could hold in your hands when you felt low. When she allowed herself to think of such things, she felt like another biblical flood was needed to fall to wash away the clogged drains of society, starting with the dictators of the world.

If she survived the rest of this seemingly ageless life, she wondered what would be left of this world at the end. Would she see the end of the civilization or, worse, the world? The thought frightened her more than anything else she could conjure.

*I need to find you. Where are you? What am I?*

Maria spent her evenings on the beach. The sound of the tumbling foamy sea eased the spiraling hopelessness of her cold search. In moments like this she would have liked to have been a dolphin or whale, sinking into the deep where creatures cohabitated in relative peace, except to feed as dictated by the natural order of things. With that thought, her belly would begin to rumble from her strict rationing.

Her gifted supply of blood was running dangerously low. The need was nearly constant. Based on how she had attacked the man at the hospital and her reaction to Esmeralda's father—and that other time in Monterrey she didn't like to think about—the hunger could make her do things she would regret to people who didn't deserve it. She didn't know the people of this city well enough to 'sing' for her supper. There were always pimps and dealers she could take from—but that was a last resort. She wouldn't kill them, only scare and drain them.

Her fingers always managed to find her turquoise cross. *Abuelita, I miss you. Lord, I need you. Hear me, dammit!* With the words out of her mouth, she'd kick a heel's worth of whatever was closest to her foot.

# 11

Maria's phone rang at ten on Monday morning.

"Hi Maria, it's Paloma from the bar. You gave me your number on a napkin."

Maria jumped from her bed, her mustard seed of hope kicking in excitement. "You have some news?"

"Uh, no, but you said you were new in town and maybe I could show you around. Your gringo could be hiding out somewhere else."

Maria fell backward on her bed. So much for signs. Maria had no other plans, so she took a chance. "Okay, what do you have in mind?"

"Meet me at the bar around two and I'll give you the grand tour."

Maria had been waiting so long for a breakthrough. What was a few more hours? She might also come across some way to score fresh blood that didn't involve sinking her teeth into a body.

Paloma pulled up in a large shiny black Mercedes G-Class wearing reflective sunglasses. To Maria, it all seemed rather extravagant for a bartender.

"Nice ride," she said flatly.

Paloma blushed, quickly responding, "It was a gift. Big birthday from my father. He has to do everything big. I have a beat-up old thing I bought myself in Austin."

Maria mentally pinched herself; she could tell she had made Paloma feel self-conscious. She really needed to work on her people skills.

"Well, I would love a gift like this. You don't even want to know how old my car is. Please excuse my jealousy!" She gave Paloma a cheerful smile, rubbing the soft leather seat as she climbed into the vehicle. This seemed to bring Paloma back into a friendly mood. Maria didn't just need blood and answers: she needed a friend.

Paloma's hair was naturally curly, falling to her shoulders and she had a curvy body which she displayed with pride in cut-off denim shorts, cowboy boots and tank top. Maria admired this woman's ability to show her dimpled thighs and the roll of flesh that puckered above her jeans. Growing up, Maria would have given anything for breasts and thighs like Paloma's. She remembered running home crying after a day of teasing for being the least-developed girl at school. Paloma seemed to have the confidence of her idol, Selena; it was the kind of confidence Maria was just learning to enjoy. Paloma felt good about herself and that was beautiful. What she liked the most about her new friend were her kind, brown eyes. She reminded Maria of Jorge with her easy disposition. Maria's mood softened.

"Ready for a little adventure?" Paloma said.

Maria chuckled inside. "I'm beginning to think I was born for the unexpected."

Paloma revved the engine and sped off. They drove through what appeared to be the nicer parts of Acapulco and out into the countryside.

"What brings you to town?" Paloma asked after a while.

But Maria couldn't speak. She was overwhelmed by the breathtaking views of the mountains and sea. Sunshine glittered on the water as if God had tossed diamonds and spun gold across the surface. The endless expanse of water, earth and sky made her feel the size of a grain of sugar. She could understand the ancestral worship of such an awe-inspiring thing as the sun.

"Maria?"

"Um... sorry, I've never seen..."

Paloma eased her pressure on the gas. "It's okay. I guess I take it for granted. Mexico is such a beautiful country. I'm a student at UT Austin hoping to get into med school. If I wasn't so interested in medicine, I might have chosen anthropology."

Maria was still in her own world. "Don't take a second for granted."

Paloma gave her a genuine smile. "You may be a woman of few words, but I can already tell you have heart and kindness. We have this moment, and it could be our last. Enjoy."

Maria inhaled a deep breath of salty air then turned the music even louder as they continued to drive. The playlist included Whitney Houston, Mana, Elvis Crespo, even a little Dolly Parton. Paloma's hair whipped in the wind as she sang along. Maria truly wanted to live again.

It was a good day with few questions for Maria while the stereo continued to play Celia Cruz and Selena loudly. If she could explain the concept of vacation, it would have been that day. They laughed about nonsense and Paloma was happy to answer all of Maria's questions about Texas. American life sounded wonderful, despite the upcoming election. Maria ached for a dream beyond survival. She had to admit to a little jealousy at Paloma's seemingly carefree existence. There were so many things out there for people, just not enough for everyone. Like the tides, her emotions and thoughts were pulled back as quickly as they floated from below.

Maria returned to her room that night pleased to have a new friend, however, she had been so distracted in her bubble of sun, sea and small talk that she had a very serious matter to think about: she was dangerously low on her stored blood. She had been able to control herself in the past because the people around her were friends, but with a stranger or someone she felt deserved to have their throat ripped open she truly feared for her ability to contain her instincts. If this journey came to nothing, if all her hopes were a futile dance to a tune not of her choosing, Maria feared what she might become. She might give up all sense of right and wrong and just live. If only there was some spell to transform her into a jaguar so she could escape to the heart of the Amazon.

A text popped up on Maria's phone.

*Diablo's tomorrow night? I had a great time today. Thanks for coming. Paloma*

Maria responded with *YES!* She wanted to get a better survey of the town to find a new butcher to purchase blood from. So far the two she had visited couldn't help her. She prayed the universe would reveal its hand soon because all she wanted to do was fold on this game.


This time Maria didn't bother with all the fuss of dressing up for Diablo's. She had officially put her "I don't give a fuck" hat back on. There were so many more important things on her mind. It was a laid-back jeans and t-shirt night. She thought she looked her best in jeans anyway.

The bodyguards didn't ask to inspect her bag when she approached the entrance, instead escorting her to a small table in the corner where a bucket filled with various soft drinks sat sweating. Maria watched the bodyguards, the dancing couples, searching for any secret door or unusual movements. Nada. Why had Tizoc had any interest in this innocent local watering hole? Maybe she was just meant to find another friend on what was a very lonely road.

Paloma waved at Maria from behind the bar. She spoke to whoever was taking over before joining Maria at the table. Maria noticed one of the bodyguards at the front of the club changed positions to stand near their table. Her temples pulsated, trying to make a constellation out of these random dots of information. This obsession was exhausting. Would anything come along to shout *Don't give up!* Maria decided to give up even just for the night. Fuck everything. She was ready to live today.

"Glad you came out," said Paloma as she grabbed a soda from the bucket. "I know it might be weird because we just met, but my family is taking a trip to Cancún tomorrow. Just for two nights. My father has business there *soooo* I thought we could go with them and see the pyramids. Have you been?"

Maria shook her head. Why did she think of Tizoc again? Maria was too embarrassed to tell Paloma she had never been on an airplane before. She took a large gulp of soda, which she would regret later, and gave Paloma a smile. "Let's go see the pyramids!"

The soda bubbled uncomfortably in her empty, aching stomach. Her vampire body couldn't digest human food or drinks, and not having enough blood in her system would only make it worse.

Paloma returned the positive answer with a big "Yes! Let's dance now!"

Maria hesitated, then allowed Paloma to drag her to the dance floor by the hand.

After a few minutes of people bumping into her to a remixed salsa jam she had never heard before, Maria remembered what it was to dance. Then there was only the beat and the bodies surrounding her. Maria fell into the same comfortable rhythm as she did with her boxing. She missed the fury of the fight and training, but she couldn't risk the exertion. When was the last time she had danced?

Dusty cowboy boots stomped until four in the morning.


The pre-dawn air was fresh when they exited the club.

"I'll send a car for you. Where can they pick you up?"

Maria snapped out of her euphoria at Paloma's question. "Uh, I'll just come here. What time?"

Thankfully Paloma seemed too high on adrenaline to notice this as odd. "Flight's at three, so noon. Can I give you a ride home?"

Maria shook her head. "I need to cool off. Don't worry, I'll be okay. See you at noon."

"Are you sure you want to be walking around alone? I don't like the idea. I wouldn't do it."

"I promise no one will fuck with me. And if they do,

I have these and I know how to use them." Maria took her brass knuckles from her back pocket.

Paloma didn't look convinced but she let it go. "You promise to text me when you're in your room?"

"I promise. Now go and sleep."

Maria waved at Paloma and walked in the other direction. After a long night of wild dancing, she pined for blood. The hunger had to be all over her face by now. She had finished the last of her stash the previous morning and she had to find a new butcher to source blood from. She walked the back streets looking for someone who might be deserving of her blood-seeking justice. Maybe someone to mess with her, just to give her an excuse to fight back and satiate her needs. Pockets of hungry guilt coursed through her veins, causing every step to feel like she was sinking deeper into quicksand. The capillaries in the whites of her eyes started to throb; the soda was acid burning a hole through the pit of her stomach. Panic seized that spot where the little seed would tell her when to worry. In her delirious state, Maria remembered the last time she had lost control, in Monterrey.

An older woman dressed in black arrived at the gym around eleven at night. Her face was a dry, hollow mask with eyes red from crying.

"How can I help you, madre?" Maria asked.

The woman burst into tears, showing her a photo. "This is my daughter—she was taken from me. She started dancing at that club off the highway, Zuma Zuma. I didn't worry at first. A lot of girls dance; no problem. They make their money to feed their kids or pay their rent and go home. My mistake thinking it was just extra cash for her. She became thin, stopped coming over for dinners. My calls to her, my prayers to God, went unanswered. I finally found out through my son that she was introduced to some poison at the club. He got the bartender drunk and found out the owner of the club hooks some girls onto poison so he can fill his brothel. He saw my daughter as a wounded animal and struck. When she became too unattractive for the club she went to the brothel where she could get all the poison she wanted. When I tried to go there, the head pimp threw bottles at me. His men came outside saying horrible things about my girl, things I can't repeat. Her body was found dumped, bruised, scarred. That story didn't have to be her story. It's my fault, I know it is! I should have made her stronger so she would resist such temptations. I should have fought for her." The mother, older than her years, began to sob.

Maria put her arms around her. "What can I do?"

The woman's heavy-lidded eyes lifted. "It's too late for my girl, but not the others. Take it down. My son says the man who supplies the poison is always at the brothel on a Monday night. He will be there tonight! I will forever pay in my heart for her fall, but those pimps and dealers... The cops won't do anything! You can! I beg you!"

Her recent feed flushed Maria's face as she wondered if Hell had decided to increase the production of scum around the world. She sent the woman home without blood payment because the small fridge in her room was already difficult to close from her supply. Maria placed the photo of the girl next to her burning sacred heart of Jesus candle. With a wrapped left hand and brass-knuckled right, Maria was ready to exact her kind of justice.

The house was well known to everyone. People steered away, pretending it didn't exist because they couldn't do anything about it. As she walked closer, she could hear music playing and see flickering lights in the windows. It brought her back to the factory; only this was a factory of another kind. How different things would have been if someone like her had intervened during the maquiladora slaughter. Her creator didn't save her; he only gave her a different hand of cards before leaving. The face of the old mother, her fate, her dead coworkers, flared her nostrils and anger electrified her fists.

With her signature booted kick the door flew off its hinges, taking down the armed guard inside. Maria seized his gun to crush it with a solid stomp before throwing him out the door. The paid muscle ran off like his life depended on it once he saw her fangs and red-hot eyes steer his way.

A few half-clothed women and men smoking or shooting poison lounged in the front room. In their surprise, the girls tried to cover up and hide in the small kitchen that faced the main room. Maria punched her way through the men who tried to fight back. They were no match for her blood-fueled strength. Maria tossed them out of the open door or nearby windows. A few ran out, thinking it was some sort of shakedown. Her fury grew as she saw the table of hard drugs. She broke the table in half with her boot, pulverizing the drugs underfoot.

When the living room was clear Maria approached the women.

"Stay here," she instructed.

Then she made her way to the back bedrooms: more cracked bones and more tossed-out customers. These girls ran to the kitchen to join the others.

When she reached the last room, a man was waiting with a shotgun while a girl no more than fifteen or sixteen sat curled on a single bed under a sheet. He cocked his gun and fired. But Maria was too quick: the bullet only blew away his back-up, who was running up behind Maria. Before he could get off another shot, she was under his legs with her fangs deep into his femoral artery.

He screamed, letting go of the shotgun. He looked at her with pleading eyes as he crashed to the floor.

"No, please don't. I have money, drugs—please don't."

But Maria was overcome by the proximity of blood. "How many small voices have told you 'no' before?"

she growled, crawling on top of the cheap-suited head pimp like a monstrous leech. She hadn't intended to kill anyone, but this rat was making it so very easy to forget her promise. Maria wanted to gift this unworthy human a one-way ticket to Hell.

"Please!" he screamed, turning his grubby attention to the girl in the bed. "Baby, help me, tell her."

Maria looked back at the girl, waiting to hear her voice. There were no words, only eyes peering past the sheet she clutched, giving all the judgment Maria needed. Maria returned her gaze to the pimp, ready to carry out his sentence with a smile.

"*We* aren't disposable, but baby bullies like you are."

The pimp spat in Maria's face. "I'll see you in Hell, bi—"

Before he could finish, Maria dug into his neck, relishing every sweet drop of blood. He tasted as delicious as Carlos.

Moments later, two men appeared in the doorway with more guns. But the sight of a bloodied Maria drinking their feared boss to a sun-dried ear of maize made them turn around and run into the night.

The house was silent except for Maria's boomeranging pulse. After her thirsty rage subsided, Maria came to herself again. The young girl was trembling under the sheet. Maria pulled the dirty cloth off the girl to see her in nothing but a t-shirt with a rounded belly. The sight of blooming life caused Maria to soften.

"Come, girl, I won't hurt you. Was this your man?

He's too old for you. Can you tell me where they keep the money and drugs?"

The girl pointed to the desk in the corner with an open safe underneath. Just like her factory. Maria wrapped everything she could find of value in the sheet. The young girl was holding her belly while staring at the drained body—possibly the father of her unborn child. Maria sat next to her.

"I'm sorry it ended like that, but you have options. That bastard, this place, was never an option. You can't raise a child here." The girl sniffled, nodding her head. Maria's heart ached for her. "May I?" The girl allowed Maria to feel her belly.

To Maria's surprise, she could feel the little life stretch and tumble. She knew she should pull away, but it was a scab over a wound she couldn't help picking. In that moment Maria thought she should offer to take this child, live her life as a mother, and walk away from the violence and her quest—damn the consequences. But deep inside her own belly she knew this was the most selfish thing she could ever do. She couldn't live with her unanswered questions or put this innocent child into danger she had created. Maria reluctantly pulled her hand away from a path that was not meant for her, no matter how much she may have wanted it.

She handed the girl a rubber-banded stack of cash. "Take this money. Buy vitamins, take care of yourself. When your baby arrives, if you don't know how you will cope, give him or her to the nurses. You have a choice but base it on what's best for yourself and your life. Okay? From today you need to think ten steps ahead. Girls like us must think ten steps ahead to survive. Promise me?"

The girl grabbed Maria's hand. "Thank you."

Maria walked back into the front room with the girl. The other women were still huddled together in the kitchen, too scared to run from the noises coming from the back of the house, watching men flee with Old Testament terror in their eyes. They didn't dare cross this angel of death.

Maria wiped her bloody face with the corner of the sheet to ease the fear of the shaken women.

"One by one, come to me in the light," she said. They edged toward her nervously and Maria gently inspected their arms and eyes. The ones that showed no signs of using hard drugs she sent off with a wad of cash. "Go home and don't look back. The rest of you, come with me to my car."

Only four women remained.

Before leaving the house, Maria set the curtains alight, pleased to be rid of this den. She hoped the foreman of Hell got the message.

One of the women walked next to Maria. "Where are you taking us?" she asked, voice shaking. "Are we to be killed for the drugs?"

Maria stopped the small group. She could only explain her intentions with a story. "My best friend in grade school, Rosemary, had a neighbor her mother would leave her and her sister with. Rosemary always wanted me to go with her to play with the neighbor, but something didn't feel right. As a kid, what do you know? You don't bother adults with bad feelings even though you should. Well, this neighbor's sodas and sweets became beer and harder stuff. When I got married, she showed up to the reception a complete mess and confessed all those terrible things he did to her and her sister as children in exchange for his gifts. She had been too ashamed to tell anyone. She didn't think anyone cared or could do anything to make the pain go away. I tried to get her to stay with me, but there was no telling her what to do that night. I never saw her again. Her sister told me she died. So, no, I'm not going to kill you, I'm going to help you do something much more difficult. Now get in the car."

Maria drove to the nearest hospital with the half-naked women in tow. As they entered the emergency room, medical staff ran up to them at the sight of Maria soaked in blood. But before they could speak, she held up one hand. "I'm not hurt, but I need you to clean these women up, detox them, get them counseling; whatever it takes to rip the poison from them for good. Keep them here as long as you can, then give them jobs—not cleaning jobs. Teach them something." Maria handed one of the doctors the sheet full of the remaining cash. "This should be enough for your time and their stay. You work for me now. Be warned, I will be back in a few months to make sure you're doing *your* job."

A nurse approached the doctor and whispered something in his ear and a hint of recognition came into his eyes. "We will both be responsible for these young women. You have my word," he said. Then he took a step closer and whispered. "Thank you, *Maria*."

Maria gave him a short nod and turned her attention to the women. "Stay strong, sisters, and please believe you can do this. This is your second chance." Maria looked at the doctor again. "I'll be watching."

Maria knew she couldn't come back, but they didn't know that. She drove back to the gym torn wide open. On the one hand, she was buzzing from the blood. On the other, she had taken a life tonight and no amount of rationalizing could clean that stain away. It struck Maria how much could be accomplished when one didn't fear an empty belly, cold on your back or death. She wondered what would happen if all of those fears were taken from the most desperate. How different it could be. The savory taste in her mouth turned bittersweet.

# 12

As Maria turned the corner, the memory of that night at the brothel still fresh in her mind, a neon cross flickered in the growing morning light. It was a church-run free clinic. Maybe she would find blood? *Jesus, Buddha, Mohammed, and the moon, I beg you, I don't want to take another life. I pray for your help.*

Through the dirty window she saw it was empty. Dizzy from hunger, Maria decided to take her chances and pushed the door handle hard enough to break the single lock. She slipped inside as quietly as possible: it took all her strength not to collapse. If she had to crawl, she would crawl. Through blurred vision she could just see where she was going. At the end of the hall she made out a biohazard sign. The blood had to be in there.

She pushed open the door and entered the room. The smell of its sticky, sweet contents was intoxicating. Agony jolted between her temples while pain bled from her gums. A refrigerator hummed and clinked in the corner of the room. She stumbled toward it and a blast of cold hit her face as she opened the heavy door. Each shelf had a label for blood type: stacks of plastic pouches filled with red liquid. Her entire body trembled with uncontrollable hunger. She snatched a bag, punctured it with her teeth, and sucked it down with greed. In the relief of the moment, she took another and sucked it down just as fast. Her belly felt satisfied. Maria took another two bags with her. Her guilt was heavy, but she knew it would be a stone around her neck if she resorted to draining or killing someone by accident. Maria kissed her cross. *Thank You.*

Dawn had arrived by the time she exited the clinic. It was time for her to go. Maria headed toward the motel to prepare for the trip. She took only what was necessary and did her best to hide anything that could reveal her secrets. Blood bottles were washed, and the rest of her belongings hidden in the few pots and pans in the kitchenette. There would be just enough time for a quick rest before she had to meet Paloma.

Paloma was sat in her Mercedes when Maria approached the club. She stopped before she got in. "Do we have a bit of extra time? Mind if we make a quick stop?"

"Sure. Did you change your makeup or do something to your hair? You look radiant."

Maria had to think of a quick response. She shrugged. "I washed my hair and put on a little extra moisturizer."

"Well, I want the name of whatever you used."

Maria directed Paloma to the clinic she visited the previous night. It was already open and filled with people waiting to be seen. Paloma parked in a space out front.

"I won't be long. Can you wait here?" Maria said, holding the door handle.

"Not a problem."

"Thanks."

A man was at the door fiddling with the broken lock. He stepped aside when she stood next to him. The heat of guilt and shame for her blood craving slapped her cheeks. But this was who she was now. She grabbed cash from her pocket and looked at it with a pang of fear. Part of her wanted to keep it just in case. Being immortal wasn't about living in a castle with family wealth. She lived in the real world with expenses like everyone else. Tizoc had chosen a dirty path: eventually she would have to find a way to live out eternity too. She had paid for the motel for another three months. Then a miracle had to happen. But she had broken the door and taken her fill last night, and it didn't feel right to not pay it back some way. The meal of stolen blood had revived her. She felt incredible. Her internal push and pull pressed her forward to enter the clinic. A nurse at the reception desk juggled a phone on her ear and typing on a computer. She looked up to Maria with an exasperated expression.

"Sorry to bother you. I can't give blood but here is a donation. Maybe it can go toward fixing the door?"

Before the nurse could speak. she placed the money on the counter and walked out.

Back at the car, Paloma looked at her with curiosity. "What was that all about?"

"I give when I can and thought it would be a good thing to donate here. Saw the place last night. Anyway, I'm ready."

Paloma placed her hand on Maria's. You have a good heart. I like that."

Maria expected to be taken to the airport, but instead they drove to a desolate patch of land outside the city with a landing strip and small jet. Only one building could be seen. They grabbed their bags from the back of the Mercedes and headed to the plane, a private plane. Maria suddenly understood why Paloma drove such a nice car. It made her wonder: who exactly was this new friend of hers?

As she climbed the steps to board the private jet behind Paloma, she heard two voices. Once inside, a man who looked to be in his late thirties dressed in dark jeans, ostrich leather cowboy boots and a white linen button-down shirt greeted them.

"Mija, my dove. I'm glad you made it." Paloma gave him a limp hug. "That's it? When you were little, you would squeeze me so tight. As you get older, your hugs get looser. Never mind. I'm grateful you accepted this invitation."

"I'm not a kid anymore, Dad, I have a life. But I'm glad I could make it here, too."

His eyes shifted to Maria, and she could feel them drink her in. "Who's your friend?"

Paloma used this question to break free from her father's grasp. "Mom and Dad, this is my friend Maria."

"It is very nice to meet you," said her father. "Let me put your bags in the closet at the front." Paloma handed her father her bag and Maria did the same. He caught her eye and gave her an intense stare as he took her bag.

Maria didn't like the way this man looked at her. It was somewhere between her own father's fake charm and Tizoc's look of a predator. Eager to avoid him, she shifted her eyes to the rest of the plane. It seated eight in comfortable cream-colored leather seats. In the middle a radiant Mestiza sat shuffling a stack of oracle cards. Her face was round with wide eyes and beautiful smooth skin.

Mrs. Castillo was dressed in a light blue linen dress that buttoned from the top to the bottom, with the only adornment on her body being a leather and silver buckled belt. Still shuffling the cards, she stared hard at Maria. Her eyes catching every inch.

Something about the situation felt inside out to Maria. Paloma's father came closer to her. Trying to stay calm, she focused on the hair peeking out of the top of his shirt and the small turquoise snake ring on his pinkie finger. She suddenly realized, *This man isn't human.* His body didn't smell like it was filled with pumping human blood.

"We are very pleased to have you, Maria. A friend of my Paloma is most welcome. Call me José, and this is Estrella."

He nodded towards Paloma's mother. He felt too close. Maria gathered enough courage to look into his eyes, and they crushed her with their intensity.

"Dad, sit down. You're being creepy." Paloma's playful manner broke the binding tension.

He sat down near to where they were standing and shouted, "¡Vámonos!"

The pilot at the front of the cabin looked back and gave him a small nod before walking to the cockpit.

"Maria, why don't we sit here." Paloma pointed to the seats nearest to her mother. The woman gripped her rosary, then returned her attention to the cards as Maria and Paloma sat across the aisle from her.

Paloma spoke in a tender voice. "Mamá, how are you? This is Maria."

Estrella's eyes flitted from her daughter to Maria. Without thinking, Maria reached out and touched the older woman's hand. Maybe Paloma's father would avoid her if she was friendly with his wife. Estrella's skin felt cold: too cold for air conditioning and too cold for life. *Two vampires and a human girl?* She would have preferred a burning agave giving her explicit instructions like a burning bush, but didn't everyone? They smiled at each other in silent acknowledgment. Maria wondered

134

if this woman was suspicious of her too. If she was, she made no indication of it. But if Maria knew about them then they had to know about her. Maria had to keep her cool and make it through the flight.

"It's nice to meet you," Estrella said in a confident tone. "I'm sure we will have so much to talk about over the next few days."

"Nice to meet you, too," Maria replied. "You mind if I close my eyes? We were out late and I'm exhausted."

"I'm so glad you said that, Maria. Same here," said Paloma.

Estrella placed her icy hand over Maria's wrist. "You two rest. Maybe I will join you."

Maria pulled her arm away gently and tipped her black hat over her eyes.

Considering this was her first flight Maria didn't feel the slightest bit of fear: that was all saved for José Castillo. As a human, she would have left sweat marks on the seat and watched the engine for the slightest spark. Diego would have held her tight and reassured her it was okay. Now, the last thing she feared was death. If the plane bucked and nosedived, she thought it might be easier to accept death, than to accept not having a purpose on a road leading nowhere or to suffer an agonizing death at the hands of a vampire. She thought she had found something meaningful in Monterrey, but that was gone. Was there anything more cruel than a feather's touch of hope on bare skin, only for it to drift away on some sudden gust of wind?

The pilot's voice filled the cabin. It was time to wake up, even though she hadn't slept, and find out what all of this really was. When Maria placed her hat back on the top of her head, she saw Estrella's eyes were fixed on her.

"Did you sleep well?"

Maria nodded but did not speak. Instead, she turned her gaze to the window as they bumped to a stop in another private airfield. An SUV with tinted windows waited for them as they deplaned. Estrella climbed into the passenger seat and José sat in the back with Maria and Paloma.

"So, what are your plans, my dear? Whatever you want to do, tell Paco and he will arrange it," said José, a little too eager to please.

Paloma scrolled through her phone as her father spoke. "Dad, we just came to see the pyramids. I don't want to entertain your old friends. You know I don't like them. That last guy gave me the worst feeling."

Maria could hear the impatience in her voice.

José put a large paw on his daughter's knee.

"My business isn't coming home. I'm conducting everything offsite, so have fun. There is one dinner I'd like you to join, just you and Maria. Mamá will be too tired."

Maria noticed Estrella's body tense in the front seat as if some nerve in her spine was severed. Paloma must have noticed too.

"Mamá, you okay?"

Estrella reached behind and touched Paloma's cheek. "I'm fine. Just a cold coming on, maybe. You know I like my books and my sleep when I don't feel well."

Paloma leaned forward and placed her hand over her mother's forehead. "If anything changes, you tell me. You always feel cool to the touch so it's hard to know."

After half an hour, they passed through a high gate and drove on a winding paved road that led to a driveway. In front of them was a house was bigger than any Maria had ever seen in her life. It was a grand, red-clay-colored hacienda with a tiled roof that peeked above the line of trees.

As they drew up outside, Paloma jumped out of the car to help her mother down from her seat. José's large hand wrapped around Maria's arm as she exited from the front.

"Maria, will you join me for a drink later?"

Caught off guard, Maria didn't know what to say. Before she could think about it, she heard herself uttering, "Sure."

A small crew of staff bustled around the house, making sure not a single candle or flower was out of place. It seemed the staff had been instructed to be ready for their arrival. Their bags were ferried away and barbequed meat was served around a low open fire pit on the patio outside. Only Paloma tucked into it.

"Why am I always the only one left eating? You people astonish me! Maria?"

The aroma of cooked meat smelled good to Maria but the last time she tried to eat solid food, many years ago, it just came back up. She had cried for days, knowing even monsters on death row get a last meal.

"I'm not that hungry, Paloma. You enjoy."

"The heat is different from the north, isn't it, Maria?" said José.

Maria didn't answer, pretending to look at the wild but manicured foliage of the large garden.

José continued to fish for more information. "So, the pyramids, why go there now?"

Between greasy bites, Paloma answered instead of Maria. "Because they are cool, Pop, and the history is like a horror story."

José frowned. "What's so horrible about offering blood in exchange for a good crop or protection? Even Christ said, 'This is my blood, drink from it.' Blood is what binds us. What are your thoughts, Maria?"

But Maria couldn't move or speak, not knowing the possible nefarious intentions behind the man's intense gaze.

Estrella spoke for the first time. "How about a story by the fire?"

Paloma appeared sleepy from the meal. She kicked off her shoes before curling into her oversized Papásan chair. "That sounds good, Mamá."

Maria was still in a state of stasis, not knowing where to look or what to touch.

José sat back in his chair and relaxed, looking at Maria as if watching a new TV show but addressing his wife. "You tell the best stories, my love."

Estrella made herself comfortable, looking into the fire like a curandera who could see the past and future. "Before the Spanish invasion, there was a king," she began. "He was a fair and honest ruler. He had an advisor by his side who was believed to be an emissary from one of their gods. This strange advisor didn't look like them: he spent his time in the king's company or kept to himself. The advisor convinced the king to limit the human sacrifices and war among the different tribes in what we now call Mexico. The king agreed and was pleased by the outcome. Not long after, this fair king became ill and his trusted advisor offered him renewed health for a price: he had to promise to continue his good reign as long as possible in this part of the world, never to waver. He had to stay strong and loyal, keep the tribes unified, even with the dark days that would befall the people in the coming times. They would need him more than ever.

"The king, like all mortals, feared death above all else, so he went ahead with the blood pact. The king regained his health and vowed to keep his people intact during their upcoming tribulation. The precarious peace among the tribes held. Then a tragedy occurred that would change everything. The king's daughter, Princess

Zuma, was struck down at just five years old with the same illness as her father. The king begged the advisor to heal her like he had healed him, but the advisor said his gift was not meant for children; they are too pure. Some laws of nature could not be defied, no matter how cruel they may seem.

"In his bitterness, the king locked his advisor alive in a stone chest. He cursed the one god his advisor worshipped. The king gave the child his blood and she died anyway.

"The tribulation the advisor spoke of was the Spanish invasion. The demons on horseback came with their crosses, their diseases, and their swords. The king knew this was what the advisor must have been referring to. The blood sacrifices performed at the temples gave the invaders the reason to conquer with their religion, and the division among the natives gave them the means. By the time the king realized his mistake, the stone chest, along with other plundered treasures, had been loaded onto one of the boats to be sent back to the Old World.

"In order to force the gods to intervene, the king began wearing a large turquoise snake necklace and built a huge turquoise snake mosaic in front of his main temple. When this display didn't work, he sacrificed one hundred of his people on that mosaic to offer his soul to the gods. A huge storm blew in that night: legend says a mysterious being rose from the blood and brought the king to his knees where he worshipped that being.

The next day the king was gone, leaving the people to their fate."

José's eyes seemed to glow in the firelight. "My love, what was the name of this king?"

"His name was Tizoc."

A maid appeared from the house, causing Maria's heart to jump.

"Señora Castillo, I am about to leave. Any instructions?"

Estrella rose from her seat. "Yes, I'm coming."

Paloma watched the fire with slits for eyes. "I'll join you. I'm exhausted. That nap on the plane wasn't long enough." Paloma began to walk inside.

Maria felt a chill in the air as it began to rain, her little mustard seed almost dragging her from that house. If there was anything to wring sweat from her body, it was this story and this man.

"I think it's time for bed," she agreed. "We danced all last night."

But José stopped Maria as she tried to follow. "Don't forget that drink later, Maria. How about in two hours?"

"I'm really tired."

"I insist."

His gaze made Maria tremble. She couldn't say no to him and give him cause to harm her. It might be his intention already. Only one way to find out.

"Fine. See you in two hours."

Maria could hear soft snores coming from Paloma's room. She hoped José would have fallen asleep but doubted it. Something told her it would be worse if she didn't keep her appointment with José, plus not knowing what the hell was going on was beginning to itch. By now, she thought she'd be used to that. Maria felt naked going into this situation. She missed the feeling of her brass knuckles in her back pocket, but it was best she had left them in Acapulco after the evening's conversation. There was too great a risk of someone going through her things and asking why she felt she needed them on a fun girls' trip.

The tiles stuck to her bare feet as she walked the corridors, the air conditioning feeling too cold for fall. Even as a vampire, she could still experience the chill. A small light illuminated double glass doors ahead of her. Maria's stomach dropped.

José sat in a large sitting room with oversized sofas made from a deep indigo-colored fabric that appeared soft to the touch. Healthy plants blossomed in all corners and Indigenous art dotted the walls. He sipped from a dark beer bottle. For an older man, despite how he made her afraid, she could see he was handsome, with smooth skin and wide-set eyes that appeared almost green. He offered her his bottle.

"Would you like a drink?"

"No thanks. It doesn't agree with me."

He got up from his seat to walk toward Maria, like on the plane, he felt too close for comfort. "Come now,

I think you will find this to be very different."

Now, José's body was almost pressed against hers.

But none of that mattered to Maria, as she smelled the perfume of human blood wafting from the bottle. She closed her eyes to control her desire and so the veins in her eyes wouldn't betray her secret or her unease.

His warm hand was on her chin. "Open your eyes. You don't need to fear me—unless you have something to hide."

With a mix of defiance and *fuck it,* Maria grabbed the beer bottle and threw her neck back. Sticky red blood juice ran down her throat.

When she looked back at José, she saw small points protruding from under his smiling lips. She stepped back. He gave her a playful wink, took the bottle back from her and drank.

Her tension eased a bit from the nip of blood and the sign that she had gained his trust.

But just when she thought he was easing his scrutiny, he turned up the pressure again. "You see, we are very much alike. My question is, why are you here? This is my territory, my livelihood, land that I've cultivated for years. The only vamps around here are the ones *I* allow. I don't know you from Adam."

That name again.

Maria knew she had to be careful. She could tell this man lived in a constant state of suspicion. Either he knew the truth and was waiting to see if she would reveal her hand, or he suspected and was waiting for her to slip up. A half-truth right now couldn't hurt. She remembered Tizoc's words.

"I've been wandering for years," she said, quietly. "Looking for the one who created me and to find others like me. The vampire life is a lonely life."

José nodded. "I understand that better than you know, especially when you are a young vampire. I was made like this in my thirties after we had Paloma. Of course, I did everything money could buy to keep it from my dear wife. It was the most miserable time of my life. She thought I was being unfaithful. I thought I would lose her, and our daughter would no longer have a mother. I convinced my wife to become what we are. I wanted to spend an eternity with the woman I met in Bible school when we were only fifteen.

"My family would stay together, no matter what I had to do. My baby girl deserved both parents smothering her with our affection. The only regret I have with this vampire life is we didn't have a son after Paloma—someone to take over the family business. Paloma is too much like her mother, you know. I spoil her with gifts and her mother spoils her with piety. When we started out, Señora Castillo and I were of one mind, so I assumed she would grow to love being a vampire as I have, letting the power take her places humans can only dream of. Instead, she spends all her time at church with priests. Huge chunks of my money are given away in charity."

Maria grabbed the bottle back from José and took

another swig, never allowing her eyes to wander far from him. Just two vampires having a quiet drink, trying to see who reached for their holster first. Lucky for her, he was the kind of man who liked to hear himself talk.

"Speaking of money," she prompted, "how do you get yours? A private plane and big house? Those require big moves."

"What creatures like us are suited for."

"And what is that exactly?" Maria wanted to know everything she could about this vampire. Was he a threat or not?

"I have business dealings in many areas. But if you want to know how legal it all is then I will let you draw your own conclusions. I have travelled to many places around the world and only fools follow the rules. We are not fools and we do not have to suffer them either. We make our own rules."

"A law unto ourselves."

He smirked. "I like you, Maria. You have a fire and fierceness none of my hombres have. I can see that. You're a deadly, beautiful package."

Maria stepped back, not wanting to give him the wrong idea.

"And untouchable, I can see." Seeing she had finished his, he grabbed another bottle from an ice bucket, offering it to her.

Maria looked at the bottle, not wanting to know where the blood came from. It was blood, and it seemed like she would need it to get through this trip—especially if José happened to pick a fight. There had been no safe way to bring blood with her.

"How did you meet my daughter?"

This is where Maria knew she had to tread with careful steps. "Like I said, I was looking for others and needed my next meal. There's a lot of unquestioned violence in Acapulco: easy prey. I went into the bar looking for some guy to hit on me and instead I met a friend. We all need friends. Simple as that." Maria forced a smile, knowing a man like José wanted that, taking it as a sign of sweetness. Little did he know she was all salt and lime inside.

José seemed, for the time being, satisfied with that answer. They clinked bottles; once again he was standing too close to her. Maria couldn't decide if this was a means of intimidation or something worse. She knew she had to indulge this man who could cause trouble.

Finishing her bottle quickly, she made her excuses and crept back into bed. Vamps never slept, only rested their constantly regenerating bodies. She lay there wondering how the next few days would unfold. Her entire life had taken a road she never imagined in her wildest dreams—or nightmares.

# 13

When morning came, the house was bustling with helpers. Downstairs, the breakfast table was filled with fresh fruit, juice, eggs, bacon, and pastries. There was a time when Maria would have dived into this selection with a healthy, human appetite.

A housekeeper approached Maria. "My dear, the boss says you prefer protein shakes, so here is one made just for you."

The tall aluminum bottle was cold. Maria took a sip and almost fainted from the sweet mixture of blood and a hint of pureed mango. She never thought to blend food with blood, but then again she didn't own a blender.

"How did my dad know that?" Paloma helped herself to a tortilla filled with potato and egg.

"I couldn't sleep last night. We just talked for a bit." In her peripheral vision she saw Mamá Castillo give her a daggered look. However, it seemed to be one more of concern than malice.

After their morning meal Maria and Paloma headed to the driveway where a gleaming blue Jeep convertible awaited them. José emerged from behind them. He placed one large hand over Maria's shoulder, once again too close, the other held a book.

"Have fun you two—I will see you at eight tonight for that dinner. Maria, here's a little something on the pyramids. It's sacred ground, you know."

Maria accepted the book. It appeared worn around the edges, with the type of cover you would find on any tourist guide.

"Alright, Papá. That's enough hounding. See you later," said Paloma as she climbed into the Jeep. Maria followed her, not wanting to spend any more time with José.

They pulled out of the drive, radio volume on maximum, leaving a trail of dust. The sun, wind, and music soothed Maria's soul like their night of dancing. For these few moments, she wouldn't think of the mess she had gotten herself into. She hoped on the sacred heart of Jesus this man was just full of talk and trying to scare her. Yes, there were coincidences, but nothing to connect it all together. Just a cluster of stars.

During the long drive to the pyramids, Paloma was her usual happy, chatty self, while Maria quietly contemplated her next move. When they arrived at Chichen Itza, all the anxiety birthing in Maria's mind seemed to vanish. If this was her last day on Earth, what a last sight!

Lush foliage surrounding rising stone filled Maria with curiosity. The previous night's rain gave the grounds a fresh tropical green smell. Although the site was long dead, it felt so alive to her. They walked along the main path, taking in the view of the largest temple in the center of the site. Tourists took photos and bought crafts from locals. Maria considered how, after they were all gone, this majestic structure would still bear the brunt of the heat, wind, and rain. When Maria started her journey, she was like these people, looking up at something they were far removed from and could not truly understand, but now she felt like she was becoming this temple. If she were to die tonight, she could die proud of her efforts. She didn't want it to end like this but so be it. It was a moment that brought gratitude back into her heart. Without Paloma's and Jorge's friendship, she would have felt completely lost.

As they stared in deep wonder at these temples, Paloma turned and took Maria's face into her hands.

"Can I kiss you, Maria?"

Maria pulled away. Paloma was left on the verge of tears, with a confused, heartbroken expression.

"I'm sorry, I thought..."

Maria realized her extreme reaction. "No, *I'm* sorry. I just—I've only been with men and haven't been into that. I'm not into anyone. The last time I was kissed someone was... If you were a man, my reaction would have been the same. Love isn't something I have time for now. Maybe ever. I'm no one you want to love anyway."

The truth was on Maria's tongue. She wanted more than anything to recount her tale to her friend. The world of secrets and silence was a burden too heavy to carry alone. She did want love but didn't feel worthy of it. Still, Maria wanted to make up for bruising a woman who deserved to receive the love she gave.

Paloma began to cry into her hands and Maria put her arms around her to comfort her.

"I don't care if you like women. I'm flattered; really, I am."

Paloma looked up. "You're just saying that. I've been told so many times it's shameful."

Maria looked into Paloma's eyes. "No! Don't ever think that. Deep down, you know you're exactly how you should be. You're smart, fun, sweet, ambitious, easy on the eyes..." With this she gave Paloma a playful nudge.

Paloma laughed as she wiped her nose and eyes. "No one knows here. I've never felt comfortable enough to say it except to a few friends in Austin. It's a different world out here. My mom is so religious. As an only child, I'm expected to get married and have kids and live life the way other generations did. I don't want to know what my parents would think."

Maria thought Paloma's mother and gangster father weren't in any position to judge. They were a pair of bloodsuckers, after all. "Aren't we supposed to love our neighbors as ourselves? I don't recall anything about gay, straight, trans or otherwise. We need to just be *nice* to each other! I think the world would be a better place if we focused on that. Besides, there's someone out there for you. She could be just around the corner." Maria embraced Paloma again, then pulled away and smiled. "I hope we can be good friends."

Paloma chuckled. "Best friends."

Maria felt like whatever strange meandering road she was on, there were still little blessings along the way to keep her going.

They walked under the shade of the floppy tree branches, stopping for their pre-packed lunch. Paloma ate her simple sandwich of ham and cheese; Maria sucked on her smoothie in silence. She couldn't stop absorbing the strange magic of this place. It felt solemn, yet familiar.

"What's on your mind? You're a little quiet," asked Paloma.

Maria snapped back to reality. She touched her neck and turned to Paloma. "You see this cross? My great-grandmother—my abuelita—gave this to me. She said the stones came from her cousin who worked on an archaeological dig in a place like this: just manual labor. He found a few of the treasures but was so angered by the greed of the men organizing the dig that he decided to keep some of the stones for himself and gave one to her. She said they were scales from a great snake, but it's just a story. Who knows what's true and untrue in those old tales?"

Paloma threw a thoughtful look at Maria. "Like the one my mother spoke about last night?"

The mango-infused blood in Maria's belly soured as she recalled the story from the previous night. Surely it couldn't be a coincidence. Maria flipped through the book given to her by José, which she had placed in her back pocket when they arrived. She found a corner turned down on a page was about the great temple El Castillo; a few pages on, another was marked where the name Tizoc appeared. He was the seventh Aztec ruler, or tlatoani. A large stone, the Tizoc Stone, was created during his reign. The large carved stone showed his military prowess and strength as a leader. His death only five years later was shrouded in mystery. It was clear to Maria that it was because he became a vampire. She struggled to keep down her smoothie.

When they finished their lunch they walked around various parts of the site to take it all in. Maria ran her fingers along the lichen-stained stones. Maybe it was just her imagination, but she could faintly detect the ghostly scent of the blood that must have flowed down these steps: blood that had covered the stones of her beloved necklace. There was no way she could avoid going back to that house without raising suspicion. Despite all her fears she *needed* to know more. She would follow this path to the very end, even if it meant the end of her.

Maria walked with Paloma back to the Jeep, glancing back at the main temple as she went. Bats were just beginning their journeys as evening approached. Maria would face whatever waited for her in that house. For the time being, she was done with this place.

# 15

The hacienda seemed empty when they pulled up. The windows were unlit with no guards or staff in sight. Fear darkened Paloma's usually bright eyes.

"Something isn't right, Maria.

Maria knew that already, but she didn't know what was waiting for them—or how to prepare herself.

"I'm sure my father would have messaged me if my mother wasn't well."

They rushed inside and found José waiting for them in the entryway. Maria could see the thick red-thread veins in his eyes.

He knew.

His gaze turned to Paloma. "My darling, I need you to leave now. This woman is not who she says she is. She is dangerous."

Paloma looked confused. "What? What are you talking about?"

"Just go!" he roared.

Paloma took a step back. Maria could see the terror on her face as she looked at her father.

"Your father is right, Paloma. You should leave, but I am not dangerous to anyone except those who deserve what is coming to them. Your father isn't who he says he is, either."

Something snapped in José and he lost all self-control.

"¡Mentirosa!" he screamed as he leaped toward Maria. But before he could attack her, Paloma blocked his way. With one swipe of his hand, Paloma crashed against the wall. She fell unconscious on the floor.

Maria bared her fangs: both hands were at the vampire's throat within seconds. She would have his blood for that. Her knee contacted his groin then an uppercut put him on his back. Maria straddled his frame, trying to dig her teeth into his neck. Then José had Maria by the throat, although he wasn't squeezing yet.

"You *are* the Jesus Enforcer!" he hissed.

Maria gave him a puzzled look and for a moment eased her frenzied attack. José took advantage of that small opportunity, pushing Maria off his body. She had thought this was just about Tizoc. Both jumped to their feet, circling each other like hyenas fighting over a fresh kill, ready to strike at any given moment.

"Don't play stupid, girl. My daughter was worried about you so she had a bodyguard follow you the other night. He caught you in the clinic, then reported what he saw back to me instead of her. It wasn't until you left that vile motel that they were able to go through your things. They brought the evidence I needed this afternoon." Maria's box of belongings lay in the corner. "My men have been bearing your mark. You also did something to my creator, Tizoc, didn't you? Tell me now or die!"

Maria's chest heaved with disbelief. She tried to regain the upper hand. "Well, if you weren't a lying, gun-smuggling, woman-trafficking, drug pushing piece of trash, we would have nothing to worry about. Just like Tizoc, you're not worth the blood in your veins."

José released a deep growl that sounded more wolf than man. "Girl, it's time for you to pay for your crimes." José used his bulk to trap Maria, grabbing her by the throat again and driving her up against the wall. Holding her by his outstretched arm, her body dangled in the air without any way to land a clear punch or kick to any part of him.

His eyes slithered up and down her body while licking his lips. "You know what I'm going to do? I'm not going to kill you. I'm going to sell you. I'm going to watch as you spend an eternity in chains on your back or knees. There's no one to save you now. Whatever fight you thought you had is nothing compared to my power."

Maria wouldn't allow it to end this way. She would rather die than fatten this pig. She glanced at a still unconscious Paloma, momentarily forgetting her own predicament. *Not like this, God, strike me down. I'm ready. Let Paloma be okay. Don't let me live for this cabron.*

It was when Maria stopped struggling that she heard the rapid slapping of bare feet on the tiled floor. Estrella ran from behind José and drove a machete through his heart.

A look of surprise, then sorrow formed on his face as his hand loosened around Maria's neck until she fell back to the floor. He couldn't see who had ripped his heart in half, but Maria could see he knew without any doubt who it had been. He fell to the ground, Estrella falling alongside him without a look of remorse. All color drained from his skin as his blood soaked Estrella's nightgown. In any other circumstance Maria would have spat on his dead body, but out of respect for Estrella's sacrifice she did not.

Paloma began to whimper in pain against the wall. Without hesitation, both women ran to her aid. Estrella cradled her daughter's face and rubbed one of her hands.

"Maria, I suspected it was you," she murmured. "The sisters whispered about your deeds in the north. You are like me, like him, but so much more."

Maria grabbed Estrella's hand. "You saved me. You killed your own husband."

Estrella's bitter glance toward José resembled a wad of spit. "I've been trying to leave him for years. You take life in vain and surely you will have life taken from you in the same way. He was not a good man: the men he did business with were far worse. They are the scourge of the Earth. If I hadn't given in to his vampire dream, he would have forced it upon me. That man, Tizoc, I have only seen once, but he brought another with him. He reminded me of El Diablo. My husband thought I just sat back, paying no attention to his business, but I wouldn't leave my only child's future in his hands. Life means nothing to the people he works with. When I saw that new man a few weeks ago, I knew some plan was brewing. For years I've been plotting how to end my husband's blood reign, but the pieces never truly fit until I heard about you. There was also Paloma to think about. None of his so-called business friends would think twice about using her for their own gains or revenge."

A constellation started to form in Maria's mind. Tizoc had been an ancient vampire who had created a network of blood crime, and José was one of his many warlords. That was all she had, but it was a start. It all seemed to weave in and out of making sense like colorful ribbon running through braided hair. Maria shook off this thread of thoughts, since the immediate danger was gone.

"How do you feed?" she asked her savior.

"The good priests of my church have been feeding me for years in the confessional. I am their patron. Every penny of my husband's money I give to them or those in need. The powers we possess are meaningless unless it makes a difference even in the smallest of ways." The vein in her forehead bulged and pink-tinged tears ran down her ageless face. Maria could see the faint lines of emotional struggle creasing her skin. "It's up to us, Maria. You gave others hope, even if you might have thought there was none left for you. You need to be here. Not the man that I once loved. It was always going to end this way between us. And my daughter loves you."

Maria blushed. "Maybe you can help me. Do the names Adam or Mordecai mean anything to you?"

Estrella ran her fingers through Maria's hair like she would her own child. "Adam will be here in the morning. I spoke with him and I believe he is the one who created you. I took the chance and contacted him to see if he knew about you. It seems you were not the only one to go through a transformation all those years ago. I also sent a message to Mordecai when we landed. I knew José was up to something: with Tizoc unavailable I thought you would have a fighting chance with a little back-up. Unfortunately, José moved too soon, but it's better he went by my hand. May God forgive me. You should go to England with Adam to meet Mordecai. Remember last night's—"

Estrella was cut off by Paloma. "Mamá?" She was now moving and trying to sit upright while rubbing her head.

"Mamá? I can't believe he hit me. What happened?"

Estrella hugged her daughter like she hadn't held her in months. "Mija, it's a mother's job to protect her child until she is ready for certain truths. I would die a thousand deaths to keep you safe."

Paloma's pleading tone turned somber as she stared at her father's body. "What's going on?"

Maria and Estrella looked at each other as they held hands. Estrella pulled out a set of fake teeth before both women showed the little white points in their mouths.

Paloma fell back. "Impossible."

"Mija, with God everything is possible and not everything happens like you think. Dinosaurs aren't mentioned in the Bible, but we know for a fact they existed. Which one do you believe?

"Your father and I are vampires. We had you when we were humans."

Paloma shook her head and squeezed her eyes shut. "All of this. Is this real? Am I in some lucid dream?"

Maria touched her arm. "We are very real. And I am sorry about your father."

Tears slid down Paloma's cheeks.

"You both need to tell me everything. I am so lost," said Paloma

"Why don't you tell her," said Maria. "You know more than me." Maria could see Paloma staring at her mother's bloody clothing. "Why don't we change first and sit in the kitchen." She turned to Paloma. "Is that alright?"

"Yes, I might put some ice on my head." As she rose to her feet she looked towards her dead father and the bloody machete next to him. Her lips quivered as she began to cry again. "I can't believe…"

Maria and Estrella glanced at each other as they stood next to Paloma. Maria walked towards a soft leather sofa with a blanket neatly folded on the back. She pulled it off and covered the body.

"Thank you," said Paloma as she wiped her tears from her cheeks.

Maria turned to Estrella. "You said Adam is going to be here? The one who made me like this?" The news made Maria's head spin.

Estrella nodded. "He has a good heart, better than he knows. But sometimes where we come from, what we are told about ourselves, and our circumstances, make it hard to believe."

"When did you meet him?"

She smiled and Maria detected a slight twinkle in her eyes. "Not long after I became a vampire. He arrived with his sister to do business. José threw a party and we talked all night. We kept in touch until… it was complicated…"

Paloma moaned and touched her head. Both Maria and Estrella stopped their conversation and helped Paloma to the kitchen and made sure she wasn't too badly injured. Then they left her with hot tea and ice for her head so they could clean up. When they were refreshed, they returned to the kitchen and related their stories to Paloma. Paloma listened wide-eyed but without interrupting. Estrella and Maria took turns talking about their lives over the years. Estrella told her about the Keepers and Adam. She didn't skip the truth of what kind of man Paloma's father had been.

"I guess we all have different stories to our lives. And that includes becoming creatures that we are told only exist in movies and books," murmured Paloma.

"Thank you for understanding and listening."

Paloma glanced at Maria then at her mother. "I have something to tell you as well. Maria already knows, but do not wait or hope for me to have a husband. I don't want one. However, maybe I will meet someone who could be my wife."

Maria clasped Paloma's hand. Estrella nodded her head then embraced her daughter. "I don't care who you love as long as you experience true and lasting love in this life."

"Thank you, Mamá."


Morning arrived quicker than any sunrise Maria could remember. This was a good thing, for the anticipation of a journey coming to an end made her want to fast forward time. She had been waiting for this moment every second of every day since 1995. The house was quiet because Estrella had given the family help a few days off. The sound of birds could be heard coming from the patio; bright sunlight streamed through the windows. The night had brought death and tragedy, followed by revelations of secrets, and now it was a new day.

When the knock she had been waiting for finally arrived, Estrella was making coffee for Paloma. She turned to Maria. "Shall I get that or do you want to?"

Maria knew it was Adam. "I will."

Estrella gave her a soft smile. "Paloma and I will give you two a little time."

Maria rose from her chair and walked slowly to the front door. It wasn't just any door she was opening: it was a chance at knowing the truth about that mysterious vampire and all the questions she asked herself for so long. She hesitated before looking through the peephole.

It was him.

All those years, all that spilled blood, and here he was. Maria opened the door to a man who was still as young as the day he created her all those years before. His hair was shorter and he was dressed like a backpacker instead of a stylish businessman. The man who stood before her was not that same sad, conflicted creature from their shared past.

"Maria. I'm glad to see you're well."

Not knowing which emotional urge to follow first, she gave him a hard slap followed by an immediate hug. "Brother, I've been searching for years. I thought you left me there to die."

# 15

When they walked into the kitchen, Estrella greeted Adam warmly and put out a carafe of blood for him and Maria. "This was a willing sacrifice from sisters and brothers at a church out of town. I will leave you two to discuss things." She left with the mug of coffee for Paloma.

Adam watched her leave the room. Then he turned to Maria who sat at the table with her arms crossed. He took a deep breath and looked like he was prepared for a punch to the stomach. "I know I don't deserve anything from you. But I have come here upon the request of Estrella. I couldn't believe you had found each other. Maybe it was destined. However, you have to believe me when I say there are plans unfolding that are beyond our little lives. After I saved you..."

Maria leaned closer to the table. "Excuse me? You didn't save me, brother. I saved myself. Every day I had to pull myself together not knowing who or what I was.

There were so many moments when all I wanted to do was disappear. You gave me your blood. I did the rest."

"You are right. I know you have so many questions. They will be answered in time."

"Time? I am so tired of that son of a bitch. My patience has been tested so very much wondering about his existence and you."

"I don't know what you have been through all these years, however, I do know how time can be atrophying when living with questions."

"How do you know Mrs. Castillo? She told me only a little."

He glanced in the direction she left. "Estella and I met one night at a party. It changed everything for me. I was miserable before that night,"

He took a sip from his mug. "There are many fewer vampires than humans in the world: we mostly know of each other. There are those who prefer the shadows, then there are those who believe we are a gift to the world and humanity. They are a clandestine group helping humans in times of crisis led by a very ancient vampire named Mordecai. I am from the fourteenth century and the Keepers existed even then as a secret society of vampires. I'd done nothing with my life but accumulate wealth. I haven't been as brave as the Keepers and put my neck on the line for others. After I changed you… I changed too. There had been a growing restlessness inside of me to find some real purpose. The Keepers have shown me that since I joined them."

Adam poured more blood into both mugs while Maria stared at him, digesting what he had just said. Then he lifted his eyes to meet hers. "José and Tizoc were only the beginning. You have done so well on your own, but now there is a bigger fight. The Keepers need all the help we can get. I'm asking you to come to England. My mentor Mordecai is waiting there with others like us. I know this is a lot so soon, but we need good people like you."

Maria laid her head in her hands, not knowing what to say in this moment because she had never seen past it. She looked up at Adam. "So... suddenly *you* are a good person?"

He smirked and sipped from his mug. "I decided to have a real purpose."

"You think I need this too?"

"I know you do. You have helped others with the power within you."

"Yes, but I have also lusted and craved human blood—killed for it."

"We still are what we are and you know this is bullshit. You are all heart."

She stared into his eyes feeling a sense of peace. Was it possible to be both giver of hope and take of life?

Abruptly, they heard the sound of shattering pottery from the back patio. They rose swiftly and rushed toward the noise. Outside, Paloma stood next to her mother, clutching her coffee, as Estrella broke flowerpots against the ground.

Among the broken shards of clay were plastic bags filled with cash.

"Here is some of the money my husband has been hiding—gardening wasn't just a hobby for me. I don't want it. It's blood money. Take it. Do some good with it. Paloma, go back to school and don't come back here. I will stay with the Sisters of Concepción in the mountains for the time being. Everything we have will be put in your name."

Paloma looked at her mother. "Wait, the Keepers are vampires? The way you spoke about them to me sounded like they were a humanitarian organization."

"I knew the day would come I would have to confess everything at some point. You are no longer a child and my differences to you would become more apparent."

"I can't go back to school and forget this. I want to know more about this world of vampires."

Estrella shook her head in desperation. "No, you want to be a doctor. You need to live your dreams. You need to finish school."

Adam stepped in. "She can still study to be a doctor. Mordecai can arrange it. He's been building a network of human and vampire cooperation for centuries. Paloma can leave at any time and live her life, helping us when we call. That is one of our rules with humans."

"Mamá, I won't go without your blessing. Please give me your blessing. I promise to finish school. This feels right. I want to help where I can."

"My fear isn't you not finishing school. I don't

want you to become so involved with immortals that you forget about living as a human. The temptation is strong. I know." Estrella turned to Maria who felt a little dazed by the turn the morning had taken. "Walk with me, Maria?"

Taking Maria's arm, she escorted her through the vibrant gardens. "I'm not your mother, but if I was I would order you to go to England and be with our kind. You've had many years to figure out who you are as a human: this is your chance to find out who you could be as a vampire. Mistakes will be made and perhaps there will be some tears, but you are a strong woman. Your days of wandering are over. Who is going to save this world if not the greater species? Just promise me, as long as Paloma is human, you will look after her. She is the only baby I will ever have."

Maria stopped their stroll as they walked from beneath the shade of a tree a few feet beyond the patio. She grasped Estrella's other arm so they faced each other. In that moment she needed to feel grounded. A veil of blinding light covered her eyes, giving her the sensation of intense pain. Ceaseless rain overcame her thoughts, then a voice as small as her mustard seed whispered Go. It wasn't a burning bush, but she took it as a sign. The determination she felt on her quest to find Adam reignited for this second unknown journey. The sacred heart within her chest felt aflame once more. Maria fluttered her eyes to see Estrella observing her.

"Mysterious ways have caught you off guard, I see.

A vision is a sacred blessing not to be ignored. Maria, you are a blessing, too."

Maria wrapped her arms around Estrella. "Thank you. You have done so much for me, and I will be eternally grateful."

"De nada. We are sisters in blood and forever bound. We take care of each other until the end, Maria. Now come help me to deal with the body."

The four of them stood over José's dead body. "This home we built will become a funeral pyre," cried Estrella. "Make sure we start the fire with your father's body, Paloma. There can be nothing left. Nothing! Especially the bones!"

Tears fell from Paloma's eyes. Her hand touched her cheek where a bruise had formed.

Adam spoke to the young woman gently. "I'll take care of it. Gather what you need, then we head straight for the airport. Is your plane still available?"

Paloma sobbed quietly and then finally nodded. "I'll call to make the arrangements. If my father was good at anything, it was having everyone on standby."

Maria and Adam did their best to clean up José's body, arranging him so he looked like an innocent father enjoying a mid-morning nap. They sat him in his favorite chair, covered in a blanket and holding a rosary. Estrella kneeled next to him.

"You know I remember the first time we met and

fell in love. Look how far we have fallen from what is important. Even with all my charity I still feel complicit. No longer. The rest of my days will be used making up for my cowardice. Goodbye, José, and forgive me."

She rose to her feet. Adam touched her hand. Their eyes locked for a moment. Estrella smiled at him and left the house.

Listening to her mother speak prompted Paloma to kiss her father goodbye, then she followed Estrella out the door. Maria watched while Adam struck a match and lit the corner of the blanket covering José's body. The flame crept up the blanket until it came to life in a hot rage. When it reached his body, his flesh scorched and turned black. The aroma of copper filled the room.

"What do you think happens after we die, considering we are predators who use other humans for sustenance?" Maria asked Adam.

He shook his head as the body burned and the smoke filled the room.

"I don't know and I hope I won't know for a very long time. I have lived long enough to be grateful for my time. But I don't think tigers or sharks care when they hunt. That's not to say we should kill indiscriminately like Tizoc or José, but we are what we are."

Maria liked that answer and she liked the idea of getting to know more vampires and their experiences.

They left when the entire body was aflame.

Estrella sat in the driver's seat of the Jeep convertible

with Paloma beside her. Once they were in the car, she pulled away, driving quickly toward the airstrip and the pilot who would take them back to Acapulco. From the backseat Maria saw Estrella leave the property without glancing once in the rearview mirror.

Paloma and her mother sat on one set of plush sofas in the lobby of the Palacio Mundo Imperial Hotel in Acapulco, Adam and Maria opposite them.

"It's done," Estrella said, taking Paloma's hands. "All the legitimate assets are yours, my darling. The rest is gifted to charity and there is some for Maria for the journey. I'm not ready to let you go, baby girl, but I know it's time. I'm glad to go to the convent. You need to start your life. If you need me, I will come to you no matter what. Don't hesitate."

Paloma wrapped her arms around her mother. "Mamá, I've packed your iPad and you have your phone. Please keep them close."

Estrella patted her daughter's cheek. "I will. We are in dark times. Give love and create some good medicine for those who need it most. You have my blessing."

Estrella's phone pinged. "Looks like my car is here."

"I will walk you out," Paloma said, and they all rose from their seats to follow.

Maria took Paloma's arm to comfort her; Adam walked next to Estrella and spoke in a quiet tone, repeating words they had all spoken many times in the last day. "Are you sure about a convent? You have so much to offer. Why don't you come with us?"

They stopped outside and Estrella shook her head. "I need to be alone for a while after what happened with José. I need to heal from that. So many years I yearned to be a widow and now I am. I need a little time."

He gave her a soft smile. "Contact me when you are ready. You know I have time... especially for you."

A slight flush covered her cheeks. "I will."

Estrella gave them all one last embrace, without lingering. The last few days had been difficult enough for everyone.

"Don't stop until you get to the convent," Paloma said to the driver. "I want a text and photo as soon as you see the sisters take her inside."

As the car merged into traffic, Paloma turned to Adam and Maria shaking off her tears. "Off to London, I guess?"

Maria looked at Adam. "Can we please make two more stops? I promise not to be long. And it will give you time to tell me more about you and the others."

"What did you have in mind?" asked Adam.

"Before I start this new chapter, I feel I need to close out the past and say a proper goodbye. And, I want to help a good friend before I leave."

"I owe you that and more."

"Why don't I meet you guys at the private airport in Monterrey. We can fly from there. You two can... catch up." said Paloma.

Maria looked surprised by this but appreciated the thought. "Are you sure?"

Paloma nodded, her eyes red from crying. "I'll be fine. This is my home and I know it well. You two go in the Camaro. I'll tie up loose ends here and call my school, then I'll take the plane straight to Monterrey. I think I could use a little time alone."

# 16

Adam continued to think of Estrella, but knew they would see each other again when the time was right. He'd have to accept the space between would be like the lingering scent of fresh blood wafting in the night air. And a vampire always knew hunger.

They drove nonstop with Maria at the wheel. They took advantage of the fact that they needed very little rest, loading the car with enough stored blood for the journey courtesy of Estrella. Adam had lived with his sister for hundreds of years, learning along the way when to leave a woman alone and when to offer his ear or advice. Maria would talk when she was ready. It was a strange feeling having his progeny sit next to him. They shared something so intimate yet knew nothing of each other. His life could fill an entire library, with the events of the last year alone filling volumes. But he suspected there were only two things she wanted to know.

Within a day of leaving, Maria asked the questions he had been waiting for. Without judgment or emotion, Maria spoke. "Why did you give me your blood and not fight for the others? Why didn't you come back?"

He sighed and with his eyes on the long empty road ahead, began to tell his story.

"Maria, I'm old. 'Born in 1338' old. Until a few months ago, I had a younger sister and we had spent centuries living a lie accumulating wealth we didn't need or share. I made a promise to our parents before they succumbed to the Black Death that I would remain by her side and look after her. Back then, that's what human women required, so I agreed. She became a vampire first then turned me.

"When I entered that factory, I had already spent weeks traveling around South America investigating new business ventures. We didn't even need the money. Making money was what I was raised to do and that was all I poured my energy into. Didn't matter who paid the price for that. The suffering I saw in the fourteenth century was the same as 1995, and it continues now. Humans think they're getting smarter, but in reality we're just getting smarter at cruelty, smarter at how to hide it: the starving, the despots, the rape, and the greed. When I saw you trying to escape that bloodbath, I imagined my sister being torn to pieces for sport. It made me sick. I thought I would give you a chance, even if it meant taking your mortal life away. As for the other women... at the time I valued my own skin above theirs. I have a long list of deeds I'm not proud of, but my selfishness is at the top. For what it's worth, I tried to come back. I saw the fire and was stopped by police before I could get anywhere close to the area. I decided to return to the airport in search of another way to atone for the things I have done. I had so little hope in those days."

Maria watched the headlights illuminate the road.

"What's on your mind? Tell me, Maria. I need to know. I can't read you at all."

Her expression didn't change and for several minutes she was silent. Eventually, she spoke. "I've imagined everything I would say to you and what you might say back. But it's all faded, like these markings on the road. Except this. You took *everything* away, not just something. I was pregnant. I have done things I'm not proud of too, but I've also done good. My husband and I were planning on paying someone to smuggle us to the States. Who's to say that journey wouldn't have killed me, even if you never walked through that door?"

Maria spent the rest of the drive telling Adam about her life before and after becoming a vampire. He listened to all she had to say, hoping to feel like he had made the right decision. In the end, Adam wasn't sure what to think, other than that he liked the woman she had become. She was a good soul.

"Where exactly are we going?" he asked.

"A place I once called home."

—

Maria drove through Juárez towards the home she once shared with Diego. When he bought it, he said he never wanted to leave. Now she would know if he had meant that. He would either be there or he wouldn't. Diego would be fifty years old now. She pulled up a little way down the street, and they sat waiting for the last of the evening light to fade away.

Adam touched her hand. "I will forever be sorry for taking you from this life, from your love. It's only now I can begin understand how that must feel. I would never dare ask for your forgiveness."

Maria looked Adam in the eye. "If it wasn't for you, I would be dead like the other women in that factory. And Diego was never the one for me. He was what I thought I needed at the time. Now I know I am so much more. He would have never allowed me to be *more*. I have already forgiven you. Just try to forgive yourself, brother."

Adam's hands began to shake. He looked away from Maria with tears in his eyes. "You don't know how much that means to me."

When darkness fell, she approached the house. She could hear multiple voices laughing and talking. She peered through the screened window. An older Diego sat at the table, looking a little heavier with the appearance of a contented man. A woman sat across from him, and there were three children between them, two boys about twelve and a young girl, maybe fifteen. Diego reached for the girl's hand.

"Gabriela, you want to say grace?"

Maria stepped back, grabbing her belly where her little mustard seed resided. Spasms of emotion erupted under her flesh. She couldn't look, but she had to. She peered through the window as they all bowed their heads while the girl prayed. Bright red bloody tears soaked her face and t-shirt. She felt very little seeing Diego. Her new start was for her and her alone. But the dream of experiencing lasting love remained. That was why she cried. The road to only needing oneself is a painful one with many lessons. She grieved the child she had lost and would now never have. Perhaps that was her true destiny. She prayed this wound wouldn't always bleed.

"Goodbye forever," she whispered. Maria ran to the car, jumped into the driver's seat and smacked the steering wheel. Maria knew there was a time to lament loss and a time to let go. She had to let go of the past: as a vampire, she would have more years than the average human to experience regret, loss, and pain.

Diego wasn't the one she missed anymore: only that dream she had willed herself to believe was her only possible path in life. It was inevitable life would go on, even after her death. Here she sat with her vampire creator and her fingertips on another handle that led to someplace only God knew. If she was honest, she kind of liked this version of Maria a little better. She had achieved more than she ever thought herself capable of. She looked forward again.

"Let's go to Monterrey. There's a gym we need to visit."

Fight Box was a welcome sight after their sixteen-hour drive. Maria smiled as they pulled up. This felt more like home than the previous stop. How far she had come from stealing blood just to survive, without a clue about her true nature as this strange creation unexplained by science or religion. Jorge had been part of her journey. *Some segments of our path are meant to be traveled alone as we develop into who we are meant to be, then others are brought in for us to truly express our inner light in the most generous and beautiful way*, she thought.

"My friend Jorge doesn't know it, but I owe him," she explained to Adam.

Adam handed Maria one of Estrella's plastic sandwich bags filled with cash. "I'm sure he would say the same about you. Take this to him: he can use it more than us considering what he's doing for the kids in the community."

Maria grabbed the bag and walked toward the gym. As she entered, she heard a familiar little voice. It was Esmeralda. The little girl thumped the punching bag while Conchita looked on, laughing and encouraging her daughter. Jorge emerged from the kitchenette, wrapping his arms around Conchita's belly. He playfully kissed her neck then looked up to see a silhouette in a hat.

Maria stepped closer to the light and put one finger over her lips. Understanding, he excused himself to follow her back outside. Maria pulled him out of sight.

"Maria! What are you doing here? Come in, everyone would love to see you."

She shook her head. "I can't stay. I just came to say goodbye. Again."

"Are you okay?" asked Jorge.

"I'm fine. Actually better than fine. I found what and who I was looking for. You know, I owe you so much."

There was an awkward silence between the two. If she had her way, they would spend the entire night getting to know each other properly without all the secrets. Jorge only knew one side of her. But if she stayed, she would never leave. She was on another path which may or may not lead back to this place.

"So, you and Conchita? It's a good match. I approve!"

Jorge gave a shy smile. "Oh yeah, she's a great woman. After you left, she spent a lot of time here for Esmeralda. We were getting closer before, but now it's more. She helped me out with the gym and after closing we spent the evenings talking. She doesn't care what I have or don't have. I just fell in love with her and Esmeralda. Well, what's not to love about that sweet girl? Things are so much better around here after your crusades, but we miss you. Esmeralda is growing so fast. She is a smart little firecracker."

Maria held out the sandwich bag. "Here's a little gift for you. I know you will put it to good use.."

He looked at the car then the sandwich bag. "I can't take this. Or your car."

Maria pressed the bag into Jorge's chest. "Yes, you will, and you're just holding the car for me. Take care of her. I will leave her at Las Palmas airport."

Before she walked away, she stopped.

"Wait—your leather jacket!"

Jorge waved her off. "Keep it! We will never forget you, Maria."

Maria peered into the gym one last time to see Esmeralda, then headed back to the car. She was finished with her goodbyes and felt ready to move forward to whatever fate had plucked from the universe for her.

"You ready for England?" Adam said as she got back in the car. He was sat at the steering wheel.

Maria felt stillness where her mustard seed usually lay. "I am now."

Adam passed her a little book. A British passport. Maria traced the gold image on the front of the book with her finger. The picture inside wasn't of her, but it was close enough to get into England. All those years of human toil, all those years of vampire purgatory, and here the dream of leaving Mexico was coming to fruition.

"I know it doesn't make up for anything you've been through but consider it a fresh start. We need someone with your strength, Maria."

Maria's emotions were a jumbled jigsaw on the floor. This was no time to organize the pieces. "Thank you. Now drive before I change my mind."

—

Adam and Maria arrived at Las Palmas, the tiny private airport, ready to depart for London. Paloma hadn't arrived yet. Adam's phone rang as they sat in the car. He glanced at the name and number then looked at Maria, confused. "It's Mordecai. I wasn't expecting him to call before we arrived in England."

Adam answered the FaceTime call. An aging bald man with olive skin appeared on the screen. "Hello to you both. Maria, I am Mordecai. I'm glad you're safe."

"It's nice to meet you," she replied. "Adam has told me about your organization."

"Good. You will learn more soon, but for now I won't waste time because for once time is not on our side. Adam, I have reason to believe Lucifer is on the move again. He's been spotted with the presidential candidate, Horace Kilburn."

Adam looked concerned. "Lucifer? That vain charlatan thinks he owns this place."

"Well. He certainly is confident in his power."

"What can I do from here?"

Mordecai turned to Maria without answering Adam's question directly. "Maria, I understand from Adam that you recently killed a very old vampire named Tizoc."

Maria touched her cross. "Yes, a total creep. He said a few things before he died. I took his iPad in case I could do something with it, but it's locked."

Mordecai put his hand up to stop her. "Can I ask what you did with his body?"

Maria was confused at this question. "I buried it there and I'm glad I did. There was a truckful of innocent girls about to be trafficked."

Mordecai's eyes darted back and forth, as though trying to connect threads only known to him.

Adam leaned forward. "You're speaking of his bones. The marrow. I have heard about it, but never witnessed it being extracted—or known anyone to take it."

Mordecai nodded. "That's because it's dangerous and we don't want it to be common knowledge. A vampire's marrow is incredibly powerful and potent if consumed by another vampire. If a human consumes it by their own free will, they will acquire abilities only someone with extreme self-control and morality can handle. Otherwise, it could send them into madness. What did Tizoc say?"

"He said the time for us was coming. That promises were being made. Something about a feathered serpent? It didn't mean anything to me at that moment. I'm sorry. I didn't know about the body."

Mordecai's kind blue-green eyes looked at Maria. "My dear, we are called the Keepers because we hold many secrets from humans as we work in the shadows. We must find that body and get the bones out of Mexico as soon as possible. Both of you must carry out this mission."

"Anything else?" asked Adam.

"If my suspicions are correct, I believe Lucifer might use the marrow of Tizoc to start a dangerous global chain reaction of events. Possibly he will offer this power to his preferred candidate in the U.S. presidential election. You see, Lucifer can't bend free will, but he is a master at using it to his advantage. He looks into the hearts of us all and massages whatever already lurks there. Estrella called me when she saw José with Lucifer, then when she overheard José talking to others about Tizoc being missing. I think Lucifer will assume you will come to London so I've called in a favor. Once you have the bones, you are to go to Las Vegas to meet Vlad to see if he knows anything and if he can unlock Tizoc's iPad. Then the bones should be brought here for safekeeping."

"You think Vlad will cooperate?" Adam asked. "He's a loose cannon and not always pleasant to be around."

"Yes, he is a trained warrior. He doesn't show his perceived weak spots, but he has a deep soul. There are always excuses not to try or hope. Humans would have died out long ago if they did neither."

Maria could see Adam's exasperation with the idea of talking to this Vlad character.

Adam sighed and nodded his head. "We are on it, Mordecai. Thank you."

"Be safe."

The old vampire ended the call.

Maria looked at Adam, she felt suddenly overwhelmed. "That was…"

"A lot," said Adam.

"Yes. Did he really say Lucifer? As in the Devil? He is real?"

"Hold on. Actually, it isn't the biblical Satan. Lucifer

is an entity, another type of creation like us. He is associated with Venus and the cosmos. Not what we have been told to believe. No red skin with horns and a tail."

"But he is evil?"

"Some would say we are evil. He probably thinks he isn't, but he knows he is superior. We need to find out what he is up to. For centuries he has popped in and out after great catastrophes. He loathes humans and the chaos they cause even if he uses them. My sister loved the idea of being a companion to him, but she valued nothing and loved no one. Everything was a great fantasy to her."

"What other... entities exist?"

Adam took a deep breath. "Demons, us, Lucifer, angels... It's all real. There are probably things we don't know about or access, but Lucifer can because he is all cosmic light and energy. That is why he is the way he is. But as you have found out with vampirism, the known entities do not exist like the movies or stories. Back in England we have an entire library dedicated to books about these things. We are a small team of vampires at Grandthorpe Hall who keep this knowledge and the balance in the world when we can."

"I need time to process all of this. But what about Paloma? She's human and we have to remember that. I want her to be safe, no matter how much she may fight our decisions. Who knows what we will find at Tizoc's club? She doesn't know we've arrived yet so I will text her that we've got one extra errand."

"I agree. We have to do this, and do it quick."

# 17

Adam and Maria parked behind Zuma Zuma. It looked different in the light, like all seedy places do. But it was better to be here before the club got busier with staff before opening after dark. No one seemed to be around just yet. The building was a concrete box, its paint faded by the relentless Mexican sun. At night, the lights cast shadows so no one noticed the age of the building or the cracks along the walls. The grand palms, illuminated in the evening to look majestic, now hung with brown leaves and names etched into the trunks. The stench of trash and alcohol lingered like a foul vapor.

Maria opened the trunk of her car, took out an old shopping bag she'd picked up from a tacky souvenir shop, then led Adam around the back of the building to the spot where she had buried Tizoc. The anxiety taxing her adrenal glands was the same as the day she had looked into the locked trunk of the Camaro for some small clue. At least this time she had help.

"Maybe someone found him, or the stray dogs got to him?" Adam said.

"I hope not, and the dogs get fed well with those dumpsters. But there's only one way to find out."

Swiftly, they pulled weeds, woody branches and bright flowers away to reach the soil. Then they clawed at the dirt with their bare hands, moving much faster than average humans. For a short while Maria was afraid his body was gone. Dirt flew in all directions the harder they dug.

Then Maria felt something solid. She grasped it and pulled it out. A human bone. Small beetles and maggots clinging to the dirt fell from her fingers.

"We found him," she said.

Tizoc's flesh was indeed gone: Adam explained it decomposed faster than a human's without a blood source. Only his worm-infested skeleton remained hidden among the dry dead leaves and dirt, like some long-lost grisly treasure. They scooped up every fragment they could find under the dirty, rotting clothing and placed it in Maria's bag.

"I didn't know. If I had, I would have burned him as soon as he died." She cursed her ignorance.

Adam halted in this gruesome task. "Maria, you've had to learn so much on your own already. There was no way you could have known. You can't apologize for something out of your control. If it's anyone's fault, it's mine for leaving you to fend for yourself with no guidance."

Maria knew he was right, but it was a mistake she wouldn't make again. She had taught herself another language, survived a personal wilderness of hunger and anger, and now she would learn everything she could about what they were and this strange entity called Lucifer. The only devils she knew were the ones here on Earth. She rose to her feet with renewed confidence and the bag in her hand. "Now that we have what we came for, we should go."

Hours after the two vampires left, evening preparations began at Zuma Zuma. Bartenders cut their limes, girls moved in and out of the dressing rooms, and the DJ checked the sound system and lights. That's when Lucifer walked in, not really caring if anyone saw him. He walked straight to Tizoc's office. The room was a sloppy, disorganized mess, which wasn't in keeping with Tizoc's personality. Lucifer also noticed what appeared to be claw marks in the carpet, and a small spattering of blood across a tacky dog painting on the wall. These pathetic humans didn't notice the simplest things because they were all so consumed with their next meal, lay, paycheck or bowel movement.

He opened the window to peer outside. He had already demanded the overflowing dumpsters be searched, but nothing had turned up. Where was the man? Tizoc was a lot of odious things, but disloyal he was not. He wasn't supposed to die, at least not yet.

Lucifer's intention was to find out all about Tizoc's business: who the vampire players were and who was human. He was taking stock: deciding who would live and who would die as he resolved to rid the world of its ugliness once and for all. The plan had always been for Tizoc to die but whoever had taken him down prematurely had mighty big balls.

Lucifer would have to use most of the little power he could muster here—but not too much. Any more would go noticed by the Almighty. Lucifer wanted to see this picture fully. He hated going from cosmic to human form. He felt so weak on Earth, chafing against the rules the gods had imposed upon him. The gods only pretended to be as silent as spiders living in the corner of some barn, but Lucifer knew that the Almighty saw and felt all, with its many watchful eyes and exposed nerve endings.

Lucifer sat behind the desk and closed his eyes. The radiation of his true form cleared the barriers of gray junk within his skull. Through Tizoc's eyes he saw a vampire woman; he felt Tizoc's immediate desire for her; he heard the names Adam and Mordecai; saw the scuffle; and, just as he suspected, Tizoc's eventual death. He also sensed Tizoc's bones were gone.

With that frustrating revelation, Lucifer shut down his use of power before it could be felt in the heavens. He wanted those bones, and soon. It wouldn't be long until some demon would claim to be the victor of the US election. Demons fought to the death to claim human leaders, their favorite hands of mischief. Now, almost all the world leaders had one of those insatiable creatures embedded in their backs, sometimes the claws dug in so deep they calcified into bone. Lucifer already knew the outcome, giving him the advantage no matter what little wrenches the heavens or demons might want to throw his way.

Horace Kilburn, his candidate, was one of the worst kinds of human: textbook narcissist, completely unaware of his personal shortcomings. When things went wrong, and they always did with these types of humans, they were the first to blame someone else. His hate was infectious. This was exactly why this pompous buffoon was perfect, as he was pliable to Lucifer's influence. His eventual descent into madness would make him disposable with the flick of a finger. What made this pawn even more attractive was that Mr. Kilburn's bloodline was just as involved in his circus of the ridiculous—a nice bit of insurance.

Tizoc's bones might be missing but he had discovered an enticing new vampire. And the repulsive Tizoc and his equally repellent protégé José, with their distasteful appetites, were dead and he hadn't had to lift a finger. He had thought that, after a few millennia, the pleasure of his unfolding plans would wear off, but it never did. Sometimes these pathetic humans made it too easy.

# Part Two

# 18

Maria felt her nerves amp up even higher as she finally boarded the flight to the U.S. from Monterrey airport. Her dream of the States was finally coming true, even if it wasn't as she had imagined all those years ago. She was a near-immortal, caught up in some cosmic fight she didn't fully understand, on her way to America, followed by England, to meet a whole bunch of other near-immortals. Maria had always doubted she had any talent or any worth, but now she felt like El Castillo: able to withstand the sun, wind, and rain.

Maria sat with a still-grieving Paloma on one side and Adam on the other. Her friend needed her more than ever. Maria believed the difficult part of her journey was ending, while for Paloma it was just beginning.

She held Paloma's hand, passed her tissues when she burst into tears, and allowed her to vent when she needed to, but offered no advice. As she knew all too well, there was nothing she could say that would ease her pain or make it right. She was also afraid to say the wrong thing at the wrong time. The little she knew of José wasn't good. The usual platitudes didn't apply in this situation. Paloma seemed satisfied with silent support: that was something Maria could provide.

Later, when Paloma closed her eyes to sleep, Maria turned to Adam.

"Tell me, Adam, what do I need to know about this Vlad? You don't seem too pleased to be meeting him."

Adam rolled his eyes and leaned back in his seat. "Where do I even begin? He isn't bad per se, and I am no one to judge. But he loves himself a little too much."

"You have to tell me more." She leaned in toward Adam.

"He is a complicated man. The last time I saw him we had to flee Russia. The Revolution was in full violent swing, which meant the party was over. Rasputin, one of the worst vampires to ever be created, had been captured, tortured, and had died several deaths. We all suspected that, once he squealed, we would be next. The smart move was to go our separate ways, but before we did Vlad took a young girl named Anastasia as his new protégé. She was as good as dead if he didn't take her with him. They were close, like family. She joined the Keepers but was killed before I was part of the organization. He abandoned the Keepers and all vampires after her death. His grief was like a blast of anger towards us. As a vampire you get used to losing people. Some hit harder than others, especially when it's another vampire and you think you have all the time in the world with them. These days, from what I know, Vlad loves social media and social media loves him—or at least the human everyone thinks he is. In reality, he is no more of a psychic than anyone else."

"Psychic? What do you mean?" asked Maria, now very intrigued.

"He has a very popular entertainment show in Vegas. He's created an irresistible image for the age we live in. It has to be bigger, better. Everything is done with no expense spared. Everyone wants a dream, and Vlad is happy to oblige a very self-indulgent one."

"That's it?"

"He's also the son of Vlad the Impaler."

Paloma turned her head and opened one eye. "See, this is why I will happily stay on this plane. Go handle it."

"Are you sure, Paloma?" Maria didn't want her friend to feel abandoned.

"Just go. I'll be alright and I'm in no mood to meet the son of Vlad the Impaler. Thank you for caring, though." She gave Maria's hand a double pat.

"Maybe it's safer. I don't want to cross your mother. Adam will come and get you when we know what is happening."

"Thank you, Maria. I don't want to weigh down important vampire business. Plus thinking about my dad, my guilt... the truth. Feels like a platter of leftover carne asada covered in flies. I could use more sleep and rest as I process it all."

Paloma rose from her seat and stretched. "My head is pounding. I'm going to the back to try to sleep properly. See you both later."

"Sleep well."

Paloma nodded before heading to the small cabin with a bed.

"Guess it's just us, Adam. I'm going to rest as well."

"Not a bad idea, Maria. Who knows what will happen next?"


They landed in Las Vegas around three in the morning. Maria checked on a still sleeping Paloma before deplaning with Adam. A black Bentley awaited their arrival, to take them to Vlad's compound in the desert. Adam opened the door for Maria then walked to the other side. Vlad's driver glanced back when they were both seated. He was a big gringo in his forties, human, with old tattoos on his hands. Their shapes had bled and faded into his skin. Country music played on the satellite radio. "I will get you to your destination as soon as possible."

"Thank you. Do you mind using the scenic route down the Las Vegas Strip?" Adam asked.

The driver nodded. "Yes, sir."

Maria watched the parade of twinkling lights covering innumerable hotels in complete awe. Each one was more beautiful than the other. Even at nearly four a.m., people flooded the streets without a care in the world, in this playground for adults with money and time on their hands. Maria wondered how it must feel to have the luxury of time and money. There were fountains, a pyramid, endless restaurants and large screens advertising pop stars performing at some hotel or another.

As they passed one large hotel Adam chuckled.

"What was that about?" Maria asked, looking out his window.

"That man on the billboard is Vlad."

Maria craned her neck and twisted to look back as they continued to drive. A massive billboard displayed the image of a man in dark sunglasses and a white suit performing card tricks. The banner read *BILLY XERXES: BLOW YOUR MIND.*

Once they passed the lights, they hit the desert again. There were strip malls and luxury car dealerships and a development where the houses looked like picture-perfect creations spit out of some giant mold. The yards were green and manicured with tall palm trees. She could make out every detail in the darkness with her sharp vision. Maria thought it looked like a commercial: the so-called "dream life".

Dawn was still in hiding when they pulled up to a solid metal gate. After a few seconds it opened to a long driveway that cut through a garden of cacti and giant agaves. Small lights illuminated the grander plants. The drive led to a sprawling modern geometric mansion, all concrete and glass. The road looped around a large fountain topped with a sculpture of a dragon spewing water from its mouth. As they approached, a red light illuminated the water.

"Classy as ever," Adam mumbled under his breath.

Despite the early hour, a woman in foot-binding-sized heels and a minidress opened one of the black double doors as they exited the car. From what Maria could tell, she appeared and smelled human as well.

"Welcome. Please follow me." She spoke with a pleasant, robotic voice. The type of tone you hear when put on hold.

The entranceway was all marble, modern art, and black-and-white photographs of a man Maria now recognized as Vlad himself in various poses. Maria was astonished by the size of the entryway, without even seeing the rest of the house. She had never seen such an ostentatious show of wealth.

The woman escorted them through the entrance that opened up to a massive sitting room featuring all-white leather furniture, including a large L-shaped couch and matching love seat. Around the entryway and the main room were various exotic plants in all sizes in decorative white pots. In the center was an enormous glass coffee table. The left side wall had a gaping fireplace with a thick, shaggy black rug laid in front of it. The entire back wall was made of large glass windows and a double door. Their escort opened them and continued to the flagstone patio.

The outside resembled an adult version of Neverland:

the extensive space contained an array of exotic plants, a neon-lit bar, DJ booth, and right in the center an illuminated pool as large as a small lake.

"Welcome to paradise!" a deep male voice boomed across the patio.

Overwhelmed by the scene before her, Maria had failed to notice Vlad himself, who was sitting in a rocky hot tub made to look like a Japanese onsen. His head was thrown back, with arms outstretched in complete relaxation. Small beads of water glistened on his dark well-trimmed beard.

"Want a drink? Thalia, can you please serve our guests? Thanks."

Thalia lifted a tray off a marble bar not far from the onsen. Frosty silver pouches with little spouts at the end stood at attention in a row. Maria could smell the blood from where she was standing. Her stomach growled and she grabbed a pouch as soon as the tray was within range.

Vlad watched Maria devour the blood with amusement. "Hello, Maria." He grinned. "Where have you guys been?" He lifted a muscled arm from the water and gestured at them. "You look like you just walked out of an episode of *The Walking Dead*. Yikes. You're both filthy. Have you been rolling in a graveyard and taking this vampire biz a little serious?"

Maria stopped mid-sip. She didn't know what this guy was talking about, but she knew she felt insulted by this asshole. Sure, he was good looking but unlike Jorge, he knew it. She was about to toss the pouch into his hot tub, when Adam put a gentle hand on her shoulder to stop her.

"Vlad, cut the act. You're not on stage. This is just business." He nodded towards the house. "Looks like the entertainment industry has been good to you."

Thalia had also served Vlad a blood pouch and he paused to respond. "Hey, we make our own luck."

Adam gave him an irritated look. "Family money doesn't hurt either, does it? Speaking of which, what brought you away from Romania?"

Vlad crumpled the used pouch to throw into a small recycling bin. "First, don't talk to me about family money. You haven't exactly been a pauper all those hundreds of years. Second, I love my homeland, but the weather sucks half the time, there was always some political conflict, and the ladies don't exactly flock to Castle Dracul—if you know what I'm saying."

He surveyed Maria, his eyes running up and down her body, and gave her a playful wink.

"I would love to know your history. You are one enchanting tumbleweed."

Maria refused to speak or smile.

Vlad turned back to Adam. "That sister of yours finally left her billionaire brother for some other billionaire sucker?"

Adam placed his empty pouch back on the tray Thalia was still holding. "Adelaide is dead, and all my assets are in the good hands of the Keepers, though it sure as hell won't buy me a place in Heaven. I found that out the hard way." He sighed. "I also want to give you my condolences with regards to Anastasia."

Vlad sat upright, the water bubbling around him. "I'm so sorry, man—I didn't know about Adelaide. Anastasia... Well," he sneered, "why don't you ask Mordecai about that?" Maria thought it was the first snippet of authentic emotion Vlad had shown since they arrived.

"Mordecai is why we're here," Adam said. "He thinks the world is on the verge of something apocalyptic."

Vlad stood up and stretched with his arms raised outwards. His large, chiseled body dripped with water and steam rose from his skin. Dark curly hair covered his chest and trailed beneath his swim trunks. He had to be at least six inches taller than Adam, who was six feet tall himself. Maria didn't want to notice his physique, but she did. He stepped out of the hot tub, grabbed a towel from a free-standing metal spike with a hook, then placed it around his shoulders. "I'm not into your Keeper bullshit anymore, but if it's in my interest to help, I will. Show me what you got."

Maria took Tizoc's dead iPad out of her bag and handed it to Vlad. "It belonged to a real nasty vampire named Tizoc who was into some bad shit. It's encrypted and needs charging. It's worth a look to see the extent of his business and who he was working with. Adam has a photo of a man we need to know more about as well."

"Yeah, I heard you killed him. That was almost

enough to get you over here. Impressive, Maria. Mordecai had to give me the details I needed to know before I agreed to help him at all." Vlad inspected the blurry picture on Adam's phone. "I might know one or two people at a certain fruit-named company, but as far as this chump, who is he? A Russian spy?"

Adam looked at Maria then paused. "His name is Lucifer."

Vlad's eyes darted between Maria and Adam with an amused look on his face. "Wait. Please tell me this guy's mom just chose a really bad name. You aren't telling me we are looking for *the* Lucifer? Horn, goat hooves, orgies with virgins?" Vlad let out a bellowing laugh.

Maria and Adam didn't share his amusement.

"That's actually a false perception of him." Adam said with a straight face.

"You're serious. You Keepers really have got into some dog's mess this time. I'll have a guy run some facial recognition software and let you know if there's a trail. Mordecai didn't mention Lucifer, but he did say my help was needed because it could be linked to the election and the wrong guy elected spells disaster backwards and forwards."

"That's why we must act fast." Adam kept his serious expression.

"You know, Kilburn is like a tapeworm. You don't know it's festering in your guts until your body starts to break down in some awful, painful way, then someone's pulling a meter of worm out of your ass. Are you sure your 'Lucifer' is interested in this guy? No way he'll be elected. Have you heard him speak?"

Adam grabbed another pouch from Thalia's tray and although appeared friendly to her face, when her back turned he looked at her with suspicion. "Can we speak so candidly with her around?"

"What? Thalia? Don't worry, man, she earns more for her silence then most people will see in their entire lives. I also sometimes add a little drop of my blood to her wine to keep her looks up. Cheaper than fillers and Botox and less painful. Not as permanent as being a vampire. She loves it… Now, go on?"

"Very well, as I was saying, Vlàd, we have lived through history. We are old enough to *be* history. We've seen this play out before. It's *because* Kilburn is unqualified as a leader that he's the perfect puppet. The guy is dangerous without any help whatsoever, but he might need a little push to start some sort of Armageddon. I can't see my way through this yet. I have to trust Mordecai."

Vlad shrugged his shoulders. "I can't stand the guy and his 'Make America Number One Again' chants. I mean, what does that even mean? But, hey, I'm having a few people over tomorrow after my show. Why don't you and the Tijuana princess make yourselves comfortable, stay a few nights. And, by all means, clean up."

Maria took a step closer to Vlad and narrowed her eyes. "Let's get a few things straight. I'm not going to work with some pendejo who can't treat me with respect. Don't talk about how I look or call me anything except my name. I'm no princess; I'm not from Tijuana. Don't put me in some little Mexican box with a tag. You don't know shit about me. Comprende?"

Adam failed to conceal his glee at Maria's admonishment of Vlad.

Vlad looked at Maria in wonderment. "You know, Anastasia would have loved you, Maria. Forgive me for thinking I'm more charming and entertaining than I really am. I like a woman who knows her own mind. I've noted your wishes, Maria. I'm a jerk. Ask everyone I know."

"Apology accepted," Maria said with a nod.

Adam cleared his throat. "There's one more thing. I have Tizoc's bones. I left them at an airport locker in case we were followed here. Maria's good friend Paloma is also waiting there as she rests. I would feel more comfortable if they were here with us."

"Sounds alright to me," said Vlad.

Maria nodded in agreement. "Sure. I'd like to rest and take a bath."

# 19

Vlad sent Adam off with his driver—still sat in the car, on call—to retrieve the bones from the airport. Vlad gave the iPad to Thalia to charge up and told her to show Maria to the guest house.

Vlad then lay in the morning sun as usual, like a sleeping Komodo dragon. The light hit his eyelids and warmed his entire body. Money couldn't buy the sensation of the desert heat blanket enveloping him like a womb while bringing his senses out of their meditative state. He always had his best ideas for the show at this time of day. Prince's 'When Doves Cry' began to play as his wake-up call. He was a diehard Metallica, Radiohead, Pearl Jam, and Wu Tang guy, but the sound of Prince's voice triggered special memories. He listened to this song, these lyrics, and couldn't help but think of those days just before he was made into a vampire, and later his life with Anastasia. She had loved Prince.

His past life was just an old, cobbled road of pain

and resentment, but he loathed self-pity. When he felt sorry for himself, he didn't have to look far to read about someone who had it far worse. His thoughts morphed again like the shapes of moving clouds. *Lucifer.* He chuckled under his breath. He didn't even believe in God. His belief had started to wane fighting in war after war, and any shred of faith was shot out of his heart after spending time in the trenches during World War One. How could he forget that sweaty pencil-dick Hitler or the napalm-scarred faces in Vietnam? He had tried to save as many of his men as he could, but there were always too many.

Fuck the commies, fascists, politicians and all the other goons who ran the show with the same results century after century. He did his part in the wars before selling his soul to himself. Now he was the hottest psychic and magician in Vegas, with an Instagram following that rivaled the biggest celebrities. He had gone by many different names throughout the years; today he was Billy Xerxes because he couldn't live life as a historical myth in the shadows. At birth he was Vlad IV, named after his father, whom he despised as much as dogshit on a new pair of shoes.

When Bram Stoker's *Dracula* was printed, he enjoyed the sweet satisfaction of knowing his father would be remembered as nothing more than a fictional character. The joke would forever be on that cruel tyrant, while Vlad himself lived a charmed life in the sunshine. He masked his ageless face with a perfectly groomed thick beard he had cultivated since before he became a vampire, and designer sunglasses; after all, he owned an entire wall of them. He became a well-defined specimen of a man, with a body built through years of training and battle, even before he was made into a vampire at the age of thirty.

Once he abandoned the Keepers and all other vampires after Anastasia's death, he began to live the life he always knew he was meant to have—starting with women, lots of women. He went through women like a man with the flu goes through tissues because love was something he couldn't explain or handle. Vlad was the keeper of Vlad, and that's the way he liked it. Once everything in his life was lost not once, but too many times to count, nothing really mattered.

His reverie was broken by the eclipse of the morning sun. The hair on his chest crinkled and shrank.

"Hello, Billy boy—or do I call you Vlad, like your father?" said a sharp sarcastic voice, unnervingly close by. *Where the fuck was Thalia*? "I see you grew a beard just like him before you were turned."

Vlad opened his eyes. He couldn't see the details of the man's face because of the blinding sun behind him. He only felt the blood in his stomach bubble with the thought of his father. His eyes slowly began to adjust to the light. "Who the hell are you?"

"Lucifer. I don't think we've met before."

Vlad sat upright, his tiny bird of paradise swim trunks pressing hard against his meaty thighs. He looked around for Thalia. "How did you get in here?"

Lucifer laughed.

Vlad could see him clearly now: He appeared like a man who came from old European money, with impeccable style from his tailored suit to his pristine shoes. Although he looked to be in his late forties, maybe fifties, he had a radiant glow of perfect health with perfect teeth, hair that had wisps of gray perfectly placed at the temples, and a strong jawline to compliment his piercing eyes.

"There's no one here," Lucifer said. "I sent your little crumpet in ridiculous heels on an errand in town. She will be gone for hours."

Vlad jumped up. "You know who you're messing with, pal?"

Lucifer stuffed his hands into his suit pockets and started to walk around the patio. "Of course I do. I know you're a womanizer, a fraud, you've got a room full of guns you will never need, absolutely hideous taste in everything, and you are the way you are because you don't believe in God and you're afraid to die."

Vlad was never without the last word, but now he knew to stay calm and quiet. He felt like Billy in *Predator*; something moved in the jungle. Lucifer's eyes had a sharp coldness; his presence emitted a dense energy.

Vlad shrugged his shoulders. "What do you want, man?"

Lucifer continued to walk around the patio, stopping periodically to listen to the birds or watch the trickling water from the waterfall on the opposite side of the pool. "I love what you have done here, though. I have to give you some credit. The lushness of the foliage reminds me of the long-forgotten Eden that this planet once was. Shame the humans had to ruin it."

"It's not a garden party and you aren't my pal. I said, what do you want, *Lucifer*?"

Lucifer turned on his heels. The click of his expensive-looking shoes on the patio stones seemed to echo. "Yes. Business. I think you should rejoin the Keepers. Everyone must pick a side. And poor old Mordecai is on the way out for good."

"We are immortal, so I doubt it... and what do you care about me and the Keepers?"

"I care because, like it or not, your kind and my kind are more like each other than we are like humans. I know you can't live without them, but it's time they received a formal eviction notice for not taking care of this place. It's time for new management before it's run to the ground."

"Management? What the hell? And if I don't join you?" Vlad walked towards Lucifer, but as he got closer, he felt his giant frame was suddenly stopped, as if an invisible force had wrapped a rope around his entire body. He was paralyzed.

Then Lucifer moved so close to Vlad that he could smell his blood and hear his heartbeat. Lucifer's eyes were like black holes, infinite and all-consuming. "Well, you may not believe in God, but you will believe in *me* when I'm through with you." Lucifer raised his chin and looked around as if he sensed something unseen. "Hm."

Vlad tried to move. "What's 'hm'? You have some other master plan?"

"Oh, nothing. I will see myself out."

Vlad watched Lucifer leave and felt the bonds loosen. He wondered what the hell he had got himself into.


Vlad retreated to his white leather living room to contemplate what had just happened. As his thoughts raced, he paced around the solid alabaster coffee table in the center of the room, surrounded by the elegant photos of himself adorning the cream-colored walls.

When Adam entered the room, Vlad didn't bother to look up. "Your boy was just here."

Adam sounded confused. "Who?"

"Lucifer. He knew all about me and wanted me to help him."

Finally raising his head, he saw all color from his recently drunk blood drained from Adam's face. "Was Maria there?" he asked.

"No, Thalia took her to the guest house to clean up."

Adam glanced at his phone. "I haven't heard from her—we need to find her." He turned to the glass doors and broke into a run as he hit the patio heading in the direction of the guest house.

Vlad chased after him and grabbed Adam's arm. "Wait, there's a camera in the room. Let's have a look first. You think she'll want two men crashing into her room? I learned my lesson earlier, pal. Plus, I get the feeling she can take care of herself considering what she did to Tizoc."

Adam paused. "You keep a camera in your guest house? What if she's changing, or, I don't know…"

"There's not one in the bathroom! And it's my house."

Adam looked at Vlad with suspicion. "Fine, just briefly. No leering. Be a gentleman."

Vlad led Adam behind a mirrored wall to a small room filled with monitors, that covered every angle of the property. The camera in the guest house was switched on. They both froze.

# 20

Maria lay in the tub, which was large enough for four, staring at the micro-light speckled ceiling. It reminded her of the star-filled nights she had spent sat on the rocks overlooking the sea in Acapulco. No constellations here. As much as she hated to admit it, this enormous room and sunken bathtub were pure heaven. It was the kind of tub she'd imagined she would have had to clean, or watch other people's children splash around in, once in the States. Enough time had passed for her to truly understand what crossing the border would have meant for her if she had succeeded in 1995. Your dreams can't thrive if other people's prejudices are like bulletproof glass. Now, all she had to do was enjoy herself and be herself.

She just needed someone sat across from her. Since Adam arrived in her life, her "fight or flight" mode had switched off. The scales that hardened her core were chipping away. Touching her lips, she remembered

Paloma's almost kiss. She had never kissed a woman before, but there was always a first time for everything. No—Paloma was a true friend, not a bit of fun. And she got the feeling Paloma was looking for something much deeper, something she wasn't ready to give. She closed her eyes at this thought, allowing her hand to slowly move from her neck toward her navel. Maria needed a release.

Soft tones of piano and bass drifted into the room. She hoped Vlad wasn't trying to seduce her because she wasn't in the mood for a fight. Annoyed, she pulled herself from the tub. Ribbons of fallen hair from her bun clung to her neck. Maria grabbed the nearest towel, wrapping it around her body and moving into the bedroom. Before she could get a single curse out of her mouth, her steps were brought to a halt by an unexpected sight.

An attractive man in his late forties sat with his eyes closed in a plush midnight blue velvet armchair, listening to every note of the lonely horn that chimed in alongside the piano. The man's hair was slicked back with flecks of gray at his temples. His skin was a windswept tan, not from hard outdoor labor, but rather the kind of bronzing someone gets from spending too much time in the sun on a sailing trip or watching the water from a yacht in the south of France. He wore linen trousers, a crisp white shirt and suede loafers.

As she stared, he opened his dark eyes to look at Maria. The intensity of his gaze struck her hard, like a spotlight.

"Who are you? Get out!" she snapped, though she wasn't sure she meant it.

"I wanted to meet you," he replied with a voice as sultry as the music. "The strength you must have in your body and soul to best a vampire like Tizoc intrigues me. I look at you and I see an abandoned, carved-out coastline of dangerous cliffs, with azure water breaking hard against its jagged rocky shore. One false step and down one might fall, never to be seen again."

Maria held her ground despite being very conscious that she was mostly naked. Her hat and boots were her armor these days. Now they lay out of reach on the bed, behind this stranger who she found herself drawn to. It was the kind of sexual alchemy that leaves your good sense with the tip at a bar and your body in a taxi, elevator or the bed of a stranger. The last man to disarm her this way was Diego. The two men couldn't be more different. This man's hands were manicured, without the black stains of motor oil. Had he ever worked a hard day in his life? But it was always the eyes and mouth of a man she noticed. She used to want kind eyes or a smile of satisfaction from something she did to please. Now she wanted the satisfaction of his lips on her skin, asking her what he should do next. She was so different from the naive girl she had been all those years ago. They stared at each other in silence as if nothing existed except their bodies. She liked the way he looked at her.

Then he broke the spell. "I'm sorry for the intrusion, but so much time has been wasted already." He rose and brought Maria a robe which lay over the back of the vanity chair. "Please allow me to help you feel more comfortable."

His politeness was baffling. She felt vulnerable in just a towel so she accepted his offer. He opened the robe and turned his face away while she slipped it on, belting it closed.

"Dance with me, Maria."

She continued to resist him despite being racked with lust. "No." She wasn't going to be as easy as Tizoc, who had made his arousal very apparent. She was stronger than that. Wasn't she?

He smiled. She cursed herself for finding its charm sexy. He held out his hand.

"Please?"

There was no sexual ulterior motive in his eyes, and if there was one thing Maria could read it was hungry men. As nice as Diego was, there was always that look of "You're mine." If anyone was thinking of sex at this moment, it was Maria. She reached out, touching his fingers. Whatever drew her eyes to him traveled to her body. She wanted him.

For years she had chosen to shut down her desire, but now some internal circuit had decided to rebel. A warm radiation that felt like the sun on her eyelids as she awoke pulsed from his body. Her intuition told her exactly who this might be, but she didn't dare to even think his name. His features roughly matched the out of focus photo on Adam's phone. He held her close.

"'Blue In Green.' Miles Davis. Beautiful, isn't it? If I sat at the edge of the universe, I wouldn't be bothered with cherubim and seraphim singing my praises. No, there would be jazz, blues and soul."

Maria gulped, trying to bring any moisture to the quicksand in her throat that hindered her voice.

"Miles Davis, Coltrane, Howlin' Wolf would play their soul-stirring music for an eternity for me, for everyone. Everyone deserves a seat at the table."

She closed her eyes, hearing the music's melodic call and understanding its visionary yearning. It was easy to move to. Perhaps she was attracted to him because he seemed as lonely as she was, or maybe it was the thought of all those sexual deeds she never got to try with Diego. She inched closer to the growing nebula of temptation, ready to gasp for air in the throes of previously denied pleasure.

He looked at Maria's face. "You don't seem frightened of me; very curious."

Maria laid her head on his chest, listening for a heartbeat as they continued to dance. He smelled of honeysuckle: she had an overwhelming desire to scratch his chest with a single fang so she could lick tendrils of his blood while he pleasured her. She wondered why he was still talking.

"Maria, we are so much alike. We have a shining light within us yet there is also something else as dark as blood. You don't need to hide yourself from me; strangely, I also feel a desire to confess to you." He stepped back to look into her eyes. "I want this planet to be as it was before humankind ruined it. I mean, it's not all the humans' fault. The gods didn't do a very good job setting humans on the road to success, did they? Telling them to believe but not showing themselves. Humans ran with their own corrupt interpretations. I'm trying to bring about a new beginning: one where I'm not your enemy, and the gods can just be the gods. Humans think I'm this evil being, all horns and sulfur. It's a story humans had to tell to excuse inexcusable behavior. In fact, I'm a manifestation of the gods."

Deaf to his words, she remained hypnotized by the distracting scent of his skin and blood. She wondered what his warmth would feel like inside her. She wasn't hungry: this need to pierce his wrist or unbuckle his belt to taste this man on her lips and in her mouth would be just for her excitement. Sea spray hitting the back of her throat, perhaps his mouth fogging the inside of her thighs; the possibilities were endless.

She managed to whisper, "Who are you?"

He smiled and moved close enough to Maria's ear that she could feel his lips on her skin. "How can you not know? I'm Lucifer."

Maria's small wet footsteps came to a stop.

Lucifer looked straight at Maria again. "How about a little Otis Redding, 'Try a Little Tenderness?' I can't think of a more appropriate song for you." Music began to play. "It's been a while, hasn't it, Maria? Since you were this close to anyone."

Maria couldn't argue with that statement. She was

so weary, just like the song sang. Breathlessly she said, "I don't know what you want with me."

Giving her the slightest of smiles, he dug his fingers deeper into the fluffy robe. "Right now, I just want this. Don't stop dancing."

Maria didn't want to stop. Of all the men, after all these years, the one she felt a spark for was her enemy. Now, like plumes of smoke from a dormant volcano, something dangerous and hot stirred inside. She trembled with years of physical loneliness.

Lucifer brought his hand to her hair, unpinning the bun while keeping in tune with her body. The blood of her most recent feed was causing her to feel flush. She hoped it wasn't arousal. She couldn't even begin to remember what excitement with another body even felt like. Desire had been a distant glimmer while she bathed and now it was glowing. A nugget of luminous coal between her legs begged to be stroked as it created moistness, like a slowly melting ice cube.

Lucifer ran his hand through her hair, then traced the side of her face, shoulders, and hips. She felt his warm hands touch her leg as he pulled the robe open. His thigh brushed against her little coal while they danced, taking her to the cliff's edge of orgasm right there in his arms. If Lucifer was the father of sin, he wouldn't mind obliging her body.

Maria reached out to touch Lucifer's smooth cheek. But he grabbed her wrists before her fingertips managed to graze his skin. They held each other's gaze.

"I find myself powerless to stop whatever you want, Maria. This kind of thing isn't meant for me."

He released her wrists, allowing her to place one hand in his hair while the other traced his features. His skin turned to gooseflesh beneath her fingertips. Maria pressed herself against Lucifer's thigh, allowing a soft moan to escape her lips. One of her hands bought his face closer to her own. Her tongue snake-charmed its way between his lips while she placed his hand on her bare thigh. The shyness of youth vanished to make way for a woman's needs. He squeezed her flesh, producing an erection she could feel. It increased her arousal. As the tempo of the music changed, Maria let her inhibitions go. His hands clasped her hips, pressing her closer with every note as they kissed and explored each other's bodies like new lovers.

"Taste my blood, Maria. You could drain me over and over and I would never die."

Her mouth moved to his neck and she scraped it with a single fang. The faintest trickle of blood trailed into her mouth. She would have liked to say this devil made her want him, but she knew, deep down, she wanted him all on her own. Maria wanted his body, breath and blood all for herself in an endless feast.


Adam couldn't believe what he was watching on the screen as he stood next to Vlad. "Mordecai was right. He is still here—and up to no good."

Vlad's eyes were wide with disbelief, "Yeah, and they're... making out?"

Lucifer was looking straight at the camera with a smile. He turned Maria toward the lens, planting a light kiss on her exposed neck before whispering in her ear. Maria pointed to her bag. He walked to it and pulled out a tube of red lipstick. On the white bedsheets he scribbled, *Hello, Adam. Bring me Tizoc's bones.*

Adam flashed a look toward Vlad. "Again, it's a long story. Can we talk and run at the same time?"

"All right then, Charles Dickens, if you can't tell me what the hell is going on, may I suggest we come up with a plan to get Maria out of trouble and send the Devil back to Hell."

"Well, how long does it take to get to the guest house?"

"You got maybe two minutes."

"I guess I'll tell you the short version."

Adam stared at Lucifer through the monitor. The Devil was sat on the bed, holding both of Maria's hands as she stood before him. If he didn't know better, Adam thought Lucifer looked like a pilgrim pleading at the feet of a saint for a miracle.

"Honestly, I'm not sure what he is playing at."

Vlad grabbed Adam's chin, directing it toward another camera which showed the inside of a small room, stacked wall-to-wall with guns, ammunition, grenades, and more firepower.

"That room is right under the guest house. I put it

there because if anything happened to my toy box of weapons, I'd be safe here, and if anything went down here, I'd be safe there."

Adam gave Vlad a puzzled look. "You are very paranoid for a vampire."

Vlad threw his hands up. "Do you watch the news? Anyway, I can remotely detonate that room, giving us maybe five minutes to grab Maria, maybe the bones too, run back to the main house then start the panic procedure that will reinforce the windows. The walls were built for artillery shells, so we're good."

Adam couldn't believe his ears. "Is that it? You make it sound easy."

Vlad paused as if shuffling through cards in his brain. "Yeah, I think that's it. Grab the bones."

"Look, we can't destroy him, but we can get him out of here for a while. It will give us time to figure out his little game."

A few minutes later, Adam was running toward the guesthouse with the bag of bones, followed by Vlad. They burst into the bedroom and Adam threw them at Lucifer's feet, knowing they stood over a basement packed with explosives. He wasn't a beast of a warrior like Vlad. He was accustomed to his weapons being money and intrigue.

"Lucifer, here are the bones. Now leave her alone."

———

Maria wiped the thread of blood from her mouth as she looked at the bag of bones. She couldn't look into

Lucifer's eyes after tasting him. But she knew what she had to do. Tightening her grip on the center of her robe to keep it closed, she moved to stand next to Adam. She couldn't indulge her temptation any longer. She knew which side she was on.

"I wasn't holding Maria ransom," said Lucifer smoothly. His eyes were on Maria as he spoke but she couldn't meet his gaze. "She could have walked away at any time. Did my little message threaten her? No, you came up with that story all by yourself. I'm disappointed in you, Adam. Your sister and I spent so many years together without you ever having any quarrel with me and now you've decided to pick a side? Where did all that nihilism go? To be honest, I can't believe you survived that cave. Maybe you aren't as weak as your sister led me to believe. Then again, you were always the nicer, softer sibling."

Maria had never seen Adam so angry. She could smell his blood sour and see his hands trembling. His voice was low and cold as he said, "Leave Adelaide out of it."

A sly smile spread across Lucifer's lips. "Do I detect you choking up with the thought of her? How sweet—she would have disposed of you without a second thought."

"Don't listen to him, Adam. Send him to Hell," Maria said, as she fought back tears of shame.

Lucifer let out a hearty laugh that horrified Maria. "I really like you, Maria, but your 'God' is like an octopus and I'm one of his many arms. You can't get rid of me that easily. We are on the precipice of a new creation. That's the way of the universe. Things have to die so life can explode again. Just let it happen. Your kind will have all the blood you could ever want. You will thrive in the chaos. I bet the Lord didn't anticipate that when he created you."

Lucifer bent down and grabbed the bag of Tizoc's bones. He tossed them at Adam's feet.

"Keep these. They possess a lot of power, so please hold onto them. I just wanted to get your attention. I don't exactly have the best reputation. What I really want is for you to join me. This is a one-time offer so think carefully. Please send my regards to Mordecai. I can sense the future of Earth, and so can he, but that old goat is dying."

Adam walked toward Lucifer. "You're insane."

Lucifer matched his stare as they stood face to face. "Destroying one's only habitat and murdering your own kind century after century for the most trifling reasons is insanity. In fact, let's just check and see if I'm onto something." Lucifer got down on his knees, raised his arms in the air and shouted, "Oh Lord, if I'm betraying your will, strike me down right now!"

The room was silent. Adam, Vlad and Maria looked at each other, afraid to move in the event some great wind would blow them all away.

Lucifer laughed. "I guess that's your answer. I'd best get back to business."

223

Adam grabbed the bag of bones and he and Vlad exchanged glances. Vlad gave him a short nod.

Lucifer studied their faces and glanced towards the floor. He smirked. Maria turned away from Lucifer, unable to process all he had so casually said. As she started to walk away, Lucifer grabbed her hand and pulled her close enough to whisper in her ear. "I'm hurt you think so little of me after what I thought was a special moment between us. You won't die by *my* hand, sweet Maria. I like you too much. Until next time, perhaps. I think your friends plan to get rid of me, but I will show you all that joining me is the only way."

Maria looked into Lucifer's eyes and, for a split second, thought she could see the vast twinkling of space in his pupils.

Then Vlad grabbed her and Adam. "Time to go."

As they stepped through the door, keeping their eyes on him as they went, Lucifer sat back on the bed as though he didn't have a care in the world.

As they left the guest house, Maria saw Vlad reach for his phone.

# 21

Maria hid with Vlad and Adam in the giant walk-in refrigerator—which also served as a panic room, Vlad explained—while Vlad's explosive weaponry destroyed the guesthouse. They hoped it would get rid of Lucifer—at least for now.

"Nothing could have survived that. We should hear sirens any minute now," said Vlad. The big man was clearly shaken.

"He isn't destroyed, just not here. He is an entity... He has survived this long because he has concealed what he really is," said Adam. "I'm sorry about your property. I didn't think we would cause this type of damage."

Vlad threw up his hands. "It's just stuff. I've lost enough homes to know you can build more. Rather a home than... someone. I'm in the fortunate position to sacrifice a house now. This is one of many properties. No problem."

Maria propped herself against the icy wall of the

fridge. Her teeth were chattering and pink tears soaked the sleeves of her white robe. "All my things—my memories—are gone. I have nothing left of my loved ones and I can't go back. I was so stupid. Why *him*?" Tears turned to muffled sobs into her hands as she cursed herself for being so feeble in body and mind. The road between right and wrong was not only narrow, it was filled with booby traps. The small cracks in Maria's carefully built dam gave way and every drop in her ocean came flooding through. Determination had held together her little broken pieces, so she didn't have to confront what she was feeling for all those years.

To Maria's surprise, Vlad kneeled next to her, still shirtless in his bird of paradise swim trunks.

"I've lived long enough and lost a hell of a lot to know the things you can fit in a bag don't mean a thing. The love you shared with those you left behind are your memories, and they can't be destroyed. You've honored them with your life. Which means you're better than I will ever be."

Maria stared at the floor with pins in her mouth, ready to pierce whoever was closest. "Easy coming from someone who has everything and loves anything in a miniskirt. I saw your photos online."

"Maybe I chase women because the ones I loved in this endless life, and everything I ever owned that reminded me of them, was taken away too. To the world, they are just little facts of history. As for that other thing: well, maybe we found Lucifer's weakness in your own. As you said before, I'm a sucker for a hot warm body in a miniskirt."

Maria looked at him with wet eyes and impulsively hugged his neck. "Sorry for being cruel." She wondered if she would ever stop being so hard on herself.

"I didn't take you for the caring type, Vlad," said Adam.

As Vlad helped Maria up, he gave Adam a serious look. "Every coin has two sides, my man. Every coin."

A large bang and the sound of sirens made them jump.

"I better get out there." Vlad said.

He opened the thick door to greet the fire services. Maria and Adam followed, stepping over broken mirrors, glass, and fallen artwork upset by the blast. Sirens blared as black smoke rose from outside the main house. Through the wall of windows facing the garden, they could see the luxury guesthouse and underground arsenal had been replaced by a gaping, smoking hole. A team of firefighters worked to put out the blaze.

Vlad put his arm around Maria's shoulders. "I'll tell you what, Miss Maria, we'll replace everything that was destroyed today. My treat."

She glanced at his arm. "No thank you. I can't accept you buying me clothes."

Vlad was taken back by this statement. "You can't go around kicking ass in a bathrobe. It's nothing for me to do this."

"But it's something to me. I can borrow Paloma's clothes until I find work in England."

Adam interceded. "How about I give you an advance on the work you will do with the Keepers? Believe me, they are never short of hard work. Deal?"

Maria could live with that. "It's a deal, brother. I guess I'm a paid-up member of the Keepers now."


Lucifer's formless being rocketed to the great void. Echoing laughter reverberated in between the indiscernible language of the choir of the gods. Lucifer grumbled as he always did after changing forms. *I'm almost there*, he thought. His mind shifted to his encounter with Maria, so unexpected and titillating. And it was she who took the lead. He wanted to melt into her brown dew-dropped skin to see what was inside. Since first becoming aware of his existence, it never crossed his mind to think or feel these things for another being or creature. Attachment was reserved for the lower creations. It was a mixture of bewilderment and exhilaration.

The urge to be inside her was an unmistakable call, louder than the voices of the gods on his day of condemnation. But not now. With this human-vampire female, Lucifer understood how the first creations in this solar system decided to go through the painful process of clipping their wings to know the women of Earth who gave birth to those ill-fated Nephilim. In the old days, this woman would have been exalted as a bronze-skinned warrior goddess. He thought back to the other women he had happened upon. Jezebel took his poison too readily; Cleopatra was full of teary fear when she placed her hand in his basket. One bite and that was the end of her.

This Maria would have dumped him out of the basket and stomped the life out of him. She wasn't educated in the way humans uphold like gold, or wealthy, or from a family with a name. Despite all of that she commanded an audience and obedience. Maria took her little dusty, insignificant, human life in the universe and moved mountains. No one after all these millennia had been this close to him before. It felt good to Lucifer. Too good—like a trap.

# 22

As Paloma waited on the plane, she closed eyes that felt like they were in a constant state of puffiness. Her head throbbed from dehydration: she was too exhausted from grief to get up and grab a drink. She curled into the leather seat, a light blanket covering her entire body in the hope that cashmere had the power to shield her from the world.

Two hours later, Paloma awoke drenched in sweat and screaming, unaware that she had been dreaming. With a shaky hand, she reached for her phone and messaged Adam and Maria.

*I don't care what I'm risking, I have to see you guys.*

Adam messaged her back immediately. *I will have Vlad arrange a car to pick you up.* She grabbed her handbag and a large bottle of water and quickly deplaned. As her feet reached the hot tarmac, Adam messaged again: she would have to wait about fifteen minutes. The sun and fresh air felt good. It calmed her nerves and cleared her mind. She took deep breaths as she realized her nightmare was over. By the time she had finished her water, a black Mercedes pulled up.

They headed straight to Vlad's compound. She wanted to believe her bad dream had been brought on by the trauma of losing her vampire gangster father to her vampiress mother, but she knew deep down this was the same excuse Ebenezer Scrooge used when meeting the Ghost of Christmas Past.

When Paloma arrived at Vlad's elaborate home, a young woman in soaring heels escorted her to where Adam, Maria and a large man in very small swimming trunks were drinking what she assumed must be blood from delicate china cups. They were sat around a huge glass coffee table in a room furnished in white leather. She was so disturbed by her dream that she barely noticed that the house was an overturned wreck, with wall art on the floor and plants overturned, soil scattered across the rugs.

Adam looked startled at her appearance. "Everything okay? Your message had me worried. When I texted you earlier you said you wanted to sleep more?"

Paloma sat next to Maria and grabbed her hand. "Whatever's going on, I think I'm part of it."

As she spoke, the young woman walked in with a steaming teapot, and a flute of champagne which she handed to Paloma. She placed the champagne bottle on the table nearby. The flute was empty before Adam had brought his cup of blood to his lips.

The large vampire, who she assumed was Vlad, smirked. "I like this girl." He leaned forward and poured her another glass.

Paloma took another drink of champagne. She felt the soft buzz of the alcohol soften the sharp edges of her panic, took a deep breath, and spoke. "You may think this is strange, but on the plane I had a dream like no other dream I have ever experienced. It was more like a vision. When I woke up, I had to see you right away— the images are already fading."

"Take your time," reassured Adam.

Paloma nodded. "First, I saw a large American flag waving against a bright sky. Then that wretched Horace Kilburn smiling and punching his bloated fists in the air. His minion adult children, his niece and her husband were clapping by his side. They looked like wax figures— not too far from what they look like now. Then they opened their mouths and they stretched really wide— and small snakes, worms, and insects started pouring out. The people below kept on chanting Kilburn's name, even as all this was happening. They carried torches of some kind. Tiki torches, I think. It was so weird."

She took another long drink then stared at the champagne bottle, trying to gather her thoughts. She took another deep breath. "Then they started to reach for the tiny wriggling things, which burrowed into their skin. Next another larger snake was crossing the

United States, coast to coast, hissing while its tongue lashed out at people who tried to hack off its head, striking them down.

"Suddenly its scales became metal and it was no longer an animal... The metal snake began to bleed over the land, into the ground. I saw acres and acres of dead land, dead crops, dying animals; rows of hospital beds with men, women, and children, all sick. Trucks of water were being brought to schools by the military. There were food shortages, riots, cities becoming shells because those who could afford to leave do so, and those who were left simply died or lived in squalor."

She squeezed her eyes shut and shook her head. Maria put a comforting arm around her shoulders. Paloma opened her eyes and spoke again. "I saw Horace Kilburn saying it was sabotage, he was blaming someone... I don't know who... I just saw troops, lots of troops and lines and lines of coffins covered in flags. That's all I can remember. There might have been more, but I don't know."

"Well, that's fucking horrifying and apocalyptic," said Vlad. "Makes me think of that song 'Head Like a Hole'."

Paloma looked at Vlad in confusion. "Huh?"

Vlad and Maria answered, "Nine Inch Nails," at the same time.

Maria allowed Vlad a small smile. "I need a Bible."

Vlad brightened. "Not only do I have a Bible, I have a Gutenberg Bible!"

Adam smirked. "Of course you do, Vlad."

"Why do you need one anyway? It's just one big fairytale to keep humans in line." said Vlad.

"Most people think we're fictional beings," said Maria. "Turns out the tales had some basis. My grandmother was religious; Paloma's nightmare made me think of her."

Vlad crossed his arms. "Alright. Follow me."

As Vlad led them to a small elevator, Paloma turned to Maria. "What happened back there? The place is beautiful, but a mess!"

Maria glanced towards Adam. "You might as well tell her," he said.

"Paloma, we had a little run in with Lucifer."

"As in *the* Lucifer? The Morning Star?"

All three vampires nodded at once.

"Yep," Maria said, "and this story just keeps getting weirder."

"You mean reality," quipped Paloma.

"Ladies first," said Vlad when they reached the elevator.

They crowded inside and it dropped them two floors to a room which looked to Maria like a museum. The space was decorated in a deep shade of red. Glass cases enclosed various military uniforms from throughout the ages—some in better condition than others. They were displayed along with what she assumed were the corresponding weapons of their times, plus photographs and other surviving trinkets.

Paloma moved through the room with an expression of awe on her face. She ventured to the case that housed a British First World War uniform—a bloodstained, shredded rag which Vlad had clearly taken the time to display with care. But what interested Maria was in the center of the room: a large, leather-bound Bible sat in another glass case with a single light illuminating it. Paloma stood next to her. "What does Lucifer have to do with anything right now?"

The sensation of the wetness of his mouth returned to Maria's thoughts, but also his coldness towards humanity. "That's what we are trying to find out, but I promise I will keep you safe."

Maria turned to Vlad. "Can we take it out of there?" she asked.

Vlad looked astonished at this question. "Absolutely not! It's climate protected and well secured. I'd probably lose a hand trying to get it out. I saved this because it seemed like a cool thing to have."

Maria rolled her eyes. "Do you have a Bible we can read, not one for show?"

Vlad had to think about this. "Next door is my office and library. There… there might be one on one of the shelves, but no promises. Not my kind of reading. We can also use Google."

Her eyes moved to another case containing a book with a worn brown leather cover. Some of the letters had worn away from the title.

"What is that book?" she asked.

"That is *The Lesser Key of Solomon*," replied Vlad. "It's a few old grimoires all about magic and reveals the seventy-two known demons."

She looked toward Adam. "You mentioned they're real."

"Yeah, according to Wikipedia it was written by an anonymous writer," said Vlad, "but really it was by a vampire named Lars."

Adam peered at the book. "That is true... I must commend you, Vlad, for keeping such a treasure. Demons are as mysterious as they are powerful. Lucifer is one of the most widely known—and most active."

"Good to know." Maria leaned forward to examine the sigils and drawings. They were like nothing she had seen before. She wondered what it said about Lucifer. The thought of him made her fangs subtly grow and her thirst long for his blood again.

Vlad nudged Adam. "We can talk about that another time. Follow me."

Adam and Maria followed him out of the room, leaving Paloma to browse Vlad's treasures.

The office was a square room with wall-to-wall books and a small desk in the center. She couldn't see a Bible, but this didn't stop Maria from thumbing through the collection, wanting to fill her robe with this treasure trove.

"No luck over there? Why do you need it, anyway?" asked Vlad.

Maria looked up from examining an old copy of *The War of the Worlds*. "Abuelita used to tell me Bible stories at bedtime. When I was old enough, I received a picture book of all those stories for Christmas. Whenever I felt scared or unsure at night, I would go through the pages thinking of all the heroes. At the end of the book there was a large picture of Jesus on a white horse with a blazing sword and fiery heart. Unlike the other stories, the final chapter had no other pictures. I would beg my grandmother to explain it to me, but she refused until I was about ten or eleven.

"Then she told me of the broken seals: horrible things that would happen in the end times, the beast trying to eat the pregnant woman, and a falling star with a very weird name. I never gave any of it another thought until I was stuck in my search for Adam. I taught myself English: one of my first English books was the Bible in the motel where I worked. It's funny; all the others were in Spanish, it just so happened I chose the room with an English version. Paloma's vision reminds me of those stories. What if it is real?"

"For lack of a better term, I must play devil's advocate here," Adam said. "We know those stories in the Book of Revelation were a conversation about what was happening at the time it was written. It doesn't necessarily mean it's a vision of the future. However, I can't deny the connection."

Vlad opened a little drawer in the desk and withdrew a miniature, beaten-up black leather Bible. He touched an embossed faded letter *A* in the corner. "This was Anastasia's. It just sits in this drawer so we might as well get some use out of it. It's the only thing I have left. It was my gift to Anastasia when she was learning English."

Maria whipped her head toward Vlad. "I thought you said you didn't have anything from your lost love."

Vlad could only shrug his shoulders. She could tell this piece of memory was painful. He handed her the little book without meeting her eyes.

Maria held it carefully. She skipped to the Book of Revelation and then read out loud. "Revelation 8:10–11: 'The third angel sounded the trumpet, and a great star, blazing like a torch, fell from the sky on a third of the rivers and on the springs of water—the name of the star is Wormwood. A third of the waters turned bitter and many people died from the waters that had become bitter.' That sounds a little like Paloma's dream."

Vlad raised his eyebrows. "That's a very literal translation. What about trumpets one and two?"

Maria rubbed the smooth stones of the crucifix between her fingers, trying to understand its significance. "When it was written, it wasn't obvious. The Book of Revelation is like a collection of pictures a child draws on a rainy afternoon."

Adam nodded in agreement. "Maria, you aren't as old as us, but Vlad and I have seen the slow death of belief in God and the Devil. Science can explain most of the things that were once considered mystical. What we do know is that Horace Kilburn can't be trusted on his own, so under the influence of something malevolent, he will be even more dangerous."

Vlad paced with his hands behind his back. "Okay, before you guys start speaking in tongues, remember that is one line from a lot of text, Maria. That vision your friend had can't be discounted, but I personally think the Bible is bullshit."

Maria handed the Bible back to Vlad. "So what do you think is going on here?"

Vlad shook his head. "The entire family and entourage of Horace Kilburn is questionable. What a freak. I don't think they will purposely bring this country to ruin or World War Three, but I do think they are all *American Horror Story*-esque characters who are unscrupulous enough to allow it to unfold before our eyes. I mean, the man thinks his own daughter is hot. Fuck him, his wife, his VP, and his dog."

Maria looked at Vlad with concern trying to understand the gravity of it all. "I think this is one of those moments where we must wait."

"Yeah, I fucking hate that shit," said Vlad as he stroked his beard.

"Believe me, I spent too long doing just that," Maria said remembering the years trying to find Adam.

Paloma entered the room. "Are you guys still trying to interpret my dream? I want to just forget it all. Maybe they'll peel off their skins to reveal Predator-like aliens trying to take over the world."

Vlad threw his head back and let out a loud laugh.

"I don't think so, chica—even the Predators had a code. I've got the entire collection if you need proof."

Maria had to admit, sometimes Vlad could be charming. She loved *Predator*. She had watched it many times late at night in the motel in Monterrey.

Maria sat in the desk chair. Thinking aloud, she said, "Lucifer wants humans to be controlled, yet he wants vampires on his side to bring about the destruction. I figure, like nature, things happen in their own time; they evolve. The passages before the falling star describe the seven seals being broken, which unleash different maladies onto the world. I think one through five have already happened. You two are old enough to testify to that. The first is conquest; the second is discord and the slaying of men; the third is greed and unfair commerce; the fourth is famine, plague, and violence; and the fifth is the murder of believers. Only six and seven remain. Then there is all that mess that's written after the description of the seals—the Antichrist."

The four were silent for a few moments as they thought about what she'd said.

Vlad stroked his beard. "Damn, when you put it like that... I've kind of seen all of that in my lifetime. Adam?"

Adam slapped his hand on the desk in frustration, causing the group to jump. "What have I done with my life all these years? Maybe I could have saved my sister."

"Hey man," said Vlad gently, "regret is a rotten apple you sometimes have to stomach until you shit it out. But you're still here helping Mordecai teach his faithful believers how to build fires and can peaches. I'm sure it will all work out."

The dull but loud drip of wasted time was something Maria knew all too well. "You may be king of Las Vegas right now, but how about king of a decomposing world? There will be nothing left!"

Adam smiled. "Thank you, Maria; that's just Vlad being Vlad."

"Hey, I'm just trying to lighten the mood. I'm the biggest asshole you will ever meet. No hard feelings." Vlad raised his hands in defense.

"This isn't social media, Vlad—we're not your audience. You don't need to try so hard. You don't need to be slick around us," said Adam.

He seemed to have regained his composure. Maria believed in second chances and wanted to give that grace to Adam. He had made it known he wanted to walk a different path. She knew the courage it took to do this.

"Maybe Lucifer is setting the stage," Maria said. "Slowly putting his pieces in place by whatever convoluted means. Using a loudmouth criminal to lead an influential nation is how he starts the process." Maria placed her hands over her face as if they could shield her from the hailstorm of arrowed thoughts. "Horace Kilburn has to win first. It's all speculation until that happens."

Paloma's stomach growled loudly. "Sorry guys, but according to me the only predators in this room are you. Speaking of the food chain, this human is starving."

"I don't have anything, I'm afraid," said Vlad. "The kitchen doesn't actually have any food or any way to cook food, but I can order anything you want from the best chefs in Vegas. Thalia loves this."

Vlad led them back to the ground floor. Smoke still lingered outside and there was water everywhere but the fire had been extinguished.

"Why don't you guys stay a few extra days to rest and so we can get Maria what she needs. I'll also get that iPad cracked open for you. I'll cancel my shows. I have the best meme. It's the Terminator saying, 'I'll be back.'"

Adam opened his mouth to speak but Vlad spoke over him.

"And I'll have the best stylists grab Maria whatever she wants. Make yourselves at home. *I'll be back*!"

Vlad left them standing in an empty kitchen.

"Is it just me, or does he secretly like our company?" said Adam.

# 23

The following day Maria was shocked at how many people arrived with trunks of clothes and shoes for her to choose from. Paloma helped Maria sort through the endless piles. It seemed to be a welcome distraction for her grief-stricken friend, so Maria was happy to play along.

Vlad knew all the salespeople by name and they showered him with compliments. One of the personal shoppers arrived dressed in the kind of clothes Maria was pretty sure you couldn't find off the rack. Her black blazer with gold buttons fit shoulder to waist perfectly, matching her black stiletto boots with gold spikes across the toe. She measured Maria's hands, feet and head, then called someone and loudly told them to get it all done yesterday. Vlad's cavernous home was overflowing with voices and people eagerly anticipating his next directive. Maria could tell Vlad liked to make things happen. He was restless, like her.

Adam sat in the background, permanently attached to his phone. Since Lucifer was out of the picture for now, Tizoc's bones would be taken back to England. Maria spied Adam smiling as he typed when a little ring tone alerted him to a message coming through. She suspected it wasn't Mordecai giving Adam the look of a helpless deer. Otherwise he had a look of concern and was deep in thought.

That night, Maria couldn't rest. She stared at the ceiling trying to make sense of Lucifer's contradictory messages and her attraction to him. Eventually, she gave up and pulled on a pair of new soft gray fleece tracksuit bottoms that matched the sports bra she was already wearing.

She wandered the cool halls admiring the design of the home. In amongst the chaos of personal shoppers and clothing deliveries, Vlad had had the property thoroughly cleaned and repaired after the explosion. She could hear music playing at the end of the main hall, which had the living room, kitchen and games room adjacent to it. Maria followed the sound and found herself in Vlad's home gym, which neatly housed every piece of equipment one would need to maintain a body like his. He sat on a bench doing bicep curls to the beat of the music. He stopped when he caught sight of her in the doorway.

"Hey, help yourself. I'm wired, too."

Maria only had eyes for the punching bag and gloves.

"Thanks, I like the music."

As Maria walked across the room, she passed an elaborate sound system. The display read 'Bound for the Floor' by Local H.

It had been too long since she last boxed. She slipped on a pair of smaller gloves and started to throw punches, feeling stronger than ever before. Then again, she had human blood on tap pumping life into her veins again. Gone were the days of rationing—but her hunger changed to another form. Her fully charged body had a hot energy that had to be exerted. Untouched skin wanted to be explored.

She moved around the bag as the thoughts that had kept her wide awake marched through her head. She continued to see that sexy son of a bitch Lucifer, with his sweet-smelling skin, feeling like the end of the world dripped from between her legs. He was excitement and doom. She could almost feel Lucifer's fingertips tracing the lonely curves of her body under a loose tracksuit, slipping into the places she needed him most. As she pummeled the punching bag, Maria imagined throwing Lucifer down, grinding every particle of pleasure from his flesh while the world burned outside. How silly she was to think she could maintain celibacy for a husband who had moved on years ago! She might be a vampire, but she was still a woman of flesh and blood. It was imperative that she beat this desire from her thoughts. The blood circulating through her body made it difficult for her to ignore the siren between her legs calling out to invite someone in—not just someone but the Devil himself. She was entering some unexplored cenote in the middle of the jungle. With one last punch, the bag ripped open and fell to the floor.

Maria looked at the fallen bag then Vlad. "I will fix that."

He clapped at her. "Now, I would pay big money to watch you fight. This is Vegas after all."

Maria didn't stop herself from chuckling. She liked this quieter version of Vlad. Maybe he was starting to feel comfortable enough to reveal his true self.

"We'll be out of your hair tomorrow. You will have Vegas all to yourself again and you can go back to your shows."

"I guess."

Maria slid next to him on the bench. "You'll find your way home. We all do."

He gave her a puzzled look. "What do you mean? I am home."

She gazed into his eyes with their red-ringed pupils. "I thought the same thing. Anyway, sorry about the bag. I'm going to head back to my room. See you tomorrow."


By sunset the next day, an Escalade was packed with so much luggage that the rear window was blocked. Before they left, Vlad topped off his generosity by replacing the phone Maria's friend Jorge gave her, which was destroyed in the explosion, with a new smartphone preloaded with all Maria's favorite artists, plus a few new ones he had handpicked for her, as well as an enormous sum of iTunes credit.

"This is very generous. I don't…" she began.

"Just take it and enjoy. That is the best way to thank someone."

Maria accepted his final gift with a shy smile. "You know where to find us when you're ready."

Maria and Paloma both hugged him, planting kisses on his furry cheeks before getting into the car.

Adam extended his hand. "Thank you. You sure you don't want to join us? You aren't alone, Vlad. You don't have to be Billy Xerxes for us."

Vlad couldn't look Adam in the eye. As much as he hated to see them go, he felt the time wasn't right. "I would just piss everyone off. Mordecai is running his little Mafia just fine without me. Besides he already has a *consigliore*, Adam."

Adam laughed. "Yeah, and her name is Elizabeth."

Vlad watched the Escalade pull away and was satisfied with his decision to stay in Vegas to keep an eye on things from his bunker. He always had been a trench warfare kind of guy. If this so-called Lucifer wanted a fight, then a fight he would get. How many years had passed since he had gone to battle? Unlike the conflicts, filled with blown-up soldiers' bodies and scorched earth, this one would be played out differently. It would be subtle. They would have to be smart, keeping their eyes on the media for any small story or hint of behind-the-scenes movement. The internet made information like that easier to come by, but it also was easy to get a watered-down or convoluted version of the truth. If you wanted to defeat a snake, you had to think like one.

One thing was certain: any spectacle Lucifer had in mind would be available for the entire world to see. Vlad could put on a show like no one had ever seen and might not ever see again. This could very well be his last battle. Despite all this, he still wasn't fully convinced he was ready to return to the Keepers. Vlad wanted to see the outcome of the election before he would meet with Mordecai. While they weren't enemies, they were far from friends.

He liked the man Adam had become. Anastasia would have liked this improved version. That was enough to offer his hand if called upon. It was a shame about Adam's sister, Adelaide; she had been hot in a kind of twisted, scary way. He would never tell Adam, but it was probably better this way. She would have been the death of him at some point.

And then there was Maria. Maria hadn't noticed, but Vlad had stopped his workout the previous night to watch her at the bag. She had started off slow, then her punches became faster and harder. He thought she moved like the flame of a candle with the power of a bulldozer. Vlad couldn't imagine what she could do to the body of an enemy—or a lover. Her eyes were dark, like deceptively deep shadowed pools that could suck the strongest to the very bottom. She was like a comet in the night sky: beautiful to behold but watch out if you happened to be in her path. He felt that woman could crush a soul with one stomp, punch—or a single kiss. She was awesome in his book, even if he feared her a bit.

From what little Adam had told him of Paloma, that young woman was in deep mourning. She was going through a seismic transition, beginning with the death of her father, that would forever change her life. He knew something about dying fathers, so he would like her until she gave him reason not to.

All these thoughts echoed in the now-empty house. As hard as he tried, he couldn't concentrate on new tricks for his show. The silence weighed heavy on his shoulders.

"Thalia!" The high-heeled assistant walked swiftly to Vlad's side. "Call the usual crew and tell them… impromptu pool party tonight. I want champagne, snacks, and robes at the ready." Thalia nodded and turned to leave. "Oh, and Thalia—remind them it's bikini optional."


Maria was finally on her way to England. Paloma was asleep before take-off. She had told Maria that the prophetic nightmare had robbed her of the ability to close her eyes for the last few days, even with vampires ready to defend her. Biology still won in the end.

Maria kicked off her new dusty boots to put her feet up, her new black cowboy hat placed snugly next to her.

It felt good to have one of her own; one that fit only her head. She adored her new brass knuckles—also a perfect fit. It was the one gift she had readily accepted. Instead of +*JESUS*+, Maria's own name was engraved with a little stamp of a mustard seed. Tracing her name with her fingers reminded her how she had touched Lucifer's face. She needed to forget that man or whatever he was.

There was also Vlad.

She looked at Adam for a distraction. "Tell me more about how all this business began."

Adam was already leaning back in his seat deep in thought, which seemed to be his usual state. "It's a long story."

Maria punched his arm in jest. "Isn't this a ten-hour flight?"

Adam looked at the roof of the plane, smiling with a small twinkle in his blue eyes. Maria knew that look and suspected love was involved. He turned to Maria, seeming more assured and confident than she had seen him before.

"Well, for me, it all began with a vampire named Mordecai and an organization called the Keepers."

# 24

Maria stepped off the plane to a wet drizzle and a thick fleece of gray clouds covering the sky. The chill seeped into her bones. Maria was grateful that Paloma had suggested a large parka for her until she adjusted to the temperature. *Maria, you're not in Mexico anymore,* she thought to herself.

Adam seemed pleased to be back in England, and after his tale she could understand why. Maria was only two hours away from meeting Mordecai and starting this new chapter in her life.

Grandthorpe Hall was a magnificent mansion: all stone, crawling ivy and endless windows situated on ten acres of land. The three of them entered the main salon to find the vampires who lived in England waiting for them with trays silver-colored pouches of blood and an elaborate cream tea which Maria assumed was a thoughtful gesture for Paloma.

The large room was a far cry from Vlad's modern, slick, monochrome mansion. There were busts on pedestals, what looked like original pieces of art from centuries ago, and old-fashioned dark wood furniture. The sofas and armchairs were a deep crimson color that appeared slightly worn in the seats and arm rests. Heavy curtains, the same color as the furniture, draped the windows.

A moment later, a vampire with a bald head and light eyes followed them in. Maria recognized Mordecai from the call in the airport in Mexico. He was much shorter than she expected—especially after being around Adam and Vlad. He seemed agitated, blinking rapidly and with a forced smile on his face.

"Hello, hello, it's wonderful to have you here," he said in a rush. "There is so much to discuss. Why don't you all refresh yourselves, meet everyone, have a wander around."

Seeing Mordecai in person for the first time, Maria realized he was the first vampire she had met who didn't appear fully human. No eyebrows or eyelashes framed his unusual eyes. His faded olive skin was creased like an aging human man, but there was a warmth that made it impossible for Maria to guess his age. He dressed in wool trousers and a thick knitted sweater, with soft leather gloves on his hands. Maria had thought the oldest of the vampires wouldn't feel the cold.

Mordecai turned his attention to Paloma. "I'm so glad you could join us. The few human apprentices that live on the estate are not here at the moment. They are visiting small farms, learning how to raise and slaughter animals, but you will meet them soon. I must go now, but please enjoy the scones. I made them myself. Adam, I believe we need to talk in private?"

Paloma smiled. "Thank you for having me. And I'm sure I'll love them. No breakfast yet."

He patted her hand before gesturing for Adam to follow him and leaving.

Paloma watched the ancient vampire depart with Adam. She was grateful for his warm welcome. Feeling chilled despite donning light sweaters in preparation for the English weather, she sat in a springy, antique chair next to the fireplace and turned her attention to the steaming pot of tea. The fire was at its peak, but still the room felt only a few degrees above freezing. While the vampires talked to Maria, Paloma poured tea into a delicate china cup and grabbed a freshly baked scone. She smeared strawberry jam and clotted cream over one side and then sank her teeth into its soft sweetness.

She was just beginning her second one when a young woman in a lab coat and head-to-toe Adidas garb took the chair across from her.

"It's so good, right? I'll just enjoy watching you eat that scone."

Paloma smiled through her crumbly bite, covering her mouth while she nodded her head. The young woman poked the silver bowl of clotted cream and licked her finger.

"Mmmmm, you never stop missing food."

Paloma frowned. "Eating that doesn't bother you?"

"Well, in small and smooth quantities, no, but you have to build a tolerance. Same goes with alcohol. Those first fifty years, stay away, and after that, do not overdo it. Imagine your worst hangover then add every hangover you have ever had on top of that. Not good. Anyway, I'm helping myself to your food, but haven't introduced myself. I'm Darcy. Biologist, doctor and part-time DJ for fun."

Darcy was tall with endless limbs and a pixie cut that only someone with her delicate features could pull off. Paloma wiped her fingers clean to shake her hand.

"Paloma. I'm a student, as of last year. I hope to go to medical school. This is the first time I've crossed the Atlantic and I've just been through the strangest few weeks of my life." Maybe it was the jet lag, missing her mother or another bout of delayed grief, but Paloma's eyes started to gather tears.

Darcy wasted no time kneeling in front of her. "Hey, hey... whatever it is, it's going to be okay. We're a family here—human and vampire. If you need to talk, I've got ears. How 'bout we take a walk and see some cool stuff? When you're up for it, London has some of the best museums. And they're free!"

Paloma wiped her nose and laughed. "Thank you. That's really nice of you. A walk would be good. It's that or a nap, and it's way too early to sleep. I guess this is jet lag. To be honest, being in the presence of so many vampires is daunting, considering I'm your food source."

Darcy gave her a warm laugh while preparing another scone for Paloma to take with her. "I promise we don't bite..."

Paloma couldn't help but to giggle. "What has brought you here?"

"I was orphaned during the Second World War. Children in London were shipped to the countryside. Mordecai took me in. As I got older, I discovered the truth about this place and made the decision to become one of them."

"Wow. My mother is... like you, but I just found out about it."

Darcy gave her a warm smile. "Why don't we take that walk to make you feel more comfortable here."

"I would like that." Paloma rose from her seat and followed Darcy for a tour of the grounds, including the room Paloma would later call her own.

Maria watched Paloma exit the main room with the younger-looking vampire woman. She knew her friend was in good hands: Adam had given her a little background on the Keepers who lived at Grandthorpe. She hoped it would be a positive experience for Paloma. She had left everything behind. Maria knew that feeling all too well.

The next morning, Maria gave herself time to wander the vast property. Her emotions simmered as she thought of her encounter with Lucifer. Her mind also wandered to Vlad. She didn't want to think about either, but fantasizing was far better than thinking about the end of the world. As she explored the vast mature garden, she found Mordecai also walking the stone pathways.

He looked towards her as she approached and gave her a warm smile. "How are you today?" he asked.

"I'm alright. It's such a big change."

"Did you rest last night?"

"Yes, thank you. Though it's not always as relaxing as a good human sleep. Like not all blood being the same. For a long time, I tried to only feed on animal blood."

"You must be careful with that. As a young vampire, if you drink only animal blood for long enough, you will eventually die. Through careful training, the very old vampires like myself have learned to delay our human blood feed and survive on animal blood—or nothing at all."

"May I ask how old you are?"

He chuckled. "I'm ancient. Time is something we all must face and it changes us all. Some of the other ancients you might find a bit frightening. They are the hardest working, preferring their own company. I guess thousands of years will do that to a soul. If you go to the archives, there are photographs of most of the vampires."

"I know we can see our reflections…"

"Yes, we can have photos taken also. We were flesh and blood once. We exist in the material world like everything else. There is no reason why we shouldn't."

"Transformation? We change?"

"Yes, you can see for yourself. Over time the old ones have become androgynous, their eyes and skin have lost their pigment, their nails have become thick, hard, almost wood-like. If left uncut, a vampire's nails can be a serious weapon. The ones who don't go through the effort of masking their appearances mostly operate at night. I'm guessing that may be where the myths come from."

"You mean vampires that can't withstand sunlight? I was surprised myself when I didn't burn in the sun," said Maria. "But if they can't blend in anymore, then what do they do?"

"You know all those desperate situations around the world—natural disasters, war, famines—where the impossible happens? That's usually one of them. They are true miracle workers. They don't often venture abroad these days because travel in the twenty-first century is very different from stowing away on a ship. You will only see them if it's an absolute emergency. By night they move like nocturnal animals—digging wells, providing food, leaving supplies in hospitals in locations human rescue workers don't dare to go if they value their lives. Historically they are on high alert in wartime, helping when they can."

"But not all vampires are good. Like Tizoc and Paloma's father."

"Are all humans good? Are humans shaped by trauma and this world? So are vampires. We are all products of the world we live in."

Maria remained silent for a moment as she thought about this. "Why do you care about humans so much? Tizoc and the ones who attacked the factory I worked in couldn't care less. For them, humans are things that exist for pleasure or sustenance."

"Without humans we die, and if we abuse our position there is no guarantee they won't actively hunt us all down and destroy us. There are more humans than vampires. Too many vampires and we will run out of blood. Like nature, there is a delicate balance that must be respected."

This made Maria think of Lucifer and his place in all of this. She felt it best to leave the conversation there.

"Thank you, Mordecai. You have given me much to think about." She turned to walk away.

"Of course. I am here when you need me."

# 25

Returning to the house from the garden, Maria cruised the halls of the old stone property, which was even larger than Vlad's modern mansion. It felt like a castle, though it was in fact a stately home. According to Adam, it had once belonged to one family for generations.

The wood floors had been kept in pristine condition with a dark lacquer. Each room had its own decorative theme, whether color or art. All the furnishings appeared comfortable in size and fabric. A winding, wide staircase climbed up four floors. As she wandered, Maria took in the faces and voices of her new home, her new family. She didn't go to college but from the movies she had seen this new arrangement was the closest she would get. She passed a small table with a newspaper laid on it. The headlines were about the U.S. election. As the days narrowed, the cockfight was becoming dirtier. The deep battle wounds that scarred the American landscape were surfacing. She didn't want to hear about it anymore. Kilburn was a nasty man.

As she turned to continue her self-guided tour, Adam appeared through a door on the left side of the hallway. "I've been looking for you. Tizoc's iPad has arrived from Vlad's contact. It's unlocked. We're going to look at it together."

Maria followed Adam up more wide stairs to the top floor.

"What do you think of it here?" he asked.

"It's beautiful and old. I feel like I am in the setting of a book."

"Yes, England is filled with such places. And many are haunted with the ghosts of the past. Don't forget to visit the library."

He stopped to let Maria go ahead of him into the large study. In the center stood an ornately carved mahogany desk surrounded by comfortable chairs and sofas. The rows of windows let in the muted English light. Paintings from different time periods decorated the walls, creating a beautiful collection that could have come straight from a museum gallery.

Mordecai sat with hands clasped in front of a large computer screen with the stolen iPad on the desk. Maria was nervous just looking at it.

Mordecai cleared his throat. "I received a somewhat unexpected message. I needed to meditate on it before I took any action. As the humans say, I have good news and bad news. The bad news is Tizoc's iPad contained nothing regarding Lucifer's plans. However, he was meticulous in recording the grotesque details of his business. Maria, you saved those women in the truck from a terrible fate. By killing him, you have saved even more beyond Mexico. Your instinct and courage are things that can't be taught. I've alerted authorities we can trust to break up as much of his trafficking ring as possible.

"Now, this second piece of business; the message I received this morning: Lucifer has called a meeting of the vampire community leaders at Lake Como in Italy."

Adam huffed. "Already? We just obliterated him! I didn't think he could do whatever he does to reappear again so quickly."

Mordecai nodded. "He is a powerful entity. He was not born of flesh and blood like us vampires. Demons are the same. They abide by a different set of rules. Even when an entity is banished, say in a possession, it is not destroyed. Our reality is only one of many in existence."

Adam and Maria looked at each other as if their world had become that much smaller with this knowledge.

Adam turned back to Mordecai. "Do we really want to entertain him? Why should we do this? We cannot discount he might summon demons to aid him. They are harmless if they get what they want and are satisfied. But any perceived slight can set them off to cause trouble. They know how to hold a grudge and keep score."

Mordecai nodded. "I understand your hesitation, Adam, but we need to know his true intentions. More can be accomplished with cooperation for the time being. I will stay here, it is time others started to take more of a lead in the organization as I age. I also think we should involve Vlad. I think he cares more than he lets on."

Mordecai dialed Vlad on his computer screen, seemingly uncaring about what time it might be in Las Vegas. When Vlad answered the video call, Maria saw on the screen that he lay on his stomach and was being massaged by two women in short skirts.

"Hope this is important. I'm busy," Vlad drawled.

Adam leaned in to speak first. "Well, you perked up pretty quickly. Did you receive the invitation from our friend?"

Vlad began to turn onto his back as he spoke. "I did and it freaked me out. I thought that explosion would take him out for longer. He was extra nice in asking for my attendance. I think he wants something from me, which is why I won't go. You should send Maria. Think he's got a thing for her."

Maria's neck and cheeks went warm as Mordecai and Adam turned to look at her.

"That man is definitely hot for teacher. Send Maria. Let me know how it goes." Vlad ended the call.

"I will go alone." Now they were all staring wide-eyed at Maria.

Adam shook his head in agitation. "Mordecai, please let me go with her, even if I don't attend the meeting."

Mordecai's eyes never left Maria. "Maria will go

alone. I can tell that is what she wants. Adam, you will be on standby. Maria, you will keep a tracker on you at all times. Okay?"

Adam went to protest but his resistance was defeated by the older vampire's intense gaze. "I will respect your wishes on this," he said eventually.

"I appreciate that. And I hear you. Now, may I have a moment alone with Maria?"

Adam nodded. "I'll be looking at the accounts if you need me." He glanced at Maria before leaving the office.

Maria remained with this strange man, who wielded so much power yet seemed uncorrupted by any of it. If she felt like El Castillo in Chichen Itza, this man was one of those ziggurats of Persia made long before the pyramids, eroded by the heat and sand until consumed by the very thing that created it in the first place.

When the door closed behind Adam, Mordecai addressed Maria. "The meeting is in two weeks' time. Until then relax, explore the estate, and learn about our what we do."

"I'm very glad to be part of this organization—it seems like you do good work here." She hesitated, then added. "Also… could I go to Italy a day early, if possible?"

Mordecai leaned forward. "May I ask why?"

Sitting in front of the old vampire as if in confession, she clutched her cross. "I don't get the feeling he will hurt me. Like Vlad says, Lucifer made it clear he likes me. Maybe I can get more out of him one on one. He did say he wanted us to join him and not to fight."

This was true. Maria wanted to help the Keepers because she didn't want people like Jorge, Conchita and Esmeralda to suffer, but she also wanted to know more about this mysterious being.

Mordecai continued to study her face as if he could read her heart. "I see... Very well. Go early. But Maria... please remember he may look and feel like a man, but he is something else entirely. We all go through trials and lessons."

Maria left the office feeling like she was moving through the impenetrable fog that sometimes covered the English countryside in the morning. She didn't want to bother Paloma with her troubles while she was enjoying Darcy's company. They were heading to London to see the museums and go on some Jack the Ripper tour. From what she heard, he was a vampire who went nuts then decided to disappear. She was happy for Paloma. Adam was busy too, spending his time with the Keepers' accounts. Humanity's ever-growing, desperate needs never stopped. They were as constant as the planet's orbit.

Maria had free time on her hands and her curiosity about the books and photos of the oldest of the vampires led her to the library.

Her movement triggered a sensor, causing small lights to illuminate an entire wall of framed photographs of the oldest vampires. These vampires were frightening, just as Mordecai had described them. Even so, the photographer still managed to capture that small spark of humanity that remained in their eyes no matter how different they looked. She moved towards the books with black hardcovers. Each one had names printed on the spine in gold lettering: Sitri, Amon, Bathon, Zepar, Belial. The names seemed endless. She took one off the shelf and carefully flipped through it. These were the names of demons. There were sigils, a description, and how to summon them. She placed the book back and started to look for a book about Lucifer. She looked everywhere, scanning the shelves until her eyes hurt, but there wasn't one. She wondered why. But then again she didn't need a book to tell her about a man she knew.

That night Paloma knocked on Maria's open door, peered around it and then walked inside.

"Maria, I missed you today—we need to catch up! Do you have a minute?"

"Of course!" cried Maria, getting up to embrace her friend. "I've missed you too. Tell me about London! And have I been replaced as best friend?"

Paloma flopped onto Maria's bed. "Of course not! But I *really* like her. She is this crazy mix of music and brains and curiosity. We listened to Christine and the Queens in the hotel room before going out. Almost held hands wandering through Whitechapel. She knew the history behind everything we saw."

"And she's cute," Maria added.

Paloma's face illuminated with that thought and then she sighed. "I know. It's very distracting. I don't know what to do. I don't think I could handle another rejection… you see, I met this beautiful woman named Maria and she turned me down." Paloma gave Maria a sarcastic grin and tried to hold back her laughter.

Maria playfully threw a t-shirt at Paloma. "You're something else, Paloma Castillo."

The two women laughed like not a moment was spent apart.

"What else? You talked to your mom?" Maria asked.

"She messaged that she's fine and sent me photos. I hope she is happy, and I do wonder when I will see her again. But she just tells me to get on track with the project here and school."

"She wants you to live your life, and you are. I'll be gone for a few days soon. I assume you will be alright here—with a little help from Darcy."

Paloma sat upright in the bed. "Yes, but will you? Be careful, Maria. You really want to dance with the Devil?"

"I need to know. He is like a magnet. Maybe another lesson I have to learn, but I need to know what the hell exists beyond this flesh and blood."

"I won't tell you what to do, but know I'll be here when you get back if you need me."

Maria gave Paloma a warm smile. "I know. Thank you."

—

Maria was still deciding what to pack the night before she was due to leave for Italy. It would still be warm there, so she decided on a floral black button-down dress with ballet flats. For the meeting with the rest of the vampires, she would dress like usual in her jeans, t-shirt, hat and boots.

Paloma and Darcy knocked on her door. "I've got *Fright Night* or *The Lost Boys* if you're interested in a movie night?" said Paloma.

Maria looked up. She felt too distracted to watch a movie or be a third wheel. Darcy had her arm lovingly around Paloma's waist. "I'm okay. You enjoy—maybe I'll join you later."

Paloma turned around and mouthed, "Thank you."

Maria felt her pulse quicken as she turned back to her suitcase. She remembered how good it felt to have Lucifer's hands and lips on her body. The absolute oblivion of desire had been so intoxicating in his presence. What was she thinking—going on this solo mission to be alone with Lucifer? She had packed enough clothes, but she couldn't help overthinking things. She had to know what this strange magnetism meant.

She lay on the bed to calm herself and perhaps come to her senses, but her restlessness would not cease. She got up to join Paloma and Darcy after all. Part of her wanted to confide in her best friend and be talked out of what she was about to do. She would let fate decide.

But when she entered the room, the soft glow of the TV shined on Paloma and Darcy kissing beneath a blanket. This was good for her friend; she could be who she was without fear of reprisal or judgment. Fate gave its answer like a hand of tarot cards laid before her.

# 26

The view across Lake Como was the type of landscape you would see in a painting. The mountains, covered in thick green fur, rose to dramatic heights toward the sky. Maria felt like she could reach out to run her fingers through the lush forests. The lake was a placid layer of shining silk cradled at the feet of the mountains.

Despite all this beauty, she sat fidgeting in the backseat of a small green Fiat taxi. The driver played Italian pop music at a low volume; she could smell the floral deodorizer used to clean the fabric of the seats. The longer she sat, the more her excitement grew. She ached between her legs while her racing, well-fed heart wished the car would keep up. Lucifer didn't know she was on her way. Maybe her unannounced appearance would anger him, causing him to reveal horns and yellow eyes, or maybe he wouldn't care and would tell her to come back the next day. Maybe something else would happen. She had to find out for herself.

When the car pulled up to the old, pale-yellow villa, Maria thought she should turn around—but she didn't want to. The winding road leading up the hillside was empty, with no other homes around, as they were high above most of the other properties. If she left that instant, there would be no trace of her. For nearly two weeks she had laid in a duvet cocoon, resting, replaying the moment they first touched, the sensation of his hot tongue in her mouth.

The door was in front of her. Her fingertips were on the bronze handle in the shape of an unfurling fern. She didn't remember getting out of the taxi. To her surprise, the door opened as she pressed on it. She passed the threshold to see a large room filled with fresh flowers and antique bowls overflowing with fruit. The prince of darkness had taste. She walked across a marble floor that made the inside of the house feel cool. The silence was a stark contrast to the bustling property in England.

As she was about to call out for Lucifer, she turned to her left toward a double love seat. There he was, on a wide terrace that stretched the entire length of the villa with an unobstructed view of the lake. His hands rested on a stone balustrade as he stood watching the last of the evening light in nothing but thin white linen drawstring pants. The curves of his shapely ass could be seen through the gossamer material. His hair was no longer groomed, but loose around his face. What the hell was she doing here with this man, who for the first time looked like a fallen angel?

Below a wall-mounted TV, Maria attached her phone to the stereo. Nina Simone's 'Don't Let Me Be Misunderstood' began to play. She dropped her bag and slipped off her shoes to join him outside.

A light breeze blew underneath her flimsy dress, cooling off her otherwise naked body. She was as accessible as she needed to be. Lucifer looked back as the music drifted onto the terrace.

"Maria. I thought you wanted to blow me to Hell— in fact, you did. What brings you here today?"

Maria stepped closer, reaching for Lucifer's hand. "If you are who you say you are, then you deserve to be in Hell—but so do I. Can I show you why I'm here? I think you might know." Maria placed his hand on the side of her thigh. "Do you want this, too?"

Lucifer withdrew his hand. "I have never experienced intimacy with any creature in my existence. Yes, I want to know, and I want that with you."

Lucifer allowed Maria to guide his hand up her thigh until it reached her engorged little parcel pulsating with blood. Their fingers intertwined as she guided him to the kind of rhythm she liked. Lucifer smiled at her as he allowed her to lead him.

"Yes, show me exactly what you need from me. You can have it all."

She could feel his body responding to his arousal as he stared into her dark eyes. He scooped Maria up in both arms, ready to carry her inside.

"You know, before I took this form, I watched the

first humans from the bushes as they joined together. It was the most curious thing to me."

Maria scratched his neck with one fang to lick his blood for pleasure instead of hunger. "Take me to your bed," she said in a low growl.

Lucifer did as instructed. Maria pulled off her dress. She stood naked before this man she craved, and had thought of every night since they first met. She pulled at his pants impatiently before leading him onto the bed. Lucifer allowed Maria to guide him inside her and rock him to a beat that would extract the most pleasure out of their bodies. Her body was open to him, as soft and vibrant as an orchid in full bloom. With every thrust she squeezed him inside like they might float away if she forgot to do so. The unknown sensations that accompanied every tight pulse rippled through his skin.

Lucifer offered his wrist and whispered, "Drink me."

Maria's excitement flooded to her nipples. Flesh and fantasy blurred all her thoughts, and now his blood would take her to a place not of this Earth. She pricked his skin and took him inside of her once again. She could feel an orgasmic hot flush in her face while her body became slick with Lucifer's sweat. The friction of his body against her erect nipples made her want to cry out. Maria had to let go of his wrist before she took it too far.

Like a vampire, he took her nipples into his mouth, sucking with just enough pressure to cause her to moan and bite his shoulder. She reached down, keeping the tension going, bringing herself to orgasm. The tight coil of twenty-five years of celibacy cracked in two. Maria shuddered, unable to scream out from the overwhelming delight springing from deep within her body. Volcanoes, earthquakes, thunderstorms that sweep in at midday erupted within each of her cells, hailing a supernova to destroy it all. Hijole, she needed that.

Lucifer watched her cheeks turn deep red as she licked the remaining blood off her fangs.

Her shivering body gripped him tighter as she bit him again, as he squeezed her breasts. His breath quickened with every gulp of blood swallowed. "My love, you make me feel... feel light-headed... I don't know how long I can wait..."

His body spasmed as he cried out. He buried his head in Maria's hair.

They lay in limp post-coital exhaustion next to each other for hours, neither knowing what to say after an experience so intimate. Maria relished the feeling of someone close to her, holding her tight.

Lucifer was the first to move. He turned toward Maria and her closed eyes. "I think I have found a new god with you."

Maria turned to face her lover. "Don't say that. It's just sex. Tell me: you taste like a man, you feel like a man. What are you really?"

Lucifer ran his fingers through long hair that covered her now-softened nipples. "Like humans, I don't have any memory of my beginning. One day I was just aware of my existence. But unlike humans, I know exactly where I come from. I lived in constant contemplation and praise of my creator.

"From the moment the gods sneezed out this corner of the universe, I was in awe. I had not seen such a thing before. The effort, love and joy that went into creation left me and all my kind in worshipful applause. We watched as the cold, formless void blossomed in a beautiful violence that evolved into something pure and worthy of our adoration. I wanted to create, too. I envied this power and wanted a creation of my own. As all the heavenly know, there is nothing greater than the gods; defiance is not an option.

"Then came the great beasts. How large and fierce they were, ruling the Earth. But the gods were not satisfied. These beasts were grand, but they lacked any sense of who made them or what they meant to their creator, so another was created. This new creation would be like us, self-aware. I was sent to destroy the great beasts to make way for the new.

"Two prototypes were created of what they hoped man would become. This was nothing new to the gods, but it was to me. Adam and Eve. I disliked them from the time they could speak. They were too much like us. They didn't deserve a gift such as Earth. God heard my argument and decided to place a tree in their midst as a test.

"Once again, I said this was absolute folly. How can you place what they shouldn't have right in front of their faces and expect them not to be curious? I accused God of being an arrogant, short-sighted fool. I said I could have done better given the chance. As punishment I was sent to test them as a small and lowly beast, a snake. I thought I would prove Him wrong and He would allow me to destroy these two prototypes. I set all my will to their failure. Fail they did. God not only punished the humans, but I also had to stay in my beast form. Because of these wretched humans, I was stuck on my belly in the dirt."

Maria covered her body with the sheet, her skin turned to gooseflesh even though she wasn't cold. The human curiosity that had brought her to his bed in the first place wanted to know more about his story but it unnerved her.

"Maria, I can tell you're scared. I won't hurt you."

"You want to hurry along the apocalypse because you hate humans."

Lucifer rolled onto his back, placing his arms behind his head. "Don't take any of what I'm about to say personally. Yes, humans are the worst thing to happen to this jewel of a planet, to this system designed for life. I could see it before anyone."

Lucifer's handsome face began to darken. "Since that first step into the wild their impulse has been to dominate. They murder, rape, torture. They putrefy the grand oceans with their plastic; spread their waste, cause pestilence. There is no respect for creation or each other; they use God to justify their selfish agendas; they allow their innocent young to be defiled and that defilement is sent over the globe; animals are slaughtered for a toenail; their evil saturates the Earth. Each generation just as cruel as the last. They only live for whatever sick impulse takes their fancy in the moment, damn all the consequences."

Maria could see his eyes growing paler as his voice went from just above a whisper to a near shout. His skin turned red like a man who has just drunk half a bottle of tequila in one go. She was startled by his hate.

Maria touched his chest. "I need some air."

She walked onto the terrace where the sky was starting to lighten. Had they really spent a night in bed making love and chatting about Genesis? Little lights dotted the mountains around the lake. All those souls would be gone if he had his way.

Then Lucifer was behind her, wrapping his arms around her body. Her hands found his arms.

"You know," she said, "it was selfish human impulse that brought me here. I couldn't stop thinking about you: when the opportunity to see you again arrived, I took it."

Lucifer kissed her neck. She pulled away.

"Please, Maria, this is very different. We are not like them. There are no spouses or children wondering where we are. We are adults agreeing to this enjoyment; we can't create unwanted life. I know I frightened you. You have to know that humans were never promised forever: it is by their own hand they have accelerated the process."

What angered Maria more was she agreed with

everything he said. She remembered the rescued, sweaty girls in the back of the truck and all the desperate stories that kept her up at night in her motel room exile. She hated human savagery as much as he did. There was one question she had to ask.

"What do you really look like? Show me."

"I wish I could, but you would die in an instant. At first I was a fragment of energy, then a snake, and now a man. God chose a burning bush to present himself. Our kind can't exist in our true form here. Maybe I can try something else."

Lucifer led Maria into the pool on the terrace and they slid into the water. It felt refreshing after their revealing conversation. Lucifer pulled her close.

"I wish things could have been different, but in the end, I serve God and I have committed crimes against my creator. Someone must always pay. I see you as an unexpected gift I don't deserve."

"There is a lake of fire? And you go from 'gods' to 'God'. Which is it? What is out there? I must know what the hell this all is about."

Lucifer led her to the edge of the pool. "The only lake of fire I know of is the sun. It will die as all things must and implode, creating a hole where nothing can ever escape or look upon the glorious peace of God. There is one energy with many extensions. We are one of its manifestations. There are others, godlike, as well. They can wield more of this energy like the one universal energetic source. God and gods."

Lucifer lifted Maria out of the pool. "Watch the sunrise. Your eyes will start to weep then burn. Please keep them open as long as possible." Lucifer parted Maria's legs, placing them over his shoulders. She leaned back onto her arms to watch the sleepy sun peek through the darkness like a yellow cat's eye. Maria pressed her palms into the concrete as the tip of Lucifer's tongue found its way to the only place it belonged. She wanted to watch him but kept her eyes on the sun as it continued to bleed into the sky. Sunlight cast warm rays on her body as she dug her heels into Lucifer's back. The softness of his tongue as he brought her closer to heaven. She had forgotten how much she loved this. The embarrassment she once felt in this position no longer existed.

As the sun rose to its daily glory she struggled to continue to view its splendor. Her retinas were burning, as was her body. The light became blinding as her desperation to orgasm took control of her thoughts. His mouth continued to explore every tender fold and opening between her legs, sucking and digging, like having that first taste of ripe watermelon in summer. She hoped he would go all the way to the rind. There was not a twinge of reluctance when Lucifer flickered in and out of the puckered little space Diego never dared to go. What was the point of being scared or shy? This pleasure was like every Christmas present being ripped open at once.

She moved her hips while holding the back of Lucifer's head. Lucifer lapped at her with a fevered thirst, giving her what she asked for without words. She didn't want this sex to end. Maria fell back, letting all the screams out of her lungs; her body crushed by those giant waves back in Acapulco. He sucked until her tide of joy receded.

Lucifer climbed out of the pool and lay next to Maria. His body was still aroused, and she couldn't resist taking more pleasure from him. She climbed on top, moving like a cobra responding to the snake charmer's flute.

Lucifer gripped her fleshy hips. His eyes flashed with excitement as she moved and moaned. The way his body tensed, she could feel he was on the edge of orgasm. He clenched his jaw as he held back and pulled at her ass as he stiffened inside her once again. She ran her fingertips across his chest. He had no choice but to release as he cried out in ecstasy. She reached between her legs to bring herself to orgasm once again while Lucifer was still inside her. The pleasure made her feel alive as it ignited every cell in her body.

After the sensation subsided, Maria flopped at his side, satisfied. She knew she could never give her body to Lucifer again. Sex was the easiest, most dangerous trap. Another's body was God's greatest gift and curse. Whatever was coming—and she believed the end was approaching—she would need a clear heart and head.

"Please drink from me," he said. "You need to heal your eyes to relieve your pain."

Maria could feel his wrist on her lips. She took only enough to ease the pain of her retinas.

He looked at her as she drank from him. "I can still taste you. As the sunlight fell behind your head you looked like a painting. A haloed saint born from blood, with your long, wet hair clinging to your body. You make me understand what it means to be human."

She didn't want to say it out loud, but making love to him made her feel the same way.

"Thank you," she whispered, leaving a parting kiss on his punctured flesh.

They lay side by side with the sun on their naked bodies, legs dangling in the pool.

# 27

It was the day of the meeting. Maria had at least ten missed calls and texts from Adam. She messaged back that she was okay, just distracted. Lucifer busied himself with connecting his computer to the enormous flatscreen TV and tapping swiftly on a tablet. Maria dismissed herself and wandered into the small village that sat next to the lake. It would take her forty-five minutes by foot but she had time and didn't tire easily. She watched the crowds eat their gelato and drink their coffee. Buses of tourists passed every five minutes en route to Villa Carlotta, congesting the narrow mountainside roads. Maria imagined what it might be like without a soul in sight.

At five in the evening, Maria returned to the villa. Lucifer was outside again, enjoying the view. He sat barefoot in linen trousers and a plain white t-shirt. All her desire came back, knocking at her door and begging to be let in. But this was the time for discipline, not indulgence.

Lucifer extended his hand to her as she walked across the terrace. "Please sit with me and just take it all in."

Maria allowed herself to be pulled onto his lap. She felt her little beacon tingle and throb. God, he excited her. Beneath her thigh, she could feel he felt the same.

"You know this is where it ends with us," she said in a low voice.

Lucifer kissed her hand. "Is it so bad that we enjoy each other's bodies? After all this human nonsense is over, I want to make love to you in all my favorite places. No one around, just us."

Maria felt his hand crawl underneath her Metallica t-shirt to tease her nipples. The weak spot he already knew. She started to kiss his neck. She would have him one last time.

They were too engrossed in each other to hear the footsteps.

"I guess this is a bad time."

Maria looked up to see Vlad and Adam in the doorway. Vlad was smiling and nodding his head, while Adam appeared confused.

Maria jumped to her feet, caught off guard and feeling slightly embarrassed. "What are you doing here? I said I was fine! I don't need a chaperone or saving. You should have trusted me when I said everything was okay." She turned her attention to Vlad. "What are you doing here?"

"I wanted to make sure you were alright. By the looks of it I didn't have to worry."

Vlad walked around Lucifer to the edge of the terrace. "Not bad! I can see how this place would get the ladies."

"My door was locked; how did you get in?" said Lucifer in a flat tone. He didn't seem bothered by their presence.

Vlad continued to admire the view. "Oh, we broke in through a side window. Sorry."

Adam's cheeks turned pink with embarrassment. "We didn't want to run the risk it wasn't you messaging back. You wouldn't call, so we thought the worst. After my sister..."

Maria felt the first pang of guilt. Isn't it a friend's duty to worry? "You're right. I should have called. I often act before I think."

"Obviously," Vlad chimed in drily.

She shot him a look. Their eyes met for a moment.

Lucifer excused himself and returned with three silver pouches of blood. "Well, you are most welcome even if it was not a convenient time for *us*." His fingertips rested on the small of Maria's back as he said this. "However, gentlemen, we have business to discuss. I'd like the details to be revealed in front of everyone."

"Hey, I'm sorry we interrupted what looked like a very hot moment. I mean, that would drive me crazy."

Maria gave Vlad a *shut the hell up now or else* glare while breaking away from Lucifer's touch. She stood awkwardly between the three men, not knowing where to place herself.

Adam refused Lucifer's offer of blood, instead moving to the other side of the terrace.

Vlad patted her shoulder gently. "Hey, he'll simmer down. I got your back, Maria. Lust is a bitch."

She gave Vlad a small smile.


The other vampires began to arrive half an hour later. Maria was astonished at how different they all were from each other. She wondered how their vampire lives began and who had created them.

One man approached Adam. He had brown hair that fell to his shoulders and light brown skin. His hazel eyes emitted a friendly warmth.

"Brother, I'm so very sorry about Adelaide," he began, in what she thought was a New York accent. "We lost touch, but I never stopped loving her in my own way. She was a lot of terrible things, as I found out. Even still, I can't forget what she did for Martin and our friends."

Adam embraced the man. "Thank you. I wish I had seen more of the side she shared with you. Daniel, this is Maria Muñoz. Maria, this is Daniel Perez, a business partner and friend. Those silver pouches of blood? That was Daniel's idea."

"Adam is leaving out that it was his investment that made it all happen. If I recall, he's still waiting to make a profit." The men shared a relaxed laugh.

"I'll be disappointed if I ever do. Keep doing what you're doing."

So, Adam had a business partner. There was still so much she didn't know about him, or Vlad, or this new life. She greeted the newcomers politely and quietly surveyed the vampire crowd. This community was the family that didn't have to die or become ill during their usually very long existences. How strange and big the world was. From what Lucifer had told her the previous night, the universe was just as diverse and intricate. They all introduced themselves to her and stated where they were from. A few even thanked her for dispatching Tizoc. He had been feared and hated by these vampires. They stood around the room, quickly filling it, with some forming smaller groups.

Lucifer stepped to the front of the room to get everyone's attention. "Thank you all for coming." He gave what she knew to be a phony smile and turned on the screen.

A Black woman with large clear eyes and curly hair to her shoulders appeared, staring into the camera. Maria couldn't begin to guess her age. She looked powerful and regal.

"This better be good—I'm a very busy woman," she said in a slightly exasperated tone.

"I'm grateful for your time, Sandra."

She let out a sarcastic chuckle. "Thank Mordecai. What am I supposed to do when I get an email from some guy calling himself Lucifer? I've got a city to run and this election has people going crazy. It's not called the White House for nothing. America has shown us that."

Lucifer began to move around the room, passing each vampire in turn. "The time has come to weed out the villains in the vampire community and for the same thing to happen to the humans. They had their chance and they failed. Now we will rip off the fetid carpet of humanity and watch all the cockroaches and fleas finally face justice. A series of not-so-pleasant events will soon occur that will reduce the world's population to a mere one hundred and forty-four thousand. These last few humans will see things that will scare the respect and fear of God back into their worthless hearts.

"Now, I would never allow these humans to be left to their own devices. They would simply procreate and start the cycle of self-destruction all over again. I want you, the vampires who have lived so many lifetimes, to guide these humans. I need you, the greater and wiser species, to take over. Give them real gods to worship."

Maria hadn't expected this; from the stunned silence in the room, neither had anyone else. She tried to catch Lucifer's eye but he refused to look at her.

After a moment's pause, he turned back to the screen and continued.

"Sandra, I know you have your heart set on Sandra Wilson for Congress, then Sandra Wilson for President. But how about Sandra Wilson, leader of the vampires and humans in New Eden? You are experienced, the very popular mayor of Philadelphia, smart, no nonsense, compassionate. Anyone who meets you respects you. You will, of course, answer to me."

Sandra leaned forward. "You want me to sit back, watch the whole of civilization be destroyed, take over, then take orders from you?"

This time Lucifer allowed Maria to catch his eye but he quickly looked away. "It's true, you will have to watch it all fall down but, imagine, no more opioid zombie apocalypse on the streets. Generations never knowing slavery or genocide of any kind. The clock set back to zero, without the terrible history that has shaped humanity. I know it's a price I am willing to pay."

Daniel spoke up. "And where will this New Eden be located?"

"Ah, Daniel, I was about to get to you and Vlad. The remaining few will be relocated to Nebraska. I want you to build a new blood processing center on a plot of land I have purchased. The humans will supply you with blood through donation, as you have arranged around the globe. Vlad, I need you to replicate your Vegas compound on a much larger scale to house the survivors. Eventually we will build communities all over the world. Humans will never again hold decision-making positions."

"Horace Kilburn. You're very close to him. What's your plan there?" asked Adam, who watched Lucifer's every move.

"I want to know that as well," added Sandra.

"Yes, he and his followers want humanity to return to the Dark Ages—but on their terms, of course. He will accomplish nothing but chaos. I will deliver exactly that to him, then laugh as he cries out for help and receives none. If I allowed him to destroy the world, nothing would survive. I will do it in a way that at least lets us to rebuild."

Maria saw Jorge and his new family clinging to each other under a table while they awaited an inevitable death. "How can we watch innocents die? There are a hell of a lot of scumbags out there, but so many innocent people too!"

Lucifer looked at her coldly. "They will no longer suffer. Imagine all the evil on the planet ceasing at once. Those that hide their depravity will finally pay. Are you not a champion of justice, Maria? Does your heart not burn for it? Have you not killed for it?"

His words had bite. She remembered wanting to kill Esmeralda's father and so many others like him. She did like retribution. She wondered if that made her like Lucifer.

"When will this happen?" Adam asked, urgency in his tone.

Lucifer threw his hands up. "No one knows the day or the hour. I'm just stacking the blocks. I'm a mere servant. A whipping boy."

"Let me get this straight," interjected Sandra. "You want us to drop everything and hole up in Nebraska—*of all places*—for something that could happen fifty years from now? Sorry, but I'm not joining that cult or drinking that Kool-Aid. I'm not sure where you're from, but across *this* nation, this globe, people wake up to Armageddon every day."

The crowd started to talk among themselves. Lucifer seemed unruffled. "I think you are overreacting, San—"

"Excuse me. Do *not* call me a hysterical woman. I will become a nasty woman and cut you off right here and now. *You* sought *me* out."

For the briefest of moments, Maria saw panic cross Lucifer's face. "Listen to me. What I'm trying to say is most of you are old enough to know when things start to change. You have heightened senses. All I ask is that you remain alert and gather when the time comes. Do you not feel overstretched, moving from one desperate human situation to another? The only ones who need to start work now are Vlad and Daniel."

Lucifer handed Daniel several folders filled with documents. "Here is the deed to the land, plus the details of the bank account to pay for it all. I've already hired architects and contractors. All I need is your expertise to coordinate it." He turned back to the screen. "Sandra, take your time to think about this. I know there is no better leader than you. Your drive will be needed for human survival."

Vlad was standing against a wall with his arms crossed. "And what if there's a unanimous decision *not* to go along with whatever this is? You'll destroy us all?"

"If you sit back and do nothing, everyone will perish. You won't survive without enough humans, and they won't survive without your guidance or protection. Maybe a god will intervene, but if I were them, I don't think I would tolerate any more human mess. There are worthier creations. How many chances do humans get? Go in peace and be vigilant. I will expect an answer soon."

Lucifer watched the vampires talk among themselves as they left the villa.

When they had all departed, Adam and Vlad approached Maria, who sat at the back of the room.

"Are you ready to leave, Maria?" asked Adam. "I can't tolerate another minute in this man's presence. I've recorded the entire meeting on my phone and I'm eager to get Mordecai's opinion on all this."

"Can you guys give me a few minutes alone?"

"Do what you need to do. We will see you outside."

Lucifer came over to Maria and pulled her close.

"Thank you for showing me something new and wonderful. I do hope we have the pleasure of each other's company again."

He still smelled sweet, but the alluring perfume had worn off just enough for her not to feel as intoxicated by him as before. "I would say 'maybe next lifetime,'" she replied, "but I get the feeling this is the only shot we get."

"You're right. You only get the breath of life once as vampires, even if it's for a lot longer than humans. We all return to the light from which we were formed for judgment. I want to offer you a gift, though. I don't often get to do such things. I want to give you four human lives that will be counted in the end. Take care with your decision: whomever you choose could be gone by the time the tribulations begin." Lucifer then lent down and kissed Maria's lips, face and hands. "Goodbye, Maria."

Maria grabbed her bag and walked out the door to the car. She sat in the passenger's seat next to Vlad and he gave her a smile as she buckled her seatbelt. "Five more minutes and I thought I might have to go in blindfolded and pull you off each other. Let's get going. Maria, please tell me where you get your balls from, because I might need a new pair after that."

"Are you okay?" Adam asked Maria. The anger seemed to have left him.

Maria slumped into her seat, pulling out her phone. "I'm fine. I'm done with him, but I wanted what I wanted. It had been so long... Thank you for asking, though. And Vlad, thank you for having my back."

In the end, Mordecai was right. The experience was a mix of blissful awakening and realization that she could never let her guard down. She felt somehow exorcised of her obsessive lust and thoughts of Lucifer. What was done was done, without anyone getting hurt in the process. Or so she hoped.

# 28

"We will reconvene after the election. Until then, any questions from our fellow vampires must wait. I will contact them all with my final opinion. It's not what Lucifer says that one should worry about; rather it's the things he chooses to omit."

Vlad rolled his eyes when Mordecai finished speaking, then he stormed out, slamming the door and pulling out his phone to call an Uber to the airport.

Adam followed him out of Mordecai's office.

"That son-of-a-God-I-don't-believe-in hasn't changed, has he? It's always about waiting and timing and meditating on it. Sometimes we need action." Vlad spoke at a volume he hoped would reach Mordecai's ears. "I'm tempted to start this little project in Nebraska by myself just to spite him."

Adam took Vlad's phone out of his hands gently. "He is the oldest we know of. He hasn't survived this long or built this organization without being able to think through every single detail. I know you blame him for Anastasia's death. But she made a choice as an adult to enter a war zone. If you could have seen all the people she helped, you would know her life was not lost in vain. I loved her, too. For Anastasia, please stay and see this through. If you still don't agree with Mordecai after the election, then go back to your desert palace and do whatever you think best."

Vlad took his phone back and paced along the corridor with a smirk on his face. "I knew that if I walked into Grandthorpe again, I would find it difficult to leave. I don't believe in God or destiny, only the blood of birth and dirt of death, but here I am, somehow in the place I promised never to return to."

"Maybe because you belong here. You are wanted here. I was a lone wolf for so long and it made me miserable, but I was too prideful to admit I needed others. And I couldn't let go of the past."

Vlad stopped his caged tiger steps. His eyes caught Maria passing by with Paloma. She didn't see him. "Fine. I'll stay. But just until the election."

Lucifer paced his terrace, listening to Nina Simone and swigging an eight-hundred-euro bottle of red wine. He had thought another human delight he had never experienced would bring him some comfort. It hadn't. He shouldn't have bothered with tasting notes and gone straight for the snakebite sting of tequila. There was only one taste he wanted on his tongue. Maria.

Never before in all the cycles of the universe had he felt this morose. He had only felt awe and worship of the gods—or outrage. Lucifer wondered if this had been part of his punishment all along: placing something he truly desired right in front of him, knowing he could just have a taste, but could not possess it for long. Damn God and His insufferable obsession with the forbidden fruit.

Maria's taste still lingered in his mouth. Remembering the suppleness of her body in his hands made him want to dash back to the heavens just so he could forget. But he couldn't bear to part from the place where Maria existed. He seethed with anger at God's will and stupid punishments. If only there was some other way...

'I Put a Spell on You' began to play as he stared at the calm water of Lake Como, thinking back on their brief but unforgettable time together. He would rather throw himself into a sun flare than go back on his knees to wait for the final phase of his punishment. The helplessness of this moment left him feeling humiliated. His creator would not get away with this. Not this time. Maybe he could cast a spell of his own. The power was there. He would have to ask for help from demons, but he could always dispose of them later. Maybe he could convince the demons to get rid of the last of the vampires who didn't deserve to be counted in the remnant. Better still, maybe he could give the demons the power to start the tribulations to make way for a new God. Lucifer thought it was time for outright rebellion.

He walked into the bathroom and turned the shower

and sink taps to the hottest temperature. The small room quickly filled with steam. Lucifer stood in front of the mirror with closed eyes.

"Leviathan!" he began. "I ask you to come to my aid. Amon! I call on you to sow discord. Sitri! I call on you to enflame the love of a divine creature named Maria. Zepar! I call on you to bind Maria and I. Furfur! I call on you to create chaos on the Earth and in the atmosphere." The steam surrounding him took on a distinct unpleasant odor of decay. As he wiped the condensation from the mirror, the steam formed into the shapes of humans. Yellowed eyes stared at him.

"It is I, Leviathan. Ha! If it isn't the greatest of the fallen ones," the demon rasped. "I thought we were all beneath you."

Lucifer held his temper. "You know I despise your antics, inciting the worst of the humans. However, I do know your power."

Yellow eyes glowed orange in contempt. It laughed in such horrible delight that it made even Lucifer shiver. Desperate times, desperate measures and such. Lucifer knew he had to play nice to get what he wanted from this demon.

"I've decided to stay here for good," he continued. "Forgive my original disregard. I can't begin my plans without your help. I want you to bring me a particular woman. A very special woman. She must come to me unharmed and with no resistance, stop anyone who tries to dissuade her. Not a single scratch on her body, else I will cast you into the sun myself. I have called on each of you for this specific task. "

The form placed a misty hand over Lucifer's shoulder.

"A woman? Careful now—you saw how Baal's ego-stroking got that New York Congressman into a bit of a pickle. If you consider five to ten years in prison for texting a sixteen-year-old a pickle! Humans just can't help themselves. And *we* are the villains!" The demon laughed even louder. "If I *was* interested, what's in it for me? No such thing as a free lunch, as the humans say."

Lucifer had to be careful here. Deals with demons were dangerous. Some were unpredictable in their recklessness. Their power was derived from belief.

"I will allow you to continue to exist after I take over this Earth," he said carefully. "Until then, I won't interfere with any of your vile plans, whatever they may be."

"We like to cause trouble. However, one last tiny matter to ponder. What of the Creator? We've been struck down once. What if it happens again—or worse? It's such a greedy thing and doesn't like to share."

"Please. This little rock among the vast net of the heavens means little. How else can you explain your ability to move around as you do? They have surely moved on to other creations with temperaments worthier of grace. Do you feel the Creator's presence?" Lucifer gave the demon a sly smile. He would have his way for certain.

The demon moved closer to Lucifer's neck, taking

in his honeysuckle scent. Lucifer had to hold his breath to avoid choking on the smell of fermented sewage that prickled his nostrils.

"I will possess this woman and bring her to you. Call my name and I will respond. I hope this is the beginning of a more... *symbiotic* relationship."

"And the rest of you?" Lucifer asked.

There was a pause followed by an echo, "Aye."

The misty forms disappeared. Now all Lucifer had to do was lure in Maria.

# 29

It was very early morning when shock, followed by denial, filled Grandthorpe as the new President of the United States was confirmed. Even the newsreaders were in disbelief. A former entrepreneur turned game show host could now add President to his sketchy resumé. Mr. Kilburn stood in front of a waving American flag in a massive stadium where his supporters waited for their newly elected leader to speak.

Shortly after the announcement, Vlad stomped into Mordecai's office without knocking. "Alright, old man, get talking. The election is over."

Mordecai was kneeling in front of his sofa in silent prayer. He rose to meet Vlad.

"We are going to go along with Lucifer's plan; I hope you will build the compound. It doesn't mean we are following his orders; rather think of it as taking over his idea. The future is so very opaque now. But I shall summon him to me."

Vlad looked at the ancient vampire: he seemed suddenly even older and his body appeared smaller than before. Part of him felt sorry for Mordecai. God knows how long he had lived and what the burden of that had done to him.

Satisfied, Vlad left the office to say his goodbyes. If some shitstorm was coming their way, whether now or in fifty years, he needed to be near the blood supply. *Nebraska could be fun*, he thought. It meant no more shows, which wasn't a terrible thing; he'd grown bored of having a set schedule in Vegas. The parties and the social media love would have to stop, too. It didn't matter. No one on Insta would give him a kidney if he needed one. All those friends would soon forget about him as he slipped away from the feed. He had been Billy Xerxes long enough.

He was going from social media megastar to biblical Noah, building the twenty-first century version of the Ark. The best of his architects and contractors would have to be paid a small fortune for their silence. No way he was using Lucifer's guys. He imagined all the war zones and calamities he'd seen in his extended lifetime, and what it would take to withstand every single one hitting a small colony all at once with full force. He'd spent centuries saving soldiers. It would be a cold day in Hell if he lost more.


A grinning Lucifer arrived at Grandthorpe Hall, and Adam met him outside of the doors.

"What happened to never seeing your face again? said Adam in a hard tone.

"How pleasant you are." Lucifer gave him a smug look with his hands in his pockets.

"Just follow me."

When they arrived in Mordecai's office, Lucifer made himself comfortable, sitting on the plush sofa and stretching his arms across its back. He looked at Adam dismissively. "You can leave now; I want to speak with Mordecai alone."

Adam didn't move, returning Lucifer's gaze without blinking.

Mordecai was sat behind his desk. He nodded at Adam. "I will handle this. Please tell everyone not to be alarmed."

Adam turned his attention to Mordecai. "I won't be far away if you need me." He walked out without acknowledging Lucifer.

As the door closed, Lucifer addressed the ancient vampire. "I was very pleased to hear you're going to work with me after all. Horace Kilburn's victory has you a bit spooked? I have to say it has all been so very entertaining. He's not the Antichrist, you know; just a really shitty human. He thinks it's all about him and his cronies. Not the first in history, right, old friend?"

Mordecai looked at Lucifer. "I'm a little concerned, *old friend*. Why did you come all this way? We live in a world of technology these days. A simple text message or email would have sufficed."

Awkward silence filled the passing seconds.

"How is Maria doing?" Lucifer's voice had all the shine of an oil spill.

"She is not a topic for discussion. Please don't get the wrong idea. We are not joining you; we will build a sanctuary in Nebraska in which to congregate when the time comes. That is all I've been instructed to do."

Lucifer scoffed, "You want to take credit for saving the last of the humans and vampires, and I just get left out in the cold? Not a prayer of thanks or recognition?"

"Not the cold—the Lake of Fire, I believe—and we are both following orders. Except I follow because I obey, and you follow because it's part of your punishment."

Lucifer met Mordecai's stare. "I think it is time to go. There is much work to be done." He gave Mordecai a half smile.

Mordecai remained expressionless. "I will see you out."

# 30

The months that followed were strange days around the globe. The rumblings Lucifer talked about had begun not fifty years into the future, but at the current moment in history. Whatever trash fire embers glowed under humanity's feet seemed to combust all at once. And the new leader of the United States created all the chaos he promised. New desperate situations arose before the last ones could be quelled. World leaders bickered like school-children fighting over sandboxes. Five hurricanes barreled toward the Caribbean and U.S., one after the other, without mercy.

Adam worked night and day, shuffling money, resources and contacts to be at the ready when developing situations became disaster zones. He asked the oldest of the vampires to travel to the places where humans wouldn't or couldn't go. They were the strongest, with senses that could predict and calculate outcomes before humans or younger vampires had time to think. They also could go the longest without human blood. The younger vampires were sent to other desperate areas. Someone was always on hand to provide the blood they needed to prevent hunger taking over.

It was just after the hurricanes blew themselves out that an earthquake more powerful and deadly than any in Mexico's recent history struck. Paloma and Maria were frantic. Communication broke down so they decided to go in person to help with the relief efforts and hopefully find their loved ones—Adam decided to go with them to coordinate from the ground. Maria knew she could work with little rest, lifting debris or searching for survivors in the dark of the night. Darcy wouldn't leave Paloma's side, and Paloma wanted Darcy to meet her mother. The church where Estrella lived should be safe, but the roads might have become impassable from rock falls. Estrella would allow herself to starve to death before she fed on a dying or injured human.

Maria had other intentions in Mexico. She wanted to convince Jorge and his family to relocate to Nebraska. She would feel better knowing they were close to safety. Vlad had taken the project on to buy a farm in Nebraska: perhaps Jorge could get a job with him or at least borrow a room until his family was on their feet. Maria arranged the details of their relocation. She lit a candle, hoping they were safe and she could convince them to leave Mexico.

Maria said goodbye to Mordecai, wondering how he could be so absent in these times. Since his meeting with Lucifer, he seemed to have checked out entirely. He was often found sitting in the gardens alone on mild dry days or kneeling in prayer in his office. It made her want to know the history of this man, and how time really affected vampires.

Maria made her way to Monterrey while Adam went straight to Mexico City where the situation was particularly bad. Maria was heartbroken and in shock when she pulled up to Jorge's gym. The front door displayed a sign explaining it was closed for good. She knocked anyway, hoping he still lived there.

After a few moments, Conchita opened the door. "Maria?" She threw her arms around Maria, squeezing as much as she could with a round belly.

Maria's mouth opened. "Are you...?!"

"Yes! A little Jorge."

Jorge followed behind with sadness in his eyes, even though she knew he was pleased to see her. "Maria! I thought we would never meet again. Please come in. Esmeralda is at school right now, but she will be excited to see you."

The gym was a dark, dusty room. It hurt Maria's heart to see this once vibrant place empty.

"What happened here?" she asked as they sat around the small table in the casita.

Jorge shrugged. "Things were really good for a while, then someone moved in on the territory again. They wanted twice what the previous guy demanded. I told him I have a family and it wasn't happening, so we shut down."

"I'm so sorry, Jorge. I have money if..."

"No, I still have some of what you left us. I'm not sure how long it will last, but we'll manage. Your car. He wouldn't leave us alone unless we gave him the car. Please forgive me." Jorge's eyes were gathering tears and his voice cracked as he spoke. Conchita placed her arm around him.

Maria thought of her brass knuckles, waiting patiently in her back pocket. That scum. But she wasn't here for that.

"Don't apologize, it's just a stupid car. I have a big favor to ask. You may say no. But be aware I won't leave until you say yes."

Jorge wiped his eyes. "Whatever it is, consider it done."

"Good! You're relocating to Nebraska in a week. I've got visas, medical insurance, cash, and a contact for your family when you arrive. I beg you to leave this place, and to leave now."

Jorge stood up almost knocking over his chair. "What? This is our home! Our family is here and the baby is due soon. This is too much."

Conchita sat in silence, rubbing her belly as she looked around the empty gym. Maria thought she might be the one to make the decision.

Jorge looked at Conchita. "Conchita, please tell Maria we love her, but it's out of the question. The States don't need another Mexican landscaper or farmhand.

Besides, people like us are no longer welcome there. It's been made very clear by that President and his followers."

"Jorge, I want to go. We can start over. Start another business. We will be back. We should trust Maria. She would only ask if it was very important."

Jorge took a deep breath to calm himself. "Building a life in Mexico for myself and my people is my dream."

"I know," said Maria, gently. "But the world is about to change, and I want you protected. All of you. I would not ask you to leave if your lives didn't depend on it."

Maria placed a backpack on the table. "Everything you need is in here. I'm heading to Mexico City now. We have a private plane there to take to us all to Nebraska in a week's time. I've left a little money, so please use it for a doctor to check on you and the baby and make sure it's safe to fly. I beg you to come with me. I will leave you now to talk about it."

"Can you give me more details at least?" asked Jorge.

When Maria had listened to Lucifer's plan, the vision of them cowering under the table had left her with a feeling of loss for days. That ugly turmoil returned. "Not now. Just please trust me."

Conchita hugged Maria. "Take care of yourself. We were lucky to only experience a few aftershocks. I've seen on the news so many others were not so fortunate. We will pray for them."

Jorge also gave Maria a hug despite his evident unease at her request. Then she sped off as if she was on her way to save the world.

# 31

Mordecai looked out his office window. He wore a robe one of the younger vampires at Grandthorpe had made for him while sipping tea with a thimble of marrow powder. Its rotting floral scent filled the room. 'The End' by The Doors played on his stereo. He had felt cold this morning, so he'd lit his fireplace and turned the radiators up high. He watched the desolate gardens, wondering how different it could all be. How did humans go so wrong? Could all this pain and hellish division have been avoided? He was only one man—the longest living of his kind, but that's all it takes, right? If he hadn't seen it with his own eyes, he would believe in nothing. He shut his eyelids tight, trying to flick away the buzzing insects of self-doubt and loathing before their larvae could invade his head and hatch.

Lost in thought, he didn't notice the shadow passing through his doorway.

"This place is like a sweat lodge," came Lucifer's

unwelcome voice. "And what is this music? It's a bit dramatic even for you. I think you're losing your grip, old man."

Mordecai continued to look out the window, sipping his tea.

"I thought our business was concluded," he said eventually, his voice hoarse and just above a whisper.

Lucifer walked around the office admiring the art collection. "I thought so too; let's just say I had a change of heart."

Sighing, Mordecai turned to face Lucifer. "You don't have the luxury of having a heart. You are not a man after all—or have you forgotten that? I'm not going to let you murder everyone now."

"You don't look so great, Mordecai. Your fangs are yellow, the tips are chipped, and your skin is spiderweb thin. Time to sleep for good. They don't need you anymore."

"State the real reason you are here, Lucifer."

"Where is Maria? I have come for her."

"She's elsewhere, and that's all I will tell you. Why don't I see you out?"

Lucifer smirked. "There are other ways." He snapped his fingers. 'I Am the Black Gold of the Sun' by Rotary Connection began to play. "You are a man, and I am everything you wish you were."

Suddenly Lucifer grabbed Mordecai by the arms and turned him toward the sunlight. Mordecai allowed Lucifer to manhandle him: he saw no point in resistance.

It wasn't his time yet. This knowledge did not prevent the teacup rattling against the saucer as Lucifer brought the cup to Mordecai's lips.

"Drink and see. We *will* be everything." Lucifer forced the rest of the tea into Mordecai's mouth, causing the old vampire to sputter.

Mordecai dropped the cup and saucer as he looked directly into the sun. His eyes glazed over and widened as he watched some unseen play. He couldn't pull himself away, even as a drop of sweat rolled down the side of his face.


Lucifer walked to his vintage convertible, parked on the driveway just outside Grandthorpe, pleased with the grains of information he had procured. How wonderful it would be to have a child of his own, with his celestial bloodline and its mother's beauty! The combined power inherited by their offspring would be magnificent. He or she would be a true force of this Earth. The best part was that he could spend his days cultivating this world as he pleased, and the rest of the time making love to his wife. He had decided that the real problem with humans was they had no real sense of God. Instead of some invisible force dividing the world, he and his Maria would be living, breathing gods who walked among the people. She would be adorned in feathers, gold and jewels. Their subjects could touch their feet and feel their wrath. If any human dared to harm another or pluck a single hair from a creature's back without permission, they would pay a dear price for all to see. Forget Nebraska: the blood-soaked temples of Mexico would be the center of New Eden—*his* New Eden. The Earth would heal itself and the weapons of old would all be gone. He couldn't think of a better place to spend eternity. The insufferable God that people couldn't see, smell or touch would be all but forgotten. Lucifer could feel himself becoming aroused. If only his sweet Maria were there to welcome him inside her.

He drove with the wind in his hair, pleased with his decision. It was time to find his goddess queen. Lucifer parked at Heathrow Airport, allowing his true form to expand and travel to her. This would disrupt the heavens, but he had to see her, claim her. He hoped it would work. If it didn't, he would return and kill whoever he had to for the information he needed.

# 32

The day before Maria and Adam were due to leave Mexico, Conchita called Maria to tell her she had convinced Jorge to leave, even though he was still concerned about their life as immigrants in a country that had begun the process of "Making America Number One Again," starting with making immigrants Public Enemy Number One. Conchita was given the okay to fly by a doctor—a few weeks later it would have been too late.

While Paloma and Darcy remained in Mexico with Estrella, continuing the aid work, Maria and Adam traveled to Valentine, Nebraska with Jorge and his family. Adam wanted to see the site where this human Ark would be built.

Esmeralda's eyes grew large when she saw the plane that was just for them. It was her first flight. She jumped upon seeing Maria. "Can I sit next to you? I want to know all about England and the queen."

"Yes," said Maria, giving her a hug, "as long as you promise to let your mamá rest."

Esmeralda smiled and nodded.

The stewardess fawned over the inquisitive girl, bringing her juice and treats throughout the journey. Conchita took this opportunity to put her feet up while Jorge massaged her swollen legs. Maria could see a sadness in his eyes, but at least this way he would stay alive. She tried not to think about the millions of others who would die. She couldn't understand the unfairness of it all. Who or what made up this design and the rules?

Vlad greeted them at the airport. Maria gave him a wide grin when she saw him standing at Arrivals with a dark brown cowboy hat and weathered boots. She liked the look on him.

"May I?" Vlad asked as he reached for Maria's bag.

"Sure... Thank you. How are you?"

He gave her his usual confident smile. "You know me, I am half tank and half vampire. It takes a lot to stop me."

"Well, it's good to see you." She touched his arm and followed him along with the others to their hired nondescript cream-colored van. Vlad drove them through a wide open, flat landscape decorated with Walmarts, Targets, Dairy Queens and farms.

The two-story house that came with the land he purchased was situated on a farm much like those they had passed along the way. It was a rustic, tidy place with land as far as they could see. There were apple trees, a children's play area, and a small vegetable garden. To the left of the farm was a paddock with four horses. Chickens pecked at the ground in the adjoining fenced area, with one rooster strutting among them.

When the doors to the van opened, Esmeralda squealed at the sight of her temporary home. "Are you ready for an adventure, Papá?"

Jorge smoothed the hair on the top of her head. "I am if you are."

When Vlad emerged from the big house, Esmeralda was frightened by his size and clung to Jorge.

"It's okay, mija. These are our new friends," he said gently.

Vlad gave her a smile. "Hey, do you want to see the horses?"

She glanced up at Jorge.

"It's up to you," he said with a shrug. "I'm okay with it."

She shyly nodded her head and held out her hand for Maria to join them.

While Conchita rested, Jorge, Esmeralda and Maria followed Vlad to the paddock.

"The small brown one is named Finn," said Vlad, "the white one is called Polly... and I can't remember the other two!"

Polly walked over to the gate and sniffed around. Esmeralda stood on the middle rail of the fence while

Vlad held out his hand and let Polly nuzzle his palm. Esmeralda grinned at Vlad and did the same.

"Do you know how to ride a horse?" he asked.

Esmeralda finally spoke to him. "No, but I think it would be nice."

"Okay. Well, maybe we can do something about that."

Jorge gave Vlad a smile. "Thanks. This is a big transition for us."

Vlad nodded and glanced at Maria. "Yeah, I know what you mean."

The following day, a woman in riding gear arrived at the house asking for Esmeralda and Jorge.

"Jorge, what is this all about?" Maria asked.

"I don't know. Maybe ask the big guy," Jorge said with a smile.

Maria watched the three wander to the paddock. She turned to the front door to see Vlad with a large smile on his face.

"What is this? Did you arrange this?"

"I have no idea what you are talking about."

She shook her head and nudged his arm playfully. "Of course you don't."

He looked at her. "Maybe you should learn too?"

"Me? On a horse?"

"Yeah, if the world ends in some apocalypse, it might be helpful."

"We're trying to prevent that."

He nodded his head. "We are… but maybe it's meant to happen?"

Maria looked at the serious expression on his face and how the tone in his voice changed. She looked back at the paddock and hoped to God that wasn't the truth.


A few weeks later, Vlad caught Jorge watching Esmeralda ride. A look of pain shadowed the former boxer's face. He stood with lowered shoulders and his hands deep in his pockets. His naturally tall square body seemed to have shrunk.

"You and Maria go way back?"

"Yeah. If you can believe it, I gave her a job, taught her how to box. But what she did for us doesn't even compare. I just wish I could find a stable job here to provide for my family. And keep me busy."

Vlad lent on the fence next to Jorge, his eyes on the laughing girl as she learned to trot. "Look, I talked to my foreman; if you want a job, he's willing to start you on the basics. You can float around, see what you enjoy, and learn a trade." Vlad hoped Jorge wouldn't be too proud to take him up on his offer.

"Thanks, man, I'd appreciate that. It's so nice living here, but we need a place of our own. I've been looking at rents and it's not going to be easy." Esmeralda was shouting at them to watch her ride. They clapped and whistled in encouragement. "Just seeing how happy she is," Jorge continued. "I know this was the right decision. The world must feel so big for her now. She's going to hate moving from this place."

A smile spread across Vlad's face as he watched the young girl. "What if you didn't have to leave?"

"What do you mean? The closest property is still a drive away."

"The Keepers have purchased land as far as your eye can see. If you want something for your family, we can build them a house. The idea is to connect all the houses above ground to that huge construction site over there, but that's way down the line so it doesn't have to concern you right now. I'll get a guy to meet with you in the next few days to go over the plans."

Jorge looked as though he couldn't believe the words coming out of this almost-stranger's mouth. "I can't afford any of it, you know. And I've accepted enough charity. Thank you. It's tempting to say yes, but I can't."

"Yes, you can. I've been where you are," said Vlad, turning to look the other man in the eye. "Believe me. I had to literally do battle to take back what I could to thrive. I didn't do it alone. I'll tell you what: I'm here for the long term too. Let's set something up in one of the barns—you can train me when you aren't doing construction on your own home. When that's done, I'll be happy to invest in new boxing facilities in town. I don't recall seeing any place that's any good. That's not charity. It's business. After seeing Maria at the punching bag... man, her technique is fantastic. I lived in Vegas for years and I've seen a lot of fights. You got skills as a trainer."

Esmeralda ran over to them, hair wild and clothes covered in dirt. She climbed onto the fence to be near Vlad and Jorge. "Did you see me go? I love the horses, Papá. Thank you for bringing us here."

Esmeralda wrapped her arms around Jorge's neck, kissing his face. She moved to Vlad, doing the same while rubbing her hands in his beard. Vlad let out a bellowing laugh.

Jorge turned to Vlad, "So why Nebraska?"

Vlad shook his head. "I guess it would be a place large enough for a lot of people and isolated from large cities. Easy for people up and down the Americas to get to—no big mountains or bodies of water to cross. The seasons are stable and the temperatures not too extreme. Very in the middle."

"I can see that. And fertile land."

"Believe me, I would have preferred Italy," joked Vlad.

Once again, Maria found herself restless in the middle of the night. Like in Vegas, she found Vlad also alert. He was clearing out space in the barn to use as a temporary gym.

"Need some help?" she offered.

Vlad's body was dusted with dirt and hay from his work. "Absolutely. You can help me hang the punching bag."

"It's about time you start taking credit for playing Santa Claus around here. Jorge told me about your offer."

Vlad grinned. "I have no idea what you're talking about."

When the bag was secured from the rafters, Vlad offered Maria a blood pouch. She accepted, thinking this was as good a time as any to find out more about Vlad. She found a hay bale and sat down. He joined her.

"I wanted to ask you something," she began. "You don't have to answer, but would you feel able to tell me what happened to Anastasia? Adam said you all met in Russia during the Revolution."

Vlad ran his fingers through his beard, removing stray bits of straw before answering.

"Yes. Her father—the tsar—and all her family were murdered. She escaped and I found her in an alley, bleeding from a gunshot wound to the abdomen. The streets were chaos. When I saw her, I knew exactly who she was: Adam and I had been to a ball thrown by her father. I carried her to my apartment and asked if she wanted to live. She was just a teen. She reminded me of my mother and sisters. I looked after her like a daughter after that."

Maria placed a hand on his knee. "Poor girl. And the rest of the story?"

"Congo 1996 is what happened. I've been a soldier all my life. It was my birthright and legacy—at least until I got sick of it all. After that I needed something light and easy. Most vampires have degrees upon degrees, following some intense intellectual spark I've never felt. I guess I just wasn't born or raised with that, but I can't resist a battle cry. I've always fought for the side I felt was right, then left when I sensed I wasn't needed or when the cause was no longer something I believed in. After Vietnam, I'd had enough. I took a break for a while; Anastasia studied agriculture and pharmacology. She loved what the Keepers stood for. She had big dreams.

"When I got bored of peacetime I moved into intelligence. One of my missions took me to Africa. Mordecai was concerned about the state of the continent, especially the civil wars, but I warned him it was too dangerous even for vampires to operate in the open under the guise of international aid. Both Anastasia and another vampire you haven't met named Elizabeth took his side, saying there was no point to their supernatural existence if they couldn't do what humans couldn't do. They argued that, up to that point, there had been no major incidents with foreigners. I told Mordecai to leave that work to the old ones, or at least have them in the shadows. He agreed to try, then without my knowledge they left with an aid group for Congo. I can't remember where I was deployed at the time, I just know I didn't go back when I found out what had happened.

"They were tending to locals in need of medical care when a group of soldiers surrounded them. Even as vampires, there were too many for Anastasia and

Elizabeth to overpower. Naturally, they thought of the civilians first. They couldn't be shot dead, but the crowd waiting for aid could be. The soldiers wanted everything that could be sold. While the aid station was being looted, the commander told two men to take Anastasia and kill the locals. The two men—brothers—refused and fought with the commander over the killing of the villagers. Their people. In his fury at being disobeyed in front of his men, the commander said he would shoot four villagers unless Anastasia went with him as a hostage. She agreed. Then, without warning, he slit her throat with a machete and decapitated her. He then ordered the other soldiers to gun down the disobedient brothers.

"Elizabeth managed to crawl to the two brothers, the soldiers who didn't want to kill the villagers. She gave them vampire life. But there was no hope for Anastasia."

He hung his head and paused before speaking again.

"The only comfort I take from that tale is that the three vampires went to the commander's camp that night and devoured every adult, burned the weapons, and returned the stolen goods. The brothers were happy to be rid of the man who had burned their village, slaughtered their family, and made them soldiers at age eleven. James and Seth, two stand-up guys at heart, returned to England with Elizabeth and Anastasia's body."

When he had finished, Vlad and Maria sat in silence, broken only by insects singing their night symphony.

Maria's night vision was now good enough to detect Vlad's scars. She knew there was so much more to this man who was larger than life, but still a man who bled and wept. For now, she didn't want to dig much deeper.

Vlad took another swig of his blood, looking far away. Maria brought him back to the present. "I can see why you like Metallica so much."

He seemed to shake himself and turned to her. "Hell yeah. When 'One' from *And Justice for All* debuted, followed by *The Black Album* in '91 and 'The Unforgiven,' I was officially a superfan. It was like music that had been made from my story, the story of my family. Next to Pearl Jam's *Ten* I can't think of an album I've listened to more."

Maria laughed. "I'd listen to 'Enter Sandman' when I needed an adrenaline boost before taking out Monterrey's trash."

They talked until the blood ran out and the sun began to rise.

# 33

The wind was strong that Sunday morning as they worked on Jorge's house, but that wasn't unusual for the time of year. Maria liked working next to Jorge again. The manual labor kept her mind and body busy. She exchanged a few glances with Vlad, who was also pitching in, but the hard work made her forget her confusion about her changing emotions toward him.

A vehicle approached, kicking up dirt like tornadoes on the move. It pulled up, and to everyone's surprise, Mordecai stepped out. He looked older than ever and was flanked by four ancient, androgynous pale vampires dressed in blue jeans, boots, black shirts, sunglasses and cowboy hats. They were trying so hard to blend in; instead, they looked like they were pulled from some corny low-budget vampire flick you'd see at two in the morning on the horror channel, or a sketch from *Hee Haw*. Mordecai just looked like a shadow.

Adam, Maria and Vlad approached him. "Hello,

friends," he greeted the small group. "We are sorry for imposing on you without warning. We need to talk. In private"

"There is a barn we can go to." said Vlad as he looked at Mordecai's companions with intrigue. "There are a few humans here. Don't want to scare them."

Mordecai nodded. "Show us the way."

Maria also looked at the ancient vampires with curiosity but, unlike Vlad, tried to hide it. She followed Adam and Vlad to the barn while the ancients stuck close to their leader.

Inside the barn, they settled near the stacked hay bales next to the punching bag, while the old ones stood silently by the barn door.

Vlad's eyes stayed on the old ones as he addressed Mordecai. "It must be important for you to bring the Voldemort convention with you."

"I had another visit from our friend, Lucifer," said Mordecai. "He has decided he wants to take control of Earth after the tribulations, making himself a god with a wife and his own heirs. Maria, he wants you."

Maria felt dizzy and almost like laughing. "But I can't have children! This is impossible. What happened between us was nothing. Does he even know where I am?"

Mordecai shifted uncomfortably on his hay bale. "Actually, it might not be impossible. But if he wants to heal you and create seed within himself, he will have to break universal laws. He could use his true power on

Earth, but it would mean he would never go back to his cosmic form. I doubt that means much to him now. He can find you because you have some of his essence inside of you. You drank his blood."

Maria was filled with horror and anger at herself for indulging her desire with the wrong man. She could have fucked dozens of human men... maybe even Vlad. Lucifer would have never had this insane plan if she had only stayed away. It was only sex—amazing eye-opening sex, not doomsday sex. She had to make this right.

"I'll kill him. I'll get close enough to him and destroy him for good. This is all my fault. I will make this right for everyone."

"You don't need to. I will do this. My time is over: I've outlived my usefulness like the Ark of the Covenant long ago. Everything has its place in time. That is why I have brought the old ones with me. They have been generous enough to leave their good work to assist me in trapping Lucifer, to force him into his true form so he can no longer disguise himself as human. There is a risk this might cause the tribulation to begin sooner than expected. And, once the beast is unleashed, there is no turning back. I suspect, after all this, people will begin to gather here to ensure the survival of humanity. You will have to be ready to accept the humans who find themselves inexplicably drawn to the Keepers."

Maria sat on the bale of hay next to Mordecai. She put her head in her hands, struggling to come to terms with the consequences of her decision to seduce Lucifer.

Vlad moved toward Maria but Mordecai intervened. "Can you all please give us a moment?"

Everyone obeyed, leaving the two vampires alone in the barn.

Mordecai touched her hand. "Maria, I have been here since the beginning. I have certainly made my share of mistakes. You had been alone so very long. Desire is a natural calling. At its very core, life on Earth is a sensual experience. It's our pleasure and pitfall. Although God has shown me so many things, I have not always listened as I should, nor understood his message. Let me tell you something that you cannot repeat now; the others will know all in due time. How do you think Tizoc came to be?"

Maria lifted her head and looked into the ancient vampire's strange, kind eyes.

"I created him," he continued sadly. "I misread his heart in my desperation to save a civilization. That single mistake changed history and caused immense pain for generations of his victims and their families. You cannot imagine the burden of that—of what you have finally released me from. Before we are vampire, we are human—imperfect, as God created us. Go and learn. Who knows, this might have been the plan all along. Your heart may be heavy now, but it is a heart filled with good intent."

Maria reached over and hugged Mordecai. In that moment he felt like the father she never had but always wanted.

That afternoon, a storm had appeared on the horizon and was approaching fast. The workers stopped laboring on Jorge's home to secure the barns and the other houses on the property. There was talk of multiple tornadoes and high-speed winds, but it was all speculation. Until the sirens started to blare.

As the day wore on, a gauzy film covered the sky. The sun tried to break through, creating a rose gold-tinged atmosphere that left everyone with a sense of unease. Gathered in the main farmhouse kitchen, they watched the news: it claimed it was just dust particles kicked up by the storm. This explanation didn't appease anyone's concerns.

Their fear was realized when the sirens started to wail again around four p.m. Jorge, his family, and the other human workers on the property locked themselves in the storm cellar below the main farmhouse. Maria checked on the very pregnant Conchita and the excitable Esmeralda to make sure they were safe and relaxed. Vlad had food and games ready for a long wait below ground. Then she joined Adam, Vlad, and Mordecai to convene with the older vampires who remained in the barn. The ancient vampires had removed the clothing they wore to blend in. Their striking and frightening appearance would have scared all the humans.

As the sirens wailed, Mordecai glanced at each of the ancient vampires with his sagging eyes. He nodded to one of them, who helped him to his feet. With the other three ancient vampires, they walked out of the barn and into the lashing winds.

The sirens wailed while the wind blew harshly against the wooden boards of the barn. Maria stood and started to back away from the group.

"Guys, I feel strange," she said and swayed. She stumbled, falling over her own boots. She felt dizzy, like she was on the deck of a boat in a violent storm.

Vlad rushed to her side. "Maria, have you fed?"

Maria felt feverish. "I need to go to him."

"We must stay together." Vlad tried to help her to her feet. "You can't go to him. He wants to unite with you for his own selfish reasons. He wants to rule over this Earth and rule over you. What he wants to create with you is unholy."

Maria pulled away from Vlad's arms, baring her fangs.

Adam leaped up and tried to help Vlad restrain her. But she felt she couldn't let them hold her: she would fracture every bone in her body to free herself.

"Please, if I just reason with him… If I just gave him a few days with me to come to his senses." Maria's skin began to burn beneath her silver and turquoise cross. The pain made her cry out. "Take it off, take it off! It's burning me!"

Red blisters appeared on her chest and she wept bloody tears.

———

Vlad struggled to hold onto the bucking, crying Maria. He was afraid of hurting her but equally afraid to let go. A shadow emerged from behind the bales of hay. It was one of the old ones.

"This is not Lucifer. She has been taken by a demon. They are all around us. This storm is not natural," the ancient vampire rasped. "We must exorcize it. Do not let her go. The crucifix will do nothing, but you being with her can make all the difference..."

As Vlad and Adam desperately maintained their hold on Maria, the old one wrapped his bony, paper-thin-skinned fingers around her wrists. His sharp nails seemed to interlock. Maria began to hiss and thrash.

"Get off me, priest!" she yelled.

"Who are you? I know you are in there," asked the old one.

Her mouth opened wide with her fangs growing longer. A voice from deep within her chest spoke without her lips moving. "One more powerful than you. One above them all."

The wind battered against the barn at full force. "Leviathan." The vampire priest looked at Vlad and Adam. "I need both of you to open your hearts and minds. Leave your disbelief and let your light work through you. We are divine vessels. Allow yourself to focus on freeing her with whatever words you wish. It begins with a word."

Vlad felt Adam's hard glance. "Can you do this?" Adam asked him. "Put away all your grievances. Can you do this for her?"

Vlad watched Maria's body buck and twist. Her eyes were rolling inside her head and her fangs were growing. "I will do anything for her."

They all started to say their own prayers and Maria screamed, "I'm going to be a mother! Let me go! A mother of nations. He needs me!" Blood tears ran down her face and the screams morphed into sobs. "I don't want to be alone. Don't let me be alone forever."

Vlad continued to pray, asking God or whatever hovered in the atmosphere to restore her, to restore his faith. He bent over and whispered into Maria's ear, "You're not alone. We are all you will ever need, and we will keep each other safe until this Earth is gone. Come back to me, Maria. Give me faith again."

Maria turned to Vlad, spitting in his face. "You just want to fuck me and own me like all the rest. You aren't anything but a selfish, overgrown child chasing panties. Is there even a soul behind that beard?"

Vlad felt each word like a blow. The old one looked at him. "Don't listen. It is just an inverted mirror presented by the demon. It wants to torment you with its own self-loathing and sorrow. It hates humans as much as Lucifer. Mostly, it hates itself."

Adam began to pray louder and Maria turned to him. "I want my baby!" she yelled. "*Give me my baby back*!"

Adam looked away. Vlad saw the pain her words had caused him.

"Maria, if I had known, I would have never... I will always be sorry for taking that away from you."

Maria screamed a final cry before going limp.

Panicked, Vlad shook her body and placed his head to her chest. There was a faint heartbeat.


Lucifer arrived alone, determination in his eyes. He'd not felt so set on a course of action since the day he had made Adam and Eve disobey their creator. His hair was unkempt from the blasting winds, although he still wore his handmade Italian suit. The jacket opened, his white shirt turning translucent in the pummeling rain. Before reaching the barn—before reaching Maria— he was confronted by Mordecai, flanked by the oldest vampires. He would slaughter them all without remorse.

He raised his voice so he could be heard above the storm. "Are you all so tired you've decided to allow me to send you back to the Creator today? Has the burden of near immortality caught up with you? You are all too weak to defeat me."

Lucifer walked toward Mordecai with a swagger, feeling as though victory was already his. His expensive shoes sank into the wet earth with each heavy step.

Before he could reach Mordecai, the old ones intercepted him, stepping in front of their leader.

He sneered at them. "You don't have it in you... any of you. Look how you hide in the shadows like scared children because you don't want to frighten the humans. Your power is wasted on you."

One of them opened their mouth and shrieked.

The rest followed, the haunting noise echoing through the storm. They leaped forward and dug their thick nails into his flesh, leaving open, bleeding gashes. The strong gales whipped and tugged at the old ones' bodies, causing them to anchor their feet deep into the ground as Lucifer fought them off with his superior strength. He swiftly tossed each one to the ground.

As they jumped to their feet again, Lucifer glared at Mordecai.

"Maria is mine. I want her and I know she wants me, too. We will spend an eternity worshipping each other's bodies and recreating Eden. I'm going to heal her, make her fertile again. I will give her everything her heart desires and we will rule this Earth the way it should be ruled. Our offspring will be a new being, ensuring obedience."

Mordecai defied the wind and walked close to Lucifer as the vampires grabbed him and held him, their claw-like fingers squeezing his arms.

"You can't have her," said Mordecai.

Lucifer tried to lunge, ignoring his ripping flesh. His eyes went completely white as he summoned yet more cosmic strength. "I *do* have the power, and I will use it."

"You are the Destroyer, Lucifer, not the Creator. Let her go and do as you have been instructed."

The winds continued to howl, surrounding the small group. Lucifer felt the strength of the old ones fading as he began to break the rules he was bound by. The storm's violence increased around them. Mordecai was close enough now: he pulled his left arm away from an older vampire, ripping his suit jacket and shirt along with a chunk of flesh, and reached for Mordecai. His hand shredded through the thin cotton tunic he wore until he reached Mordecai's heart, nails ripping paper-thin skin, gouging bloody tissue. As his fingers tore through Mordecai's ribcage, Mordecai ripped off one of his gloves and punctured Lucifer's chest with his own hand—a hand of bone, plated in silver, with small etchings.

Both beings held each other's pumping hearts and squeezed.

"Lucifer, you have been a slithering beast in the grass," hissed Mordecai, "a man, and now it's time to take your final form as the Great Beast and Final Destroyer."

Immediately Lucifer felt the life draining from his body. Something else took over. The old vampires let him go. He and Mordecai collapsed to the ground in a final bloody union.

The sirens stopped. Vlad and Adam flew out of the barn toward the dark scene of death outside. They left Maria inside to recover. Blood saturated the ground, surrounding the gory bodies of Mordecai and Lucifer. Dirt from the wind covered their skin. Adam kneeled before Mordecai's bloody form with tears in his eyes.

"My friend, what have you done? We need you. There is still so much I have to learn from you."

Eyelids heavy, Mordecai smiled. "You have all come together. I'm so proud of you. Take care of each other and the humans. This is my end." Mordecai looked toward the breaking clouds at something meant only for him.

Then he was gone.

Vlad stared at Mordecai's body. A single red tear fell down his cheek. "I can't believe the bastard is gone. I never really hated him. He dedicated his entire life to charity and goodness. I hated I couldn't be that…"

A small groan escaped Lucifer's lips. Vlad's whole body filled with rage as he turned to confront the being who had caused all this grief and pain, then Maria's voice sounded from behind him.

"Stop!"

She walked with assured, swift steps. The red-thread veins in her eyes were pronounced and her fangs protruded.

Vlad and Adam quickly moved to form a barrier in front of Lucifer, unsure if Maria was herself or still possessed by the demon. Then Vlad saw the silver cross at her throat no longer burned her skin. He realized Adam had also seen this: together they stepped aside.

Maria gazed upon Lucifer's damaged, bloody body.

He reached for her. "My love, Maria. Look what they have done to me," he croaked. "All I wanted was for us to be together, a family. A family everyone would love and worship. You would be the adjudicator of justice and the mother of my children. Please, help me now. It's not too late. Don't tell me I've underestimated you."

Her old self would have felt a pang of doubt, maybe a little guilt. All she'd ever wanted was a family and now Lucifer offered her a miracle; however, she buried that dream. She was so much more now. The old Maria was dead. She slapped his hand away, crushing it under her boot.

A look of horror contorted Lucifer's face. "What are you doing?! Do you not love me?"

Maria placed her other boot over his throat. "Baby, you never loved me, and I never loved you. You put some horrible creature inside me to steal me for your own selfish vision of the future. Do you know the things it showed me? How it clawed at my soul? All my friends would have died or been under your control! You underestimated me. It ends here, lover. May God have mercy on your soul."

Maria pressed her boot hard against Lucifer's throat. Then she crouched down and ripped Mordecai's skeletal hand out of his broken, bloodied chest. Lucifer's pierced bleeding heart remained locked in Mordecai's bony fingers. Lucifer's human form was dead.

Maria unlatched Lucifer's heart, squeezing his dark blood over his body before placing it back in his chest. As she pulled away, a vision of rising water and burning skies flashed before her eyes. She heard Mordecai whispering *Eat and know*. Something told her this was not the end.

Without thinking she grabbed Lucifer's heart and placed it in her mouth, sucking up the last of its contents. She tore off a chunk and swallowed it whole. The old vampires were unphased by the sight. The ancient one who had exorcised the demon from her moved closer to Maria, taking the heart from her so he also could take a bite. They stared at each other in silent knowledge of what they were doing. He nodded his head before rejoining his fellows. They turned to gather wood and she knew they planned to burn Lucifer's body.

## 35

Mordecai had left two letters on his desk at Grand-thorpe Hall: one to be read as soon as possible after his death, the other later. The first letter gave instructions for his entombment. The rest of his body was to be placed underground with the other vampires.

Vlad arrived at Grandthorpe later than the others. Upon Paloma's request, her mother had made the journey to be there as well. As well as spending time with her daughter, Vlad noticed that Estrella and Adam spent a lot of time together, talking intimately with expressions of calm contentment as they gazed into each other's eyes. Vlad was happy for his old friend. And Adam had become a true friend. He looked for Maria as soon as he arrived back in England, but Adam said she had retreated to her room to process the events in Nebraska. Maria had taken Vlad by surprise from the very beginning. In Nebraska, the words spoken through her by the demon had sliced through his carefully constructed persona. He had allowed himself the pleasure of humans because he knew they left as quickly as they appeared, but now this vampire woman made him want something more.

She affected him differently from the way Anastasia had. Contrary to what everyone thought, he and Anastasia were never lovers—not even close. Anastasia was a seventeen-year-old kid he took from certain death to raise as his own. In a human life, he would have maybe enjoyed being a father. After just a few days, he already had an entire suitcase of British books, toys and sweets to take back to Esmeralda. Even when Anastasia was well over fifty years old, still looking seventeen, he could never stop caring for her like his daughter. God rest her soul.

Maria, on the other hand... she liked Metallica and could kick his ass in a fist fight, for God's sake. What could be hotter than that? After a few days of leaving her in peace, more frightened than when he had entered any battlefield, Vlad decided to knock on her door.


Maria lay staring at the ceiling in the solace and quiet of her room as she had for days now. Adam had allowed them all some time before opening Mordecai's letter. She needed that time alone. She had to try and understand what she had felt during the possession and her emotions towards Lucifer and Vlad. Usually she liked to have music on in the background, but even that felt intrusive. Her life had taken such an unexpected turn since reuniting with Adam, it gave her whiplash just thinking about it. Even as she lay still, her mind was a restless whirlwind. Then there was a knock at her door. She wasn't expecting anyone, but perhaps it was time to join the land of the living. She got to her feet and opened the door. A flutter of warmth broke out across her body. A clean-shaven Vlad stood there, his huge form filling threshold. She smiled and reached out to touch his hairless face. Their time together had changed her feelings for him. His full mouth, strong jaw and eyes came alive without the beard and shaggy hair.

"What made you decide to do this?" she asked.

He gazed into her eyes. "It was time to stop hiding. Billy was not someone I wanted to be anymore. Billy was a dick most of the time."

Maria looked off, embarrassed. "I said some awful things to you. I'm so very sorry. I didn't mean it. You've done a lot of good things. I..."

"Maria, don't apologize. You were possessed by a demon. Besides, I needed to hear it from someone I trust and value."

Maria was very conscious of his body close to hers, as his eyes studied her face. His mouth and body heat left her feeling uncomfortable: the kind of uncomfortable that made her nipples go hard. She hoped he wouldn't notice through the t-shirt she wore without a bra. Maria liked him, despite their rocky start. He wasn't perfect, and she wasn't perfect, and the more time they spent together the more she wanted to know about him.

Diego had been the protector her father should have been; Lucifer the toe-curling lover who leaves you breathless, walking home the next day with smeared makeup, regret and shoes in hand; this was something different. Was there such a thing as great lovemaking with friendship? These awakening feelings were a long time coming. She moved closer to him and embraced him. He wrapped his large arms around her and held her close. He felt good and she was happy he was there. She looked up towards his face

"Shall we get a drink and see the others?" she asked.

"You sure you feel ready?"

Maria nodded. "I think it's time."


Adam gathered the few vampires who knew what had really happened to Mordecai. They stood in their leader's old office, around his desk. No one wanted to reach for the second unopened letter, despite the vampires' desperation to know his final message. It sat like an urn in the center of the desk. Mordecai's office didn't feel the same without his presence.

Eventually it was Adam who reached for the plain cream-colored envelope with black ink on the front. *To my Family*, it read. He tore it open and took a breath before beginning to read it out loud, his eyes scanned the contents, then he stopped and looked up.

"I can't believe this. Mordecai was never who he said he was. It all makes sense now. He was our father. When I say 'father,' I don't mean he made some of us: he was the *first* of us. He says we would know him as Abel."

*Epilogue: Origins*

## THE BLOOD OF CAIN

There had been no rain for days and the crops were suffering. Cain kneeled in the dry dirt, touching the limp leaves of his harvest.

"Cursed heat. What's God playing at?"

Cain's mother lay in the shade of the large tree outside their cave. Eve had slept most of the time since he could recall. She went through her daily life as if some dark cloud was permanently settled over her head. It would be raining in her thoughts. She spoke only when necessary, leaving a great silent void.

He gave her a soured look. "Why bother living, wretched woman?" he grumbled beneath his breath.

Cain's father, Adam, was in the field with Cain's brother, Abel, looking after the flock. Adam spent time with Cain's sniveling, weak brother when he should be looking after the crops with Cain. Cain hated the lot of them and their miserable existence. Why had God even bothered to put some insufferable tree in the Garden if they weren't supposed to eat from it? Some mighty omniscient being he was. He felt his small pet stir in the hide pouch that hung across his body.

His father had first taught him how to farm when Cain was a boy. During one lesson he was creating holes with his child-size fingers to plant seeds when a bright green snake, no bigger than the handle of a small ax, crawled on to his forearm. Its small tongue tickled his skin and made him laugh. Abel would surely have tried to take this little treasure away, so Cain decided to hide it. All these years from boyhood to manhood, he had hidden and cared for his little friend.

Cain's body grew from that of a boy into that of a fieldworker. His skin was bronzed and his hands were rough and calloused. His clothes were always coated with dust or dirt, and his muscles were defined from lifting, hoeing, pulling, dragging—whatever it took to have enough to survive. Abel, on the other hand, sat and watched his animals, daydreaming the day away under a tree or chatting with his father in the field. Cain loathed them both and repeated this declaration of hate like a prayer.

It was evening when a slight breeze blew through their camp, calling for sacrifice. Cain had heard this whisper in the wind only a few times, but today it was louder and more demanding. His mother, Eve, immediately moved from her sorrowful spot under the tree and walked into their cave. Abel ran to their camp from the field with two lambs—the only lambs born recently. Their father followed behind.

"It is He!" declared Adam. "We must do as we are told. Ready your offering."

Cain was vexed by the rushing around for something worthy of sacrifice while God had made success impossible from the beginning. All this toil tasted like bitter wild weeds and rancid seeds. He walked to his meager basket of vegetation and threw it near their firepit.

Praying aloud, Abel tied his lambs by their feet then sliced open their throats. The blood seeped slowly into the ground, staining their soft snow-white fur. This sight was almost too much for Cain to bear. Perfect meat wasted.

The breeze returned and a whirlwind of leaves surrounded Abel. Within their midst a rustle of a voice could be heard saying *This is good, thank you*. Abel and Adam fell to their knees with tears in their eyes.

Cain stood over his basket and pointed a finger to the sky. "You don't like my crop? Well, make it rain then. Don't blame me for your mistakes!" His little pet stirred. Cain returned his jealous gaze to Abel and walked off. How he wished them all dead.

Cain sat on a little outcropping not far from their cave where you could see a valley of thirsty pale-yellow fields. An orchard to the left looked sad with its lack of fruit.

Rustling leaves called out to Cain. *Why are you so angry? Why are your thoughts and heart so poisoned?*

Cain refused to answer. Instead he took a bite from one of the fruits from his offering.

*You must guard yourself and your emotions. Nothing good can come from an unforgiving, closed heart.*

Cain spat out the pit and walked away in silence.

As he returned home, he saw Abel back in his field. Abel called out to Cain. "Brother, look! More of the flock are with child. It's a miracle."

Cain's anger was as sharp as the thorns of a blackberry bush. He ran toward his brother with a heaving chest and murderous rage. Abel fell over easily: he was half the size of Cain.

Abel held his hands to his face. "Please, brother, what have I done? Tell me what I can do to fix this. Anything! Take my flock if it will please you!"

Cain took Abel's head into his laborer's hands and drove it into the rocky ground. His brother looked like those pitiful helpless lambs and their spilled blood. Cain walked away without remorse or a care in the world.

Adam saw Cain return to camp. "Where is your brother? He hasn't returned yet. It will be dark soon."

Cain didn't bother to look at his father as he heaved a sheep over his shoulders, ready to eat its flesh. "Am I his keeper? You go look for him. He's your favorite, after all."

A gust of hot air blew a small cyclone of dirt between the two men. A voice came. *Cain, you have murdered your brother when he begged for kindness. He begged for his life and you took his life.*

Adam fell to his knees and cried the cry only someone who has lost a child could make.

*Leave this place, Cain*, said the voice. *You will live until the last of days for your crime. Anyone that tries to take your life will suffer me in the worst of ways.*

Eve heard the majestic voice boom from the outside of the cave. She ran from the pile of animal skins to the field where Abel lay. As twilight descended from above, Eve kneeled in the dirt and held her son's head in her lap. She looked up into the darkening sky.

"Please Lord, do not take my children away. I have sinned greatly and have paid greatly. Take my life, take my blood and pass it to him. Do you receive my gift?"

Eve took the small slate knife from the side of Abel's belt, slashed her wrists, then placed them in Abel's mouth. Eve's eyes began to flutter as the blood drained from her body. Before the heaviness of her body weighed her down, she could just see Adam running toward her in the distance.

Eve awoke to a bandaged wrist and Abel laid next to her, covered in warm fur. His head was bandaged and his breathing was shallow. But he was breathing. Adam sat next to his son, watching his every move, while Eve too looked lovingly at her son. She remembered how terrifying her first pregnancy had been, soon after they were cast from God's care. She had watched in horror as her body changed and something moved inside of her. They vaguely knew what might happen from watching the animals in the wild, but nothing could prepare them for experiencing it themselves.

Adam blamed Eve for her transformation. When God said he would create enmity between men and women as a punishment, he was not speaking without truth. Eve only wanted God or Adam's care, but she found none. She spent months growing and wondering until her body pained her far worse than any day in the field. God was surely bringing death to her for their sins. Even Adam was scared that he would be next for this ghoulish transformation, followed by pain. He took pity on his wife, holding her arms as she squatted in the dirt by the river.

They screamed in fear when their firstborn arrived. Cain. The small, wrinkled, bloody thing howled as it exited Eve's body like a little calf or lamb. Eve cradled the creature with tears streaming from her eyes and a white substance dribbled from her hardened breasts. The thing scratched for the liquid. Without thought she placed it to her breast, and the small creature was quiet. Adam cut the long snake-like cord which attached Eve to her child while more strange contents exited her body. They watched their little creation fall asleep. Whatever enmity was felt between the two no longer existed. They were both completely in wonder of their child.

By the fire they watched Abel as they had watched their two children right after their births.

The last thing Abel remembered was his body beginning to feel cold, like when the seasons first change. His mother held him close like she used to at her breast, but this time a bright light, so white and peaceful, stood behind her. He felt no fear. The light moved from behind his mother to her outstretched arm that now fed him. The longer he drank the sleepier he felt. He could feel his eyes flutter and a voice, so small, say, *Awake and go.*

Abel turned his stiff neck toward the warm fire while voices gently called his name. It was his mother and father.

"Please son, be careful. Do not strain yourself."

The trio sat in front of the fire as it flared and danced.

"It is he." Eve moved closer to the fire.

A voice both male and female called to them. *Abel, I have revived you for a great purpose. A purpose that will extend your life and eventually end it. I will make you a father of a nation, but a nation unknown to mankind. Your kind are to keep humankind. Your mother gave you new life through her blood sacrifice: it is through blood you will survive. You shall only drink from your mother and father until we speak again. Go, all of you: find Cain and the others who have been created separate from you. Cain will have taught them all I have taught you. Keep watch over your brother and the other humans. From now you are no longer Abel. You are Mordecai. When the time is right, you shall hear me again. Do you accept this gift, Mordecai? You will be void of desire of the flesh and live for the one task I have asked of you."*

Abel, now Mordecai, continued to watch the fire, unable to comprehend the meaning of anything God had spoken of. But he was an obedient man. He would accept this gift and this purpose.

# Acknowledgements

I would like to acknowledge Cath Trechman for believing in me. She is a wonderful human and editor.

# About the Author

V. CASTRO is a two-time Bram Stoker Award®-nominated author of *Aliens: Vasquez*, *The Haunting of Alejandra*, *Immortal Pleasures*, *The Queen of The Cicadas*, *Goddess of Filth*, *Hairspray and Switchblades*, and *Out of Atzlan*. She is a Mexican American expat living in the UK. As a full-time mother, she dedicates her time to her family and writing. Her official site is vcastrostories.com.

For more fantastic fiction, author events,
exclusive excerpts, competitions, limited editions and more

VISIT OUR WEBSITE
**titanbooks.com**

LIKE US ON FACEBOOK
**facebook.com/titanbooks**

FOLLOW US ON TWITTER AND INSTAGRAM
**@TitanBooks**

EMAIL US
**readerfeedback@titanemail.com**